THE KIDNAP MURDER CASE

A PHILO VANCE STORY

By

S. S. VAN DINE

Non semper ea sunt, quæ videntur;
decipit
Frons prima multos.   —*Phædrus.*

OTTO PENZLER BOOKS

New York

**OTTO
PENZLER
BOOKS**

Otto Penzler Books
129 West 56th Street
New York, NY 10019
(Editorial Offices only)

Simon & Schuster
Rockefeller Center
1230 Avenue of the Americas
New York, NY 10020

Copyright © 1936 by W. H. Wright

Manufactured in the United States of America

1   3   5   7   9   10   8   6   4   2

Library of Congress Cataloging-in-Publication Data
Van Dine, S. S.
The kidnap murder case : a Philo Vance story / by S. S. Van
Dine.
        p.   cm.—(The Philo Vance series)
1. Vance, Philo (Fictitious character)—Fiction.   2. Private
investigators—New York (N.Y.)—Fiction.   I. Title.   II. Series.
              PS3545.R846K53   1994
              813'.52—dc20   94-17842

ISBN 1-883402-93-X

CONTENTS

CHARACTERS OF THE BOOK

PHILO VANCE

JOHN F.-X. MARKHAM
District Attorney of New York County.

ERNEST HEATH
Sergeant of the Homicide Bureau.

KASPAR KENTING
A play-boy and gambler, who mysteriously disappears from his home.

KENYON KENTING
A broker; brother of Kaspar and technical head of the Kenting family.

MADELAINE KENTING
Kaspar Kenting's wife.

ELDRIDGE FLEEL
A lawyer; a friend of the Kenting family and their attorney.

MRS. ANDREWS FALLOWAY
Madelaine Kenting's mother.

FRAIM FALLOWAY
Madelaine Kenting's brother.

PORTER QUAGGY
Another friend of the Kentings.

WEEM
The Kenting butler and houseman.

GERTRUDE
The Kenting cook and maid; wife of Weem.

SNITKIN
Detective of the Homicide Bureau.

HENNESSEY
Detective of the Homicide Bureau.

BURKE
Detective of the Homicide Bureau.

GUILFOYLE
Detective of the Homicide Bureau.

SULLIVAN
Detective of the Homicide Bureau.

CAPTAIN DUBOIS
Finger-print expert.

DETECTIVE BELLAMY
Finger-print expert.

WILLIAM McLAUGHLIN
Patrolman on night duty on West 86th Street.

CURRIE
Vance's valet.

THE KIDNAP
MURDER CASE

CHAPTER I

KIDNAPPED!

(*Wednesday, July 20; 9:30 a.m.*)

Philo Vance, as you may remember, took a solitary trip to Egypt immediately after the termination of the Garden murder case.* He did not return to New York until the middle of July. He was considerably tanned, and there was a tired look in his wide-set grey eyes. I suspected, the moment I greeted him on the dock, that during his absence he had thrown himself into Egyptological research, which was an old passion of his.

"I'm fagged out, Van," he complained good-naturedly, as we settled ourselves in a taxicab and started uptown to his apartment. "I need a rest. We're not leavin' New York this summer—you won't mind, I hope. I've brought back a couple of boxes of archæological specimens. See about them tomorrow, will you?—there's a good fellow."

Even his voice sounded weary. His words carried a curious undertone of distraction; and the idea

* "The Garden Murder Case" (Scribners, 1935).

1

flashed through my mind that he had not altogether succeeded in eliminating from his thoughts the romantic memory of a certain young woman he had met during the strange and fateful occurrences in the penthouse of Professor Ephraim Garden.* My surmise must have been correct, for it was that very evening, when he was relaxing in his roof-garden, that Vance remarked to me, apropos of nothing that had gone before: "A man's affections involve a great responsibility. The things a man wants most must often be sacrificed because of this exacting responsibility." I felt quite certain then that his sudden and prolonged trip to Egypt had not been an unqualified success as far as his personal objective was concerned.

For the next few days Vance busied himself in arranging, classifying and cataloging the rare pieces he had brought back with him. He threw himself into the work with more than his wonted interest and enthusiasm. His mental and physical condition showed improvement immediately, and it was but a short time before I recognized the old vital Vance that I had always known, keen for sports, for various impersonal activities, and for the constant milling of the undercurrents of human psychology.

It was just a week after his return from Cairo that the famous Kidnap murder case broke. It was an

* This famous case had taken place just three months earlier.

atrocious and clever crime, and more than the usual publicity was given to it in the newspapers because of the wave of kidnapping cases that had been sweeping over the country at that time. But this particular crime of which I am writing from my voluminous notes was very different in many respects from the familiar "snatch"; and it was illumined by many sinister high lights. To be sure, the motive for the crime, or, I should say, crimes, was the sordid one of monetary gain; and superficially the technique was similar to that of the numerous cases in the same category. But through Vance's determination and fearlessness, through his keen insight into human nature, and his amazing flair for the ramifications of human psychology, he was able to penetrate beyond the seemingly conclusive manifestations of the case.

In the course of this investigation Vance took no thought of any personal risk. At one time he was in the gravest danger, and it was only through his boldness, his lack of physical fear, and his deadly aim and quick action when it was a matter of his life or another's—partly the result, perhaps, of his World-War experience which won him the *Croix de Guerre*—that he saved the lives of several innocent persons as well as his own, and eventually put his finger on the criminal in a scene of startling tragedy.

There was a certain righteous indignation in his attitude during this terrible episode—an attitude quite alien to his customarily aloof and cynical and purely academic point of view—for the crime itself was one of the type he particularly abhorred.

As I have said, it was just a week after his return to New York that Vance was unexpectedly, and somewhat against his wishes, drawn into the investigation. He had resumed his habit of working late at night and rising late; but, to my surprise, when I entered the library at nine o'clock on that morning of July 20, he was already up and dressed and had just finished the Turkish coffee and the *Régie* cigarette that constituted his daily breakfast. He had on his patch-pocket grey tweed suit and a pair of heavy walking boots, which almost invariably indicated a contemplated trip into the country.

Before I could express my astonishment (I believe it was the first time in the course of our relationship that he had risen and started the day before I had) he smilingly explained to me with his antemeridian drawl:

"Don't be shocked by my burst of energy, Van. It really can't be helped, don't y' know. I'm driving out to Dumont, to the dog show. I've a little chap entered in the puppy and American-bred classes, and I want to take him into the ring myself. He's a grand little fellow, and this is his début.* I'll return for dinner."

I was rather pleased at the prospect of being left alone for the day, for there was much work for me to do. I admit that, as Vance's legal advisor, monetary steward and general overseer of his affairs, I had allowed a great deal of routine work to accumulate during his absence, and the assurance of an entire day, without any immediate or current chores, was most welcome to me.

As Vance spoke he rang for Currie, his old English butler and majordomo, and asked for his hat and chamois gloves. Filling his cigarette case, he waved a friendly good-bye to me and started toward the door. But just before he reached it, the front doorbell sounded, and a moment later Currie ushered in John F.-X. Markham, District Attorney of New York County.†

"Good heavens, Vance!" exclaimed Markham. "Going out at such an early hour? Or have you just come in?" Despite the jocularity of his words, there

* As I learned later, he was referring to his Scottish terrier, Pibroch Sandyman. Incidentally, this dog won the puppy class that day and received Reserve Winners as well. Later he became a Champion.

† Markham and Vance had been close friends for over fifteen years, and, although Vance's unofficial connection with the District Attorney's office had begun somewhat in the spirit of an experimental adventure, Markham had now come to depend implicitly upon his friend as a vital associate in his criminal investigations.

was an unwonted sombreness in his face and a worried look in his eyes, which belied the manner of his
greeting.

Vance smiled with a puzzled frown.

"I don't like the expression on your Hellenic
features this morning, old dear. It bodes ill for one
who craves freedom and surcease from earthly miser-
ies. I was just about to escape by hieing me to a dog
show in the country. My little Sandy——"

"Damn your dogs and your dog shows, Vance!"
Markham growled. "I've serious news for you."

Vance shrugged his shoulders with resignation and
heaved an exaggerated sigh.

"Markham—my very dear Markham! How did
you time your visit so accurately? Thirty seconds
later and I would have been on my way and free
from your clutches." Vance threw his hat and gloves
aside. "But since you have captured me so neatly, I
suppose I must listen, although I am sure I shall not
like the tidin's. I know I'm going to hate you and
wish you had never been born. I can tell from the
doleful look on your face that you're in for something messy and desire spiritual support." He
stepped a little to one side. "Enter, and pour forth
your woes."

"I haven't time——"

"Tut, tut." Vance moved nonchalantly to the
centre-table and pointed to a large comfortable up-

holstered chair. "There's always time. There always
has been time—there always will be time. Repre-
sented by *n*, don't y' know. Quite meaningless—
without beginning and without end, and utterly
indivisible. In fact, there's no such thing as time—
unless you're dabblin' in the fourth dimension...."

He walked back to Markham, took him gently by
the arm and, ignoring his protests, led him to the
chair by the table.

"Really, y' know, Markham, you need a cigar and
a drink. Let calm be your watchword, my dear fellow,
—always calm. Serenity. Consider the ancient oaks.
Or, better yet, the eternal hills—or is it the everlast-
ing hills? It's been so long since I penned poesy.
Anyway, Swinburne did it much better. . . . *Eheu,
eheu!* . . ."

As he babbled along, with seeming aimlessness, he
went to a small side-table and, taking up a crystal
decanter, poured some of its contents into a tulip-
shaped glass, and set it down before the District
Attorney.

"Try that old Amontillado." He then moved the
humidor forward. "And these panetelas are infinitely
better than the cigars you carry around to dole out
to your constituents."

Markham made a restless, annoyed gesture,
lighted one of the cigars, and sipped the old syrupy
sherry.

Vance seated himself in a near-by chair and carefully lighted a *Régie*.

"Now try me," he said. "But don't make the tale too sad. My heart is already at the breaking-point."

"What I have to tell you is damned serious." Markham frowned and looked sharply at Vance. "Do you like kidnappings?"

"Not passionately," Vance answered, his face darkening. "Beastly crimes, kidnappings. Worse than poisonings. About as low as a criminal can sink." His eyebrows went up. "Why?"

"There's been a kidnapping during the night. I learned about it half an hour ago. I'm on my way——"

"Who and where?" Vance's face had now become sombre too.

"Kaspar Kenting. Heath and a couple of his men are at the Kenting house in 86th Street now. They're waiting for me."

"Kaspar Kenting . . ." Vance repeated the name several times, as if trying to recall some former association with it. "In 86th Street, you say?"

He rose suddenly and went to the telephone stand in the anteroom where he opened the directory and ran his eye down the page.

"Is it number 86 West 86th Street, perhaps?"

Markham nodded. "That's right. Easy to remember."

"Yes—quite." Vance came strolling back into the library, but instead of resuming his chair he stood leaning against the end of the table. "Quite," he repeated. "I seemed to remember it when you mentioned Kenting's name.... The domicile's an interestin' old landmark. I've never seen it, however. Had a fascinatin' reputation once. Still called the Purple House."

"Purple house?" Markham looked up. "What do you mean?"

"My dear fellow! Are you entirely ignorant of the history of the city which you adorn as District Attorney? The Purple House was built by Karl K. Kenting back in 1880, and he had the bricks and slabs of stone painted purple, in order to distinguish his abode from all others in the neighborhood, and to flaunt it as a challenge to his numerous enemies. 'With a house that color,' he used to say, 'they won't have any trouble finding me, if they want me.' The place became known as the Purple House. And every time the house was repainted, the original color was retained. Sort of family tradition, don't y' know.... But what about your Kaspar Kenting?"

"He disappeared some time last night," Markham explained impatiently. "From his bedroom. Open window, ladder, ransom note thumbtacked to the window-sill. No doubt about it."

"Details familiar—eh, what?" mused Vance.

"And I presume the ransom note was concocted with words cut from a newspaper and pasted on a sheet of paper?"

Markham looked astonished.

"Exactly! How did you guess it?"

"Nothing new or original about it—what? Highly conventional. Bookish, in fact. But not being done this season in the best kidnapping circles. . . . Curious case. . . . How did you learn about it?"

"Eldridge Fleel was waiting at my office when I arrived this morning. He's the lawyer for the Kenting family. One of the executors for the old man's estate. Kaspar Kenting's wife naturally notified him at once at his home—called him before he was up. He went to the house, looked over the situation, and then came directly to me."

"Level-headed chap, this Fleel?"

"Oh, yes. I've known the man for years. Good lawyer. He was wealthy and influential once, but was badly hit by the depression. We were both members of the Lawyers' Club, and we had offices in the same building on lower Broadway before I was cursed with the District Attorneyship. . . . I got in touch with Sergeant Heath immediately, and he went up to the house with Fleel. I told them I'd be there as soon as I could. I dropped off here, think-ing——"

"Sad . . . very sad," interrupted Vance with a

sigh, drawing deeply on his cigarette. "I still wish you had made it a few minutes later. I'd have been safely away. You're positively ineluctable."

"Come, come, Vance. You know damned well I may need your help." Markham sat up with a show of anger. "A kidnapping isn't a pleasant thing, and the city's not going to like it. I'm having enough trouble as it is.* I can't very well pass the buck to the federal boys. I'd rather clean up the mess from local headquarters. . . . By the way, do you know this young Kaspar Kenting?"

"Slightly," Vance answered abstractedly. "I've run into the johnnie here and there, especially at old Kinkaid's Casino † and at the race-tracks. Kaspar's a gambler and pretty much a ne'er-do-well. Full of the spirit of frivolity and not much else. Ardent play-boy, as it were. Always hard up. And trusted by no one. Can't imagine why any one would want to pay a ransom for him."

Vance slowly exhaled his cigarette smoke, watching the long blue ribbons rise and disperse against the ceiling.

"Queer background," he murmured, almost as if

* There had been several recent kidnappings at this time, two of a particularly atrocious nature, and the District Attorney's office and the Commissioner of Police were being constantly and severely criticized by the press for their apparent helplessness in the situation.

† Vance was referring to the gambling establishment which figured so prominently in the Casino murder case.

to himself. "Can't really blame the chappie for being such a blighter. Old Karl K., the author of his being, was a bit queer himself. Had more than enough money, and left it all to the older son, Kenyon K., to dole out to Kaspar as he saw fit. I imagine he hasn't seen fit very often or very much. Kenyon is the solid-citizen type, in the worst possible meaning of the phrase. Came to the Belmont track in the highest of dudgeons one afternoon and led Kaspar right-eously home. Probably goes to church regularly. Marches in parades. Applauds the high notes of sopranos. Feels positively nude without a badge of some kind. That sort of johnnie. Enough to drive any younger brother to hell. . . . The old man, as you must know, wasn't a block from which you could expect anything in the way of fancy chips. A rabid and fanatical Ku-Klux-Klanner. . . ."

"You mean his initials?" asked Markham.

"No. Oh, no. His convictions." Vance looked at Markham inquiringly. "Don't you know the story?"

Markham shook his head despondently.

"Old K. K. Kenting originally came from Virginia and was a King Kleagle in that sheeted Order.* So rabid was he that he changed the *C* in his name, Carl,

---

* Vance was mistaken about this, as Kenting belonged to the old, or original, Klan, in which there was no such title as King Keagle. This title did not come into existence until 1915, with the modern Klan. Kenting probably had been a Grand Dragon (or State head) in the original Klan.

to a *K*, and gave himself a middle initial, another *K*, so that his monogram would be the symbol of his fanatical passion. And he went even further. He had two sons and a daughter, and he gave them all names beginning with *K*, and added for each one a middle initial *K*—Kenyon K. Kenting, Kaspar K. Kenting, and Karen K. Kenting. The girl died shortly after Karl himself was gathered to Abraham's bosom. The two sons remaining, being of a new generation and less violent, dropped the middle *K*—which never stood for anything, by the by."

"But why a purple house?"

"No symbolism there," returned Vance. "When Karl Kenting came to New York and went into politics he became boss of his district. And he had an idea his sub-Potomac enemies were going to persecute him; so, as I say, he wanted to make it easy for 'em to find him. He was an aggressive and fearless old codger."

"I seem to remember they eventually found him, and with a vengeance," Markham mumbled impatiently.

"Quite." Vance nodded indifferently. "But it took two machine-guns to translate him to the Elysian Fields. Quite a scandal at the time. Anyway, the two sons, while wholly different from each other, are both unlike their father."

Markham stood up with deliberation.

"That may all be very interesting," he grumbled; "but I've got to get to 86th Street. This may prove a crucial case, and I can't afford to ignore it." He looked somewhat appealingly at Vance.

Vance rose likewise and crushed out his cigarette.

"Oh, by all means," he drawled. "I'll be delighted to toddle along. Though I can't even vaguely imagine why kidnappers should select Kaspar Kenting. The Kentings are no longer a reputedly wealthy family. True, they might be able to produce a fairly substantial sum on short notice, but they're not, d' ye see, in the class which professional kidnappers enter up on their list of possible victims. . . . By the by, do you know how much ransom was demanded?"

"Fifty thousand. But you'll see the note when we get there. Nothing's been touched. Heath knows I'm coming."

"Fifty thousand . . ." Vance poured himself a pony of his *Napoléon* cognac. "That's most interestin'. Not an untidy sum—eh, what?"

When he had finished his brandy he rang again for Currie.

"Really, y' know," he said to Markham—his tone had suddenly changed to one of levity—, "I can't wear chamois gloves in a purple house. Most inappropriate."

He asked Currie for a pair of doeskin gloves, his

wanghee cane, and a town hat. When they were
brought in he turned to me.

"Do you mind calling MacDermott * and explain-
in'?" he asked. "The old boy himself will have to
show Sandy. . . . And do you care to come along,
Van? It may prove more fascinatin' than it sounds."

Despite my accumulated work, I was glad of the
invitation. I caught MacDermott on the telephone
just as he was packing his crated entries into the
station-wagon. I wasted few words on him, in true
Scotch fashion, and immediately joined Vance and
Markham in the lower hallway where they were
waiting for me.

We entered the District Attorney's car, and in
fifteen minutes we were at the scene of what proved
to be one of the most unusual criminal cases in
Vance's career.

* Robert A. MacDermott was Vance's kennel manager.

CHAPTER II

(Wednesday, July 20; 10:30 a.m.)

The Kenting residence in 86th Street was not as bizarre a place as I had expected to see after Vance's description of it. In fact, it differed very little from the other old brownstone residences in the street, except that it was somewhat larger. I might even have passed it or driven by it any number of times without noticing it at all. This fact was, no doubt, owing to the dullness of its faded color, since the house had apparently not been repainted for several years, and sun and rain had not spared it. Its tone was so dingy and superficially nondescript that it blended unobtrusively with the other houses of the neighborhood. As we approached it that fateful morning it appeared almost a neutral grey in the brilliant summer sunshine.

On closer inspection I could see that the house had been built of bricks put together in English cross bond with weathered mortar joints, trimmed at the cornices, about the windows and door, and be-

16

low the eaves, with great rectangular slabs of brown-stone. Only in the shadow along the eaves and beneath the projections of the sills was there any distinguishable tint of purple remaining. The architecture of the house was conventional enough—a somewhat free adaptation of combined Georgian and Colonial, such as was popular during the middle of the last century.

The entrance, which was several feet above the street level and reached by five or six broad sandstone steps, was a spacious one; and there was the customary glass-enclosed vestibule. The windows were high, and old-fashioned shutters folded back against the walls of the house. Instead of the regulation four stories, the house consisted of only three stories, not counting the sunken basement; and I was somewhat astonished at this fact when it came to my attention, for the structure was even higher than its neighbors. The windows, however, were not on a line with those in the other houses, and I realized that the ceilings of the "Purple House" must be unusually high.

Another thing which distinguished the Kenting residence from the neighboring buildings was the existence of a fifty-foot court to the east. This court was covered with a neatly kept lawn, with hedges on all four sides. There were two flower-beds—one star-shaped and the other in the form of a crescent; and an old gnarled maple tree stood at the rear, with its branches extending almost the entire width of the yard. Only a low iron picket fence, with a swinging gate, divided the yard from the street.

This refreshing quadrangle was bathed with sunshine, and it seemed a very pleasant spot, with its blooming hedges and its scattered painted metal chairs. But there was one sinister note—one item which in itself was not sinister at all, but which had acquired a malevolent aspect from the facts Markham had related to us in Vance's apartment that morning. It was a long, heavy ladder, such as outdoor painters use, leaning against the house, with its upper end just below a second-story window—the window nearest the street.

The "Purple House" itself was set about ten feet in from the sidewalk, and we immediately crossed the irregular flagstones and proceeded up the steps to the front door. But there was no need to ring the bell. Sergeant Ernest Heath, of the Homicide Bureau, greeted us in the vestibule. After saluting Markham, whom he addressed as Chief, he turned to Vance with a grin and shook his head ponderously.

"I didn't think you'd be here, Mr. Vance," he said good-naturedly. "Ain't this a little out of your line? But howdy, anyway." And he held out his hand.

"I myself didn't think I'd be here, Sergeant. And everything is out of my line today except dog shows. Fact is, I almost missed the present pleasure of seeing you." Vance shook hands with him cordially, and cocked one eye inquiringly. "What's the exhibit I'm supposed to view?"

"You might as well have stayed home, Mr. Vance," Heath told him. "Hell, there's nothing to this case. It ain't even a fancy one. A little routine police work is all that's needed to clear it up. There ain't a chance for what you call psychological deduction."

"My word!" sighed Vance. "Most encouragin', Sergeant. I hope you're right. Still, since I'm here, don't y' know, I might as well look around in my amateurish way and try to learn what it's all about. I promise not to complicate matters for you."

"That's a little more than O.-K. with me, Mr. Vance," the Sergeant grinned. And, opening the heavy glass-panelled oak door, he led us into the dingy but spacious hallway, and then through partly-opened sliding doors at the right, into a stuffy drawing-room.

"Cap Dubois and Bellamy * are upstairs, getting the finger-prints; and Quackenbush † took a few shots and went away." Heath seated himself at a small Jacobean desk and drew out his little black leather-bound note-book. "Chief," he said to Mark-

* Captain Dubois and Detective Bellamy were finger-print experts attached to the New York Police Department.
† Peter Quackenbush was the official police photographer.

ham, "I think maybe you'd better get the whole story direct from Mrs. Kenting, the wife of the gentleman who was kidnapped."

I now noticed three other persons in the room. At the front window stood a solid, slightly corpulent man of successful, professional mien. He turned and came forward as we entered, and Markham bowed to him cordially and greeted him by the name Fleel. He was the lawyer of the Kenting family.

At his side was a somewhat aggressive middle-aged man, rather thin, with a serious and pinched expression. Fleel introduced him to us cursorily, with a careless wave of the hand, as Kenyon Kenting, the brother of the missing man. Then the lawyer turned stiffly to the other side of the room, and said in a suave, businesslike voice:

"But I particularly wish to present you gentlemen to Mrs. Kaspar Kenting."

We all turned to the pale, terrified woman seated at one end of a small davenport, in the shadows of the west wall. She appeared at first glance to be in her early thirties; but I soon realized that my guess might be ten years out, one way or the other. She seemed exceedingly thin, even beneath the full folds of the satin dressing-gown she wore; and although her eyes were large and frankly appealing, there was in her features evidence of a shrewd competency amounting almost to hardness. It struck me that a painter could have used her for the perfect model of the clinging, nervous, whiny woman. But, on the other hand, she impressed me as being capable of assuming the rôle of a strong-minded and efficient person when the occasion demanded. Her hair was thin and stringy and of the lustreless ashen-blond variety; and her eyelashes and eyebrows were so sparse and pale, that she gave the impression, sitting there in the dim light, of having none at all.

When Fleel presented us to her she nodded curtly with a frightened air, and kept her eyes focused sharply on Markham. Kenyon Kenting went directly to her and, sitting down on the edge of the sofa, put his arm half around her and patted her gently on the back.

"You must be brave, my dear," he said in a tone that was almost endearing. "These gentlemen have come to help us, and I'm sure they'll be wanting to know all you can tell them about the events of last night."

The woman drew her eyes slowly away from Markham and looked up wistfully and trustingly at her brother-in-law. Then she nodded her head slowly, in complete and confiding acquiescence and again turned her eyes to Markham.

Sergeant Heath broke gruffly into the scene.

"Don't you want to go upstairs, Chief, and see the room from where the snatch was made? Snitkin's on duty up there, to see that nothing is moved around or changed."

"I say, just a moment, Sergeant." Vance sat down on the sofa beside Mrs. Kenting. "I'd like to ask Mrs. Kenting a few questions first." He turned to the woman. "Do you mind?" he asked in a mild, almost deferential tone. As she silently shook her head in reply he continued: "Tell me, when did you first learn of your husband's absence?"

The woman took a deep breath, and after a barely perceptible hesitation answered in a slightly rasping, low-pitched voice which contrasted strangely with her colorless, semi-anæmic appearance.

"Early this morning—about six o'clock, I should say. The sun had just risen." *

"And how did you happen to become aware of his absence?"

"I wasn't sleeping well last night," the woman responded. "I was restless for some unknown reason, and the early morning sun coming through the shutters into my room not only awakened me, but prevented me from going back to sleep. Then I thought I heard a faint unfamiliar sound in my husband's room—you see, we occupy adjoining rooms on the next floor—and it seemed to me I heard some

---

* The official time of sunrise on that day was 4:45, local mean time, or 4:41, Eastern standard time; but daylight saving time was then in effect, and Mrs. Kenting's reference to sunrise in New York at approximately six o'clock was correct.

one moving stealthily about. There was the unmistakable sound of footsteps across the floor—that is, like some one walking around in soft slippers."

She took another deep breath, and shuddered slightly.

"I was already terribly nervous, anyway, and these strange noises frightened me, for Kaspar—Mr. Kenting—is usually sound asleep at that hour of the morning. I got up, put on my slippers, threw a dressing-gown around me, and went to the door which connects our two rooms. I called to my husband, but got no answer. Then I called again, and still again, in louder tones, at the same time knocking at the door. But there was no response of any kind—and I realized that everything had suddenly become quiet in the room. By this time I was panicky; so I pulled open the door quickly and entered the room. . . ."

"Just a moment, Mrs. Kenting," Vance interrupted. "You speak of having been startled by an unfamiliar sound in your husband's room this morning, and you say you heard some one walking about in the room. Just what kind of sound was it that first caught your attention?"

"I don't know exactly. It might have been some one moving a chair, or dropping something, or maybe it was just a door surreptitiously opened and shut. I can't describe it any better than that."

"Could it have been a scuffle of some kind—I

mean, did it sound as if more than one person might have been making the noise?"

The woman shook her head vaguely.

"I don't think so. It was over too quickly for that. I should say it was a sound that was not intended— something accidental—do you see what I mean? I can't imagine what it could have been—so many things might have happened. . . ."

"When you entered the room, were the lights on?" Vance asked, with what appeared to be almost utter indifference.

"Yes," the woman hastened to answer animatedly. "That was the curious thing about it. Not only was the chandelier burning brightly, but the light beside the bed also. They were a ghastly yellow in the day-light."

"Are the two fixtures controlled with the same switch?" Vance asked, frowning down at his un-lighted *Régie*.

"No," the woman told him. "The switch for the chandelier is near the hall door, while the night-lamp is connected to an outlet in the baseboard and is worked by a switch on the lamp itself. And another strange thing was that the bed had not been slept in."

Vance's eyebrows rose slightly, but he did not look up from his fixed contemplation of the cigarette be-tween his fingers.

"Do you know what time Mr. Kenting came to his bedroom last night?"

The woman hesitated a moment and flashed a glance at Kenyon Kenting.

"Oh, yes," she said hurriedly. "I heard him come in. It must have been soon after three this morning. He had been out for the evening, and I happened to be awake when he got back—or else the unlocking and closing of the front door awakened me—I really don't know. I heard him enter his bedroom and turn on the lights. Then I heard him telephoning to some one in an angry voice. Right after that I fell asleep again."

"You say he was out last night. Do you know where or with whom?"

Mrs. Kenting nodded, but again she hesitated. Finally she answered in the same brittle, rasping voice:

"A new gambling casino was opened in Jersey yesterday, and my husband was invited to be a guest at the opening ceremonies. His friend Mr. Quaggy called for him about nine o'clock——"

"Please repeat the name of your husband's friend."

"Quaggy—Porter Quaggy. He's a very trustworthy and loyal man, and I've never objected to my husband's going out with him. He has been more or less a friend of the family for several years, and he always seems to know just how to handle my husband when he shows an inclination to go a little too far in his—his, well, his drinking. Mr. Quaggy was here at the house yesterday afternoon, and it was then that he and Kaspar made arrangements to go together to the new casino."

Vance nodded slightly, and directed his gaze to the floor as if trying to connect something the woman had told him with something already in his mind.

"Where does Mr. Quaggy live?" he asked.

"Just up the street, near Central Park West, at the Nottingham. . . ." She paused, and drew a deep breath. "Mr. Quaggy's a frequent and welcome visitor here."

Vance threw Heath a significant *coup d'œil*, and the Sergeant made a note in the small leather-bound black book which lay before him on the desk.

"Do you happen to know," Vance continued, still addressing the woman, "whether Mr. Quaggy returned to the house last night with Mr. Kenting?"

"Oh, no; I'm quite sure he did not," was the prompt reply. "I heard my husband come in alone and mount the stairs; and I heard him alone in his bedroom. As I said, I dozed off shortly afterwards, and didn't wake up again until after the sun rose."

"May I offer you a cigarette?" said Vance, holding out his case.

The woman shook her head slightly and glanced questioningly at Kenyon Kenting.

"No, thank you," she returned. "I rarely smoke. But I don't in the least mind others smoking, so please light your own cigarette."

With a courteous bow in acknowledgment, Vance proceeded to do so, and then asked:

"When you found that your husband was not in his room at six this morning, and that the lights were on and the bed had not been slept in, what did you think?—and what did you do?"

"I was naturally upset and troubled and very much puzzled," Mrs. Kenting explained; "and just then I noticed that the big side window overlooking the lawn was open and that the Venetian blind had not been lowered. This was queer, because Kaspar was always fussy about this particular blind in the summer-time because of the early morning sun. I immediately ran to the window and looked down into the yard, for a sudden fear had flashed through my mind that perhaps Kaspar had fallen out. . . . You see," she added reluctantly, "my husband often has had too much to drink when he comes home late at night. . . . It was then I saw the ladder against the house; and I was wondering about that vaguely, when suddenly I noticed that horrible slip of paper pinned to the window-sill. Immediately I realized what had happened, and why I had heard those peculiar noises in his room. The realization made me feel faint."

She paused and dabbed gently at her eyes with a lace-trimmed handkerchief.

"When I recovered a little from the shock of this frightful thing," she continued, "I went to the telephone and called up Mr. Fleel. I also called Mr. Kenyon Kenting here—he lives on Fifth Avenue, just across the park. After that I simply ordered some black coffee, and waited, frantic, until their arrival. I said nothing about the matter to the servants, and I didn't dare inform the police until I had consulted with my brother-in-law and especially with Mr. Fleel, who is not only the family's legal advisor, but also a very close friend. I felt that he would know the wisest course to follow."

"How many servants are there here?" Vance asked.

"Only two—Weem, our butler and houseman, and his wife, Gertrude, who cooks and does maid service."

"They sleep where?"

"On the third floor, at the rear."

Vance had listened to the woman's account of the tragic episode with unusual attentiveness, and while to the others he must have seemed casual and indifferent, I had noticed that he shot the narrator several appraising glances from under his lazily drooping eyelids.

At last he rose and, walking to the desk, placed his half-burnt cigarette in a large onyx ash receiver.

Turning to Mrs. Kenting again, he asked quietly:

"Had you, or your husband, any previous warning of this event?"

Before answering, the woman looked with troubled concern at Kenyon Kenting.

"I think, my dear," he encouraged her, in a ponderous, declamatory tone, "that you should be perfectly frank with these gentlemen."

The woman shifted her eyes back to Vance slowly, and after a moment of indecision said:

"Only this: several nights, recently, after I had retired, I have heard Kaspar dialing a number and talking angrily to some one over the telephone. I could never distinguish any of the conversation—it was simply a sort of muffled muttering. And I always noticed that the next day Kaspar was in a terrible humor and seemed worried and agitated about something. Twice I tried to find out what the trouble was, and asked him to explain the phone calls; but each time he assured me nothing whatever was wrong, and refused to tell me anything except that he had been speaking to his brother regarding business affairs. . . ."

"That was wholly a misleading statement on Kaspar's part," put in Kenyon Kenting with matter-of-fact suavity. "As I've already said to Mrs. Kenting, I can't remember ever having had any telephone conversation with Kaspar at night. Whenever we

had business matters to discuss he either came to my
office, or we talked them over here at the house. . . .
I can't understand these phone conversations—but,
of course, they may have no relation whatsoever to
this present enigma."

"As you say, sir." Vance nodded. "No plausible
connection with this crime apparent. But one never
knows, does one? . . ." His eyes moved slowly back
to Mrs. Kenting. "Was there nothing else recently
which you can recall, and which might be helpful
now?"

"Yes, there was." The woman nodded with a show
of vigor. "About a week ago a strange, rough-look-
ing man came here to see Kaspar—he looked to me
like an underworld character. Kaspar took him immediately into the drawing-room here and closed the
doors. They remained in the room a long time. I had
gone up to my boudoir, but when the man left the
house I heard him say to Kaspar in a loud tone,
'There are ways of getting things.' It wasn't just a
statement—the words sounded terribly unfriendly.
Almost like a threat."

"Has there been anything further?" Vance asked.

"Yes. Several days later, the same man came
again, and an even more sinister-looking individual
was with him. I got only the merest glimpse of them
as Kaspar led them into this room and closed the
doors. I can't even remember what either of them

looked like—except that I'm sure they were dangerous men and I know they frightened me. I asked
Kaspar about them the next morning, but he evaded
the question and said merely that it was a matter of
business and I wouldn't understand. That was all I
could get out of him."

Kenyon Kenting had turned his back to the room
and was looking out of the window, his hands clasped
behind him.

"I hardly think these two mysterious callers," he
commented with pompous finality, without turning, "have any connection with Kaspar's kidnapping."

Vance frowned slightly and cast an inquisitive
glance at the man's back.

"Can you be sure of that, Mr. Kenting?" he asked
coldly.

"Oh, no—oh, no," the other replied apologetically,
swinging about suddenly and extending one hand in
an oratorical gesture. "I can't be sure. I merely
meant it isn't logical to suppose that two men would
expose themselves so openly if they contemplated a
step attended by such serious consequences as a
proven kidnapping. Besides, Kaspar had many
strange acquaintances, and these men were probably
in no way connected with the present situation."

Vance kept his eyes fixed on the man, and his expression did not change.

"It might be, of course, as you say," he remarked lightly. "Also it might not be—what? Interestin' speculation. But quite futile. I wonder. . . ." He drew himself up and, meditatively taking out his cigarette case, lighted another *Régie*. "And now I think we might go above, to Mr. Kaspar Kenting's bedroom."

We all rose and went toward the sliding doors.

As we came out into the main hall, the door to a small room just opposite was standing ajar, and through it I saw what appeared to be a miniature museum of some kind. There were the slanting cases set against the walls, and a double row of larger cases down the centre of the room. It looked like a private exhibition, arranged on the lines of the more extensive ones seen in any public museum.

"Ah! a collection of semiprecious stones," commented Vance. "Do you mind if I take a brief look?" he asked, addressing Mrs. Kenting. "Tremendously interested in the subject, don't y' know."*

The woman looked a little astonished, but answered at once.

"By all means. Go right in."

"Your own collection?" Vance inquired casually.

"Oh, no," the woman told him—somewhat bitterly,

* Although Vance never collected semiprecious stones himself, he had become deeply interested in the subject as early as his college days.

it seemed to me. "It belonged to Mr. Kenting senior. It was here in the house when I first came, long after his death. It was part of the estate he left—residuary property, I believe they call it."

Fleel nodded, as if he considered Mrs. Kenting's explanation correct and adequate.

Much to Markham's impatience and annoyance, Vance immediately entered the small room and moved slowly along the cases. He beckoned to me to join him.

Neatly arranged in the cases were specimens, in various shapes and sizes, of aquamarine, topaz, spinel, tourmaline, and zircon; rubelite, amethyst, alexandrite, peridot, hessonite, pyrope, demantoid, almandine, kinzite, andalusite, turquoise, and jadeite. Many of these gem-stones were beautifully cut and lavishly faceted, and I was admiring their lustrous beauty, impressed by what I assumed to be their great value, when Vance murmured softly:

"A most amazin' and disquietin' collection. Only one gem of real value here, and not a rare specimen among the rest. A schoolgirl's assortment, really. Very queer. And there seem to be many blank spaces. Judgin' by the vacancies and general distribution, old Kenting must have been a mere amateur. . . ."

I looked at him in amazement. Then his voice trailed off, and he suddenly wheeled about and returned to the hall.

"A most curious collection," he murmured again.

"Semiprecious stones were one of my father's hobbies," Kenting returned.

"Yes, yes. Of course." Vance nodded abstract-edly. "Most unusual collection. Hardly representa-tive, though. . . . Was your father an expert, Mr. Kenting?"

"Oh, yes. He studied the subject for many years. He was very proud of this gem-room, as he called it."

"Ah!"

Kenting shot the other a peculiar, shrewd look but said nothing; and Vance at once followed Heath to-ward the wide stairway.

CHAPTER III

THE RANSOM NOTE

(*Wednesday, July 20; 11 a.m.*)

As we entered Kaspar Kenting's bedroom, Captain Dubois and Detective Bellamy were just preparing to leave it.

"I don't think there's anything for you, Sergeant," Dubois reported to Heath after his respectful greetings to Markham. "Just the usual kind of marks and smudges you'd find in any bedroom—and they all check up with the finger-prints on the silver toilet set and the glass in the bathroom. Can't be any one else's finger-prints except the guy what lives here. Nothing new anywhere."

"And the window-sill?" asked Heath with desperate hopefulness.

"Not a thing, Sarge,—absolutely not a thing," Dubois replied. "And I sure went over it carefully. If any one went out that window during the night, they certainly wiped it clean, or else wore gloves and was mighty careful. And there's just the kind of finish on that window-sill—that old polished ivory finish—that'll take finger-prints like smoke-paper.

. . . Anyhow, I may have picked up a stray print here and there that'll check with something we've got in the files. I'll let you know more about it, of course, when we've developed and enlarged what we got."

The Sergeant seemed greatly disappointed.

"I'll be wanting you later for the ladder," he told Dubois, shifting the long black cigar from one corner of his mouth to the other. "I'll get in touch with you when we're ready."

"All right, Sergeant." Dubois picked up his small black case. "That'll be a tough job though. Don't make it too late in the afternoon—I'll want all the light I can get." And he waved a friendly farewell to Heath and departed, followed by Bellamy.

Kaspar Kenting's bedroom was distinctly old-fashioned, and conventional in the extreme. The furniture was shabby and worn. A wide Colonial bed of mahogany stood against the south wall, and there was a mahogany chest of drawers, with a hanging mirror over it, near the entrance to the room. Several easy chairs stood here and there about the room, and a faded flower-patterned carpet covered the floor. In one corner at the front of the room was a small writing-table on which stood a French telephone.

There were two windows in the room, one at the front of the house, overlooking the street; the other was in the east wall, and I recognized it at once as the window to which Mrs. Kenting said she had run in her fright. It was thrown wide open, with the Venetian blind drawn up to the top, and the outside shutters were invisible from where we stood; whereas the front window was half closed, with its blind drawn half-way down. At the rear of the room, to the right of the bed, was a door, now wide open. Beyond it another bedroom, similar to the one in which we stood, was identifiable: it was obviously Mrs. Kenting's boudoir. Between Kaspar Kenting's bed and the east wall two narrower doors led into the bathroom and a closet respectively.

The electric lights were still burning with a sickly illumination in the old-fashioned crystal chandelier hanging from the centre of the ceiling, and in the standard modern fixture near the head of the bed.

Vance looked about him with seeming indifference; but I knew that not a single detail of the setting escaped him. His first words were directed to the missing man's wife.

"When you came in here this morning, Mrs. Kenting, was this hall door locked or bolted?"

The woman looked uncertain and faltered in her answer.

"I—I—really, I can't remember. It must have been unlocked, or else I would probably have noticed it. I went out through the door when the coffee was ready, and I don't recall unlocking it."

Vance nodded understandingly.

"Yes, yes; of course," he murmured. "A deliberate act like unlocking a door would have made a definite mental impression on you. Simple psychology. . . ."

"But I really don't know, Mr. Vance. . . . You see," she added hurriedly, "I was so upset. . . . I wanted to get out of this room."

"Oh, quite. Wholly natural. But it really doesn't matter." Vance dismissed the subject. Then he went to the open window and looked down at the ladder.

As he did so Heath took from his pocket a knife such as boy scouts use, and pried loose the thumb-tack which held a soiled and wrinkled sheet of paper to the broad window-sill. He picked up the paper gingerly and handed it to Markham. The District Attorney took it and looked at it, his face grim and troubled. I glanced over his shoulder as he read it. The paper was of the ordinary typewriter quality and had been trimmed irregularly at the edges to disguise its original size. On it were pasted words and separate characters in different sizes and styles of type, apparently cut from a newspaper. The uneven lines, crudely put together, read:

If you want him back safe price will be 50 thousands $ otherwise killed will let you no ware & when to leave money later.

IF you want Him BACK

SAFE price WILL Be

50 Thousands $ other WISE

killed will ~LET you NO

WARE & WHEN to LEAVe

money Late r

This ominous communication was signed with a cabalistic signature consisting of two interlocking uneven squares which were outlined with black ink. (I am herewith including a copy of the ransom note which was found that morning at the Kenting home.)

Vance had turned back to the room, and Markham handed him the note. Vance glanced at it, as if it were of little interest to him, and read it through quickly, with the faint suggestion of a cynical smile.

"Really, y' know, Markham old dear, it isn't what you could possibly term original. It's been done so many times before."

He was about to return the paper to Markham when he suddenly drew his hand back and made a new examination of the note. His eyes grew serious and clouded, and the smile faded from his lips.

"Interestin' signature," he murmured. He took out his monocle and, carefully adjusting it, scrutinized the paper closely. "Made with a Chinese pencil," he announced, "—a Chinese brush—held vertically—and with China ink. . . . And those small squares . . ." His voice trailed off.

"Sure!" Sergeant Heath slapped his thigh and puffed vigorously at his cigar. "Same as the holes like I've seen in Chinese money."

"Quite so, Sergeant." Vance was still studying the cryptic signature. "Not illuminatin', however. But worth remembering." He returned his monocle to his waistcoat pocket and gave the paper back to Markham. "Not an upliftin' case, old dear. . . . Let's stagger about a bit. . . ."

He moved to the chest of drawers and adjusted his cravat before the mirror: then he smoothed back his hair and flicked an imaginary speck of dust from the left lapel of his coat. Markham glowered, and Heath made an expressive grimace of disgust.

"By the by, Mrs. Kenting," Vance asked casually, "is your husband, by any chance, bald?"

"Of course not," she answered indignantly. "What makes you ask that?"

"Queer—very queer," murmured Vance. "All the necess'ry toilet articles are in place on the top of this low-boy except a comb."

"I—don't understand," the woman returned in amazement. She moved swiftly across the room and stood beside Vance. "Why, the comb *is* gone!" she exclaimed in a tone of bewilderment. "Kaspar always kept it right here." And she pointed to a vacant place on the faded silk covering of what had obviously served Kaspar Kenting as a dresser.

"Most extr'ordin'ry. Let's see whether your husband's toothbrush is also missing. Do you know where he kept it?"

"In the bathroom, of course,"—Mrs. Kenting seemed frightened and breathless—"in a little rack beside the medicine cabinet. I'll see." As she spoke she turned and went quickly toward the door nearest the east wall. She pushed it open and stepped into the bathroom. After a moment she rejoined us.

"It's not there," she remarked dejectedly. "It isn't where it should be—and I've looked in the cabinet for it too."

"That's quite all right," Vance returned. "Do you remember what clothes your husband was wearing last night when he went to the opening of the casino in New Jersey with Mr. Quaggy?"

"Why, he wore evening dress, of course," the woman answered without hesitation. "I mean, he wore a tuxedo."

Vance walked quickly across the room and, opening the door beside the bathroom, looked into the narrow clothes closet. After a brief inspection of its contents he turned and again addressed Mrs. Kenting who now stood near the open east window, her hands clasped on her breast, and her eyes wide with apprehension.

"But his dinner jacket is hanging here in the closet, Mrs. Kenting. Has he more than one? . . ."

The woman shook her head vaguely.

"And I say, I suppose that Mr. Kenting wore the appropriate evening oxfords with his dinner coat."

"Naturally," the woman said.

"Amazin'," murmured Vance. "There are a pair of evening oxfords standin' neatly on the floor of the

closet, and the soles are dampish—it was rather wet
out last night, don't y' know, after the rain."

Mrs. Kenting moved slowly across the room to
where Kenyon Kenting was standing and put her
arm through his, seeming to lean against him. Then
she said in a low voice, "I really don't understand,
Mr. Vance."

Vance gave the woman and her brother-in-law a
thoughtful glance and stepped inside the closet. But
he turned back to the room in a moment and once
more addressed Mrs. Kenting.

"Are you familiar with your husband's ward-
robe?" he asked.

"Of course, I am," she returned with an undertone
of resentment. "I help him select the materials for
all his clothes."

"In that case," Vance said politely, "you can be
of great assistance to me if you will glance through
this closet and tell me whether anything is missing."

Mrs. Kenting withdrew her arm from that of her
brother-in-law and, with a dazed and slightly startled
expression, joined Vance at the clothes closet. As he
took a step to one side, she turned her back to him
and gave her attention to the row of hangers. Then
she faced him with a puzzled frown.

"His Glen Urquhart suit is missing," she said.
"It's the one he generally wears when he goes away
for a week-end or a short trip."

"Very interestin'," Vance murmured. "And is it possible for you to tell me what shoes he may have substituted for his evening oxfords?"

The woman's eyes narrowed, and she looked at Vance with dawning comprehension.

"Yes!" she said, and immediately swung about to inspect the shoe rack in the closet. After a moment she again turned to Vance with a look of bewilderment in her eyes. "One pair of his heavy tan bluchers are not here," she announced in a hollow, monotonous tone. "That's what Kaspar generally wears with his Glen Urquhart."

Vance bowed graciously and muttered a conventional "thank-you," as Mrs. Kenting returned slowly to Kenyon Kenting and stood rigid and wide-eyed beside him.

Vance turned back into the closet and it was but a minute before he came out and walked to the window. Between his thumb and forefinger he held a small cut gem—a ruby, I thought—which he examined against the light.

"Not a genuine ruby," he murmured. "Merely a balas-ruby—the two are often confused. A necess'ry item, to be sure, for a representative collection of gem-stones, but of little worth in itself. . . . By the by, Mrs. Kenting, I found this in the outer side-pocket of your husband's dinner jacket. I took the liberty of ascertaining whether he had transferred the contents of his pockets when he changed his clothes after returning home last night. This bit of balas-ruby was all I found. . . ."

He looked at the stone again and placed it carefully in his waistcoat pocket. Then he took out another cigarette and lighted it slowly and thoughtfully.

"Another thing that would interest me mildly," he remarked, looking vaguely before him, "is what kind of pajamas Mr. Kenting wears."

"Shantung silk," Mrs. Kenting asserted, stepping suddenly forward. "I just gave him a new supply on his birthday." She was looking directly at Vance, but now her eyes shifted quickly to the bed.

"There's a pair on——" She left the sentence unfinished, and her pale eyes opened still wider. "They're not there!" she exclaimed excitedly.

"No. As you say. Bed neatly turned down. Slippers in place. Glass of orange juice on the night-stand. But no pajamas laid out. I did notice the omission. A bit curious. But it may have been an oversight . . ."

"No," the woman interrupted emphatically. "It was not an oversight. I placed his pajamas at the foot of the bed myself, as I always do."

"Thin Shantung?" Vance asked, without looking at her.

"Yes—the sheerest summer weight."

"Might easily be rolled up and placed in a pocket?"

The woman nodded vaguely. She was now staring at Vance.

"What do you mean?" she asked. "Tell me, what is it?"

"I really don't know." Vance spoke with kindliness. "I'm merely observing things. There is no answer as yet. It's most puzzlin'."

Markham had been standing in silence near the door, watching Vance with grim curiosity. Now he spoke.

"I see what you're getting at, Vance," he said. "The situation is damnably peculiar. I don't know just how to take it. But, at any rate, if the indications are correct, I think we can safely assume that we are not dealing with inhuman criminals. When they came here and took Mr. Kenting to be held for ransom, they at least permitted him to get dressed, and to take with him two or three of the things a man misses most when he's away from home."

"Yes, yes. Of course." Vance spoke without enthusiasm. "Most kind of them—eh, what? If true."

"If true?" repeated Markham aggressively. "What else have you in mind?"

"My dear Markham!" protested Vance mildly. "Nothing whatever. Mind an utter blank. Evidence points in various directions. Whither go we?"

"Well, anyway," put in Sergeant Heath, "I don't see that there's any reason to worry about any harm coming to the fella. It looks to me like the guys who did the job were only after the money."

"It could be, of course, Sergeant." Vance nodded. "But I think it is a bit early to jump to conclusions." He gave Heath a significant look under drooped eyelids, and the Sergeant merely shrugged his shoulders and said no more.

Fleel had been watching and listening attentively, with a shrewd, judicial air.

"I think, Mr. Vance," he said, "I know what is in your mind. Knowing the Kentings as well as I do, and knowing the circumstances in this household for a great number of years, I can assure you that it would be no shock to either of them if you were to state exactly what you think regarding this situation."

Vance looked at the man for several seconds with the suggestion of an amused smile. At length he said: "Really, y' know, Mr. Fleel, I don't know exactly what I do think."

"I beg to differ with you, sir," the lawyer returned in a court-room manner. "And from my personal knowledge—the result of my many years of association with the Kenting family—I know that it would be heartening—I might even say, an act of mercy— if you stated frankly that you believe, as I am convinced you do, that Kaspar planned this *coup* himself for reasons that are only too obvious."

Vance looked at the man with a slightly puzzled expression and then said noncommittally: "If you believe that to be the case, Mr. Fleel, what procedure would you suggest be followed? You have known the young man for a long time and are possibly in a position to know how best to handle him."

"Personally," answered Fleel, "I think it is about time Kaspar should be taught a rigorous lesson. And I think we shall never have a better opportunity. If Kenyon agrees, and is able to provide this preposterous sum, I would be heartily in favor of following whatever further instructions are received, and then letting the law take its course on the grounds of extortion. Kaspar must be taught his lesson." He turned to Kenting. "Don't you agree with me, Kenyon?"

"I don't know just what to say," Kenting returned in an obvious quandary. "But somehow I feel that you are right. However, remember that we have Madelaine to consider."

Mrs. Kenting began crying softly and dabbing her eyes.

"Still," she demurred, "Kaspar may not have done this terrible thing at all. But if he did . . ."

Fleel swung round again to Vance. "Don't you

see what I meant when I asked you to state frankly
your belief? It would, I am sure, greatly relieve Mrs.
Kenting's anxiety, even though she thought her husband was guilty of having planned this whole frightful affair."

"My dear sir!" returned Vance. "I would be glad
to say anything which might relieve Mrs. Kenting's
anxiety regarding the fate of her husband. But I
assure you that at the present moment the evidence
does not warrant extending the comfort of any such
belief, either to you or to any member of the Kenting
family. . . ."

At this moment there was an interruption. At the
hall door appeared a short, middle-aged man with a
sallow moon-like face, sullen in expression. Scant,
colorless blond hair lay in straight long strands
across his bulging pate, in an unsuccessful effort to
cover up his partial baldness. He wore thick-lensed
rimless glasses through which one of his watery blue
eyes looked somehow different from the other, and
he stared at us as if he resented our presence. He
had on a shabby butler's livery which was too big for
him and emphasized his awkward posture. A cring-
ing and subservient self-effacement marked his general attitude despite his air of insolence.

"What is it, Weem?" Mrs. Kenting asked, with
no more than a glance in the man's direction.

"There is a gentleman—an officer—at the front door," the butler answered in a surly tone, "who says he wants to see Sergeant Heath."

"What's his name?" snapped Heath, eyeing the butler with belligerent suspicion.

The man looked at Heath morosely and answered, "He says his name is McLaughlin."

Heath nodded curtly and looked up at Markham.

"That's all right, Chief," he said. "McLaughlin was the man on this beat last night, and I left word at the Bureau to send him up here as soon as they could locate him. I thought he might know something, or maybe he saw something, that would give us a line on what happened here last night." Then he turned back to the butler. "Tell the officer to wait for me. I'll be down in a few minutes."

"Just a moment, Weem,—have I the name right?" Vance put in. "You're the butler here, I understand."

The man inclined his head.

"Yes, sir," he said, in a low rumbling voice.

"And your wife is the cook, I believe?"

"Yes, sir."

"What time," asked Vance, "did you and your wife go to bed last night?"

The butler hesitated a moment, and then looked shiftily at Mrs. Kenting, but her back was to him.

He transferred his weight from one foot to the other before he answered Vance.

"About eleven o'clock. Mr. Kenting had gone out, and Mrs. Kenting said she would not need me any more after ten o'clock."

"Your quarters are at the rear of the third floor, I believe?"

"Yes," the man returned with an abrupt, stiff nod.

"I say, Weem," Vance went on, "did either you or your wife hear anything unusual in the house, after you had gone to your quarters?"

The man again shifted his weight.

"No," he answered. "Everything was quiet until I went to sleep—and I didn't wake up till Mrs. Kenting rang for coffee around six."

"Then you didn't hear Mr. Kenting return to the house—or any one else moving about the house between eleven o'clock last night and six this morning?"

"No, nobody—I was asleep."

"That's all, Weem." Vance nodded curtly and turned away. "You'd better take the Sergeant's message to Officer McLaughlin."

The butler shuffled away lackadaisically.

"I think," Vance said to Heath, "it was a good idea to get McLaughlin. . . . There's really nothing more to be done up here just now. Suppose we go down and find out what he can tell us."

"Right!" And the Sergeant started toward the door, followed by Vance, Markham, and myself.

Vance paused leisurely just before reaching the door and turned to the small writing-table at the front of the room, on which the telephone stood. He regarded it contemplatively as he approached it. Opening the two shallow drawers, he peered into them. He took up the bottle of ink which stood at the rear of the table, just under the low stationery rack, and read the label. Setting the ink-bottle back in its place, he turned to the small wastepaper basket beside the table and bent over it.

When he rose he asked Mrs. Kenting:

"Does your husband do his writing at this table?"

"Yes, always," the woman answered, staring at Vance with a puzzled frown.

"And never anywhere else?"

The woman shook her head slowly.

"Never," she told him. "You see, he has very little correspondence, and that writing-table was always more than adequate for his needs."

"But did he never need any paste or mucilage?" Vance asked. "I don't see any here."

"Paste?" Mrs. Kenting appeared still more puzzled. "Why, no. As a matter of fact, I don't believe there's any in the house. . . . But why—why do you ask?"

Vance looked up at the woman and smiled at her somewhat sympathetically.

"I'm merely trying to learn the truth about everything, and I beg that you forgive any questions which seem irrelevant."

The woman made no reply, and Vance again went toward the door where Markham and Heath and I were waiting, and we all went out into the hall.

As we reached the narrow landing half-way down the stairs, Markham suddenly stopped, letting Heath proceed on his way. He took Vance by the arm, detaining him.

"See here, Vance," he said aggressively, but in a subdued tone, so that no one in the room from which we had just come should overhear him. "This kidnapping doesn't strike me as being entirely on the level. And I don't believe you yourself think that it is."

"Oh, my Markham!" deplored Vance. "Art thou a mind-reader?"

"Drop that," continued Markham angrily. "Either the kidnappers have no intention of harming young Kenting, or else—as Fleel suggests—Kenting staged the whole affair and kidnapped himself."

"I am waiting patiently for the question I fear is *en route*," sighed Vance with resignation.

"What I want to know," Markham went on doggedly, "is why you refused to offer any hope, or to admit the possibility of either of these hypotheses, when you know damn well that the mere expression of such an opinion by you would have mitigated the apprehensions of both Mrs. Kenting and the young fellow's brother."

Vance heaved a deep sigh and gazed at Markham a moment with a look of mock commiseration.

"Really, y' know, Markham," he said lightly, but with a certain seriousness, "you're a most admirable character, but you're far too naive for this unscrupulous world. Both you and your legal friend, Fleel, are quite wrong in your suppositions. I assure you, don't y' know, that I am not sufficiently cruel to extend false hopes to any one."

"What do you mean by that, Vance?" Markham demanded.

"My word, Markham! I can mean only one thing."

Vance continued to gaze at the District Attorney with sympathetic affection and lowered his voice.

"The chappie, I fear, is already dead."

CHAPTER IV

A STARTLING DECLARATION

(Wednesday, July 20; 11:45 a.m.)

There was something as startling as it was ominous about Vance's astonishing words. However, even in the dim light of the stairway I could see the serious expression on his face, and the finality of his tone convinced me that there was little or no doubt in his mind as to the truth of his words regarding Kaspar Kenting's fate.

Markham was stunned for a moment, but he was, I could see, frankly skeptical. The various bits of evidence uncovered in Kaspar Kenting's room seemed to point indisputably toward a very definite conclusion, which was quite the reverse of the conclusion which Vance had evidently reached. And I was sure that Markham felt as I did about it, and that he was as much surprised and confused as I at Vance's amazing statement. Markham did not relinquish his hold on Vance's arm. He apparently recovered his poise almost immedately and spoke in a hoarse undertone.

"You have a reason for saying that, Vance?"

"Tut, tut, my dear fellow," Vance returned lightly "This is neither the place nor the time to discuss the matter. I'll be quite willin' to point out all the obvious evidence to you later on. We are not dealing here with surface indications—those are quite consistent with the pattern which has been so neatly cut out for us. We are dealing with falsifications and subtleties; and I abhor them. . . . We'd better wait a while, don't y' know. At the moment I am most anxious to hear what McLaughlin has to say to the Sergeant. Let's descend and listen, what?"

Markham shrugged, gave Vance a nettled look, and relaxed his grip on the other's arm.

"Have it your own way," he grumbled. "Anyway," he added stubbornly, "I think you're wrong."

"It could be, of course," returned Vance with a nod. "Really, I'd like to believe it."

Slowly he went down the remaining steps to the lower hallway. Markham and I followed in silence.

McLaughlin, a heavy-footed Irishman, was just entering the drawing-room in answer to a peremptory beckoning finger from the Sergeant, who had preceded him. The officer looked overgrown and abnormally muscular in his tight civilian suit of blue serge. I caught a whimsical look in Vance's eyes as his glance followed the man through the open sliding doors.

Weem was just closing the street door, with his sullen, indifferent manner. A moment after we had reached the lower hallway, he turned and, without a glance in our direction as he passed us, went swiftly but awkwardly toward the rear of the house. Vance watched him pass from our line of vision, shook his head musingly, and then went toward the drawing-room.

McLaughlin (whom I remembered from the famous case of Alvin Benson,* when he came to that fateful house on West 48th Street, to report the presence of a mysterious grey Cadillac) was just about to speak to the Sergeant when he heard us enter the drawing-room. Recognizing Markham, he saluted respectfully and stepped to one side, facing us and waiting for orders.

"McLaughlin," Heath began—his tone carried that official gruffness he always displayed to his inferior officers, much to Vance's amusement—"something damn wrong happened in this house last night —or maybe it was early this morning, to be more exact. What time are you relieved from your beat here?"

"Regular time—eight o'clock," answered the man. "I was just fixing to go to bed an hour ago when the Inspector——"

* "The Benson Murder Case" (Scribners, 1926).

"All right, all right," snapped Heath. "I ordered the Department to send you up. We need a report. —Listen: where were you around six o'clock this morning?"

"Doing my duty, sir," the officer assured Heath earnestly; "walking down the other side of the street opposite here, makin' my regular rounds."

"Did you see anybody, or anything, that looked suspicious?" demanded the Sergeant, thrusting his jaw forward belligerently.

The man started slightly and squinted as if trying to recall something.

"I did, at that, Sergeant!" he said. "Only I wouldn't say as how it was suspicious at the time, although the idea passed through my mind. But there wasn't any cause to take action."

"What was it, McLaughlin? Shoot everything, whether you think it's important or not."

"Well, Sergeant, a coupé—it was a dirty green color—pulled up on this side of the street along about that time. There were two men in it, and one of the guys got out and opened the hood and took a look at the engine. I came across the street and gave the car the once-over. But everything seemed on the up-and-up, and I didn't bother 'em. Anyhow, I stood there and watched, and pretty soon the driver got in and the coupé drove away. When it went down the block toward Columbus Avenue, the exhaust was open. . . . Well, Sergeant, there was nothing I could do about it then, so I went back across the street and walked on up to Broadway."

"That all you noticed?"

"No, it ain't, Sergeant." McLaughlin was looking a little uncomfortable. "I was just coming round the corner from Central Park West, back into 86th Street again, about twenty minutes later, when the same coupé went by me like hell—only, this time it was headed east instead of west—and it turned into the park——"

"How do you know it was the same coupé, Mc-Laughlin?"

"Well, I ain't takin' no oath on it, Sergeant," the officer answered; "but it was the same kinda car, and the same dirty-green color, and the exhaust was still open. And there was two guys in it, just like before, and the driver looked to me like the same big, smooth-faced guy who had his head stuck in the hood when I first crossed the street to look the situation over." McLaughlin took a deep breath and gave the Sergeant an apprehensive look, as if he expected a reprimand.

"You didn't see or hear anything else?" growled Heath. "It musta been pretty light at that time of the morning, with the sun up."

"Not another thing, Sergeant," the officer asserted, with obvious relief. "When I first seen the car

I was headed toward Columbus; and I went on down to Broadway, and then swung round through 87th Street to Central Park West and over again on 86th. As I says, it took me about twenty minutes."

"Exactly where was that coupé when you first got a squint at it?"

"Right along the curb, about a hundred feet up the street from here, toward the park."

"Why didn't you ask some questions of them guys in the car?"

"I told you before, there was nothing suspicious about 'em—not until they went by me, going in the other direction. When I first seen 'em I thought they was just a couple of bums goin' home from a joy-ride. They was quiet and polite enough, and didn't act like trouble. These guys was plenty sober, and they was total strangers to me. There wasn't no reason to interfere with 'em—honest to God!"

Heath thought for a moment and puffed on his cigar.

"Which way did the car go when it entered the park?"

"Well, Sergeant, it went into the transverse, as if it was headed for the east side. Even if I'd wanted to grab the gorillas I wouldn'ta had time. Before I coulda got the call-box on the Avenue and talked to the fella over there, the car woulda been to hell and gone. And there was no car or taxi anywhere round that I coulda chased 'em in. Anyway, I figured they was on the level."

Heath turned with annoyance and paced impatiently up and down the room.

"I say, officer," put in Vance, "were both occupants of the coupé white men?"

"Sure they was, sir." The officer answered emphatically, but with an air of deference which he had not shown to the Sergeant. Vance was standing beside Markham, and McLaughlin must have assumed that Vance was speaking for the District Attorney, as it were.

"And couldn't there have been a third man in the coupé?" Vance proceeded. "A smaller man, let us say, whom you didn't see—on his knees, and hidden from view, perhaps?"

"Well, there mighta been, sir,—I ain't swearin' there wasn't. I didn't open either one of the doors and look in. But there was plenty of room in the car for him to be sittin' up. Why should he be lying on the floor?"

"I haven't the remotest idea—except that he might have been hiding because he didn't wish to be seen," Vance returned apathetically.

"Gosh!" muttered McLaughlin. "You think there was three men in that car?"

"Really, McLaughlin, I don't know," Vance drawled. "It would simplify matters if we knew there had been three men in the car. I crave a small pussy-footed fellow."

The Sergeant had stopped his pacing across the room and now stood near the desk, listening to Vance with an amused interest.

"I don't getcha at all, Mr. Vance," he muttered respectfully. "Two tough guys is enough for any snatch."

"Oh, quite, Sergeant. As you say. Two are quite sufficient," Vance returned somewhat cryptically. Again he addressed himself to McLaughlin. "By the by, officer, did you, by any chance, stumble upon a ladder during your nocturnal circuit in these parts last night?"

"I seen a ladder, if that's what you mean," the man admitted. "It was leanin' up against that maple tree in the garden out here. I noticed it when it began to get light. But I figured it was only being used to prune the tree, or something. There certainly wasn't any use in reportin' a ladder in a gent's yard, was there?"

"Oh, no," Vance assured him indifferently. "Silly idea, going about reportin' ladders—eh, what? . . . That ladder's still in the yard, officer; only, this morning it was restin' up against the house, under an open window."

"Honest to God?" McLaughlin's eyes grew bigger. "I hope it was O.-K. not to report it."

"Oh, quite," Vance encouraged him. "It wouldn't have done a particle of good, anyway. Some one, don't y' know, moved it from the tree and placed it against the house while you were strollin' up Broadway and round 87th Street. Probably doesn't mean anything of any particular importance, however. . . . I say, did you ever notice a ladder in this yard before?"

The man shook his head ponderously.

"No, sir," he said, with a certain vague emphasis. "Can't say that I ever have. They generally keep that yard looking pretty neat and nice."

"Thanks awfully." Vance sauntered to the sofa and sat down lazily, stretching his legs out before him. It was obvious he had no other questions to put to the officer.

Heath straightened up and took the cigar from his mouth.

"That's all, McLaughlin. Much obliged for coming down. Go on home and hit the hay. I may, and may not, want to see you again later."

The officer saluted half-heartedly and went toward the door.

"Look here, Sergeant," he said, halting and turning around. "Do you mind telling me what happened here last night? You got me worryin' about that coupé."

"Oh, nothing much happened, I guess. A phony

snatch of some kind. It don't look serious, but we have to check up. Young fella named Kaspar Kenting ain't anywhere abouts. And there was a cock-eyed ransom note."

The officer seemed speechless for a moment. Then he half gasped.

"Honest? Jeez!"

"Do you know him, McLaughlin?"

"Sure I know him. I see him lots of times coming home at all hours of the mornin'. Half the time he's pie-eyed."

Heath showed no further inclination to talk, and McLaughlin went lumbering from the room. A moment later the front door shut noisily after him.

"What now, Mr. Vance?" Heath was again resting his weight against the desk, puffing vigorously on his cigar.

Vance drew in his legs, as if with great effort, and sighed.

"Oh, much more, Sergeant," he yawned in answer. "You haven't the faintest idea of how much I'd really like to learn about a number of things. . . ."

"But see here, Vance," interrupted Markham, "I first want to know what you meant by that statement you made as we were coming down the stairs. I can't see it at all, and I'd bet money that fellow Kaspar is as safe as you or I."

"I'm afraid you'd lose your wager, old dear."

"But all the evidence points——" began Markham.

"Please, oh, please, Markham," implored Vance. "Must we necessarily lean wherever a finger points? I say, let's get the completed picture first. Then we can speak with more or less certainty about the indications. Can't a johnnie hazard a guess without being quizzed by the great Prosecutor for the Common People?"

"Damn it, Vance!" Markham returned angrily; "drop the persiflage and get down to business. I want to know why you said what you did on the stairs, in the face of all the evidence to the contrary. Are you in possession of any facts to which I have not had access?"

"Oh, no—no," replied Vance mildly, stretching out still further in the chair. "You've seen and heard everything I have. Only, we interpret the findin's in different ways."

"All right." Markham made an effort to curb his impatience. "Let's hear how you interpret these facts."

"Pardon me, Chief," put in Heath; "I didn't hear what Mr. Vance said to you on the stairs. I don't know what his ideas on the case are."

Markham took the cigar from his mouth and looked at the Sergeant.

"Mr. Vance doesn't believe that Kaspar Kenting

was kidnapped merely for money or that he may have walked out and staged the kidnapping himself. He said he thinks that the fellow is already dead."

Heath spun round abruptly to Vance.

"The hell you say!" he exclaimed. "How in the name of God did you get such an idea, Mr. Vance?"

Vance smoked a moment before replying. Then he spoke as if the explanation were of no importance:

"My word, Sergeant! It seems sufficiently indicated."

He paused again and looked back meditatively to the District Attorney, who was standing before him, teetering impatiently on his toes.

"Do you really think, Markham, that your plotting Kaspar would have gone to the Jersey casino to indulge in a bit of gamblin' on his big night—that is to say, on the night he intended to carry out his *grand coup* involvin' fifty thousand dollars?"

"And why not?" Markham wanted to know.

"It's quite obvious this criminal undertaking was carefully prepared in advance. The note itself is sufficient evidence of this, with its letters and words painstakingly cut out and all neatly pasted on a piece of disguised paper."

"The criminal undertaking, as you call it, need not necessarily have been prepared very far in advance," objected Markham. "Kaspar would have had time to do his cutting and pasting when he returned from the casino."

"Oh, no, I don't think so," Vance returned at once. "I took a good look at the desk and the wastepaper basket. No evidence whatever of such activity. Moreover, the johnnie's phone call in the wee hours of the morning shows a certain amount of expectation on his part of getting the matter of his financial difficulties settled."

"Go on," said Markham, as Vance paused once more.

"Very good," continued Vance. "Why should Kaspar Kenting have taken three hours to change to street clothes after he had returned from his pleasant evening of desult'ry gambling? A few minutes would have sufficed. And another question: Why should he wait until bright daylight before going forth? The darkness would have been infinitely safer and better suited to his purpose."

"How do you know he didn't go much earlier—before it was daylight?" demanded Markham.

"But, my dear fellow," explained Vance, "the ladder was still leanin' against the tree around dawn, when McLaughlin saw it, and therefore was not placed against the window until after sun-up. I'm quite sure that, had Kaspar planned a disappearance, he would have placed the ladder at the window ere he departed—eh, what?"

"I see what you mean, Mr. Vance," Heath threw in eagerly. "And Mrs. Kenting herself told us that she heard some one in the room at six o'clock this morning."

"True, Sergeant; but that's not the important thing," Vance answered casually. "As a matter of fact, I don't think it was Kaspar at all whom Mrs. Kenting says she heard in her husband's room at that hour this morning. . . . And, by the by, Markham, here's still another question to be considered: Why was the communicatin' door between Kaspar's room and his wife's left unlocked, if the gentleman contemplated carrying out a desperate and important plot that night? He would certainly not have left that door unlocked if he planned any such action. He would have guarded against any unwelcome intrusion on the part of his wife, who had merely to turn the knob and walk in and spoil all the fun, as it were. . . . And, speakin' of the door, you remember the lady opened it at six, right after hearin' some one walkin' in the room in what she described as soft slippers. But when she went into the room there was no one there. *Ergo:* Whoever it was she heard must have left the room hurriedly when she first knocked and called to her husband. And don't forget that it is his heavy blucher shoes that are gone —not his slippers. If it had been Kaspar she heard, imitatin' a slipper-shod gentleman, and if Kaspar had quickly gone out the hall door and down the front stairs, she would certainly have heard him, as she was very much on the alert at that moment. And, also, if he'd scrambled through the window and down the ladder with his heavy shoes on, he could hardly have done so without a sound. But the tellin' question in this connection is: Why, if the soft-footed person in the master bedroom was Kaspar, did he wait till his wife knocked on the door and called to him before he made a precipitate getaway? He could have left at any time during the three hours after he had come home from his highballs and roulette-playin'. All of which, I rather think, substantiates the assumption that it was another person that the lady heard at six o'clock this morning."

Markham's head moved slowly up and down. His cigar had gone out, but he paid no attention to it.

"I'm beginning to see what you mean, Vance; and I can't say your conclusions leave me happy. But what I want to know is——"

"Just a moment, Markham old dear. Just a wee moment." Vance raised his hand to indicate that he had something further to say. "If it had been Kaspar that Mrs. Kenting heard at six o'clock, he would hardly have had time, before he scooted off at his wife's knock, to collect his comb and toothbrush and pajamas. Why should the chappie have bothered to take them, in the first place? True, they are things he could well make use of on his hypothetical jaunt for the purpose of getting hold of brother Kenyon's lucre, but he would hardly go to that trouble on so vital and all-important a venture,—the toilet articles would be far too trivial and could easily be bought wherever he was going, if he was finicky about such details. Furthermore, if so silly a plot had been planned by him he would have equipped himself surreptitiously beforehand and would have had the beautifyin' accessories waitin' for him wherever he had decided to go, rather than grabbin' them up at the last minute."

Markham made no comment, and after a moment or two Vance resumed.

"Carryin' the supposition a bit forrader, he would have realized that the absence of these necess'ry articles would be highly suspicious and would point too obviously to the impression he would have wished to avoid—namely, his own wilful participation in the attempt to extort the fifty thousand dollars. I'd say, y' know, that these items for the gentleman's toilet were collected and taken away—*in order to give just this impression*—by the soft-footed person heard by Mrs. Kenting. . . . No, no, Markham. The comb and the toothbrush and the pajamas and the shoes are only textural details—like the cat, the shawl-fringe, the posies, the ribbon, and the bandanna in Manet's *Olympia*. . . ."

"Manufactured evidence—that's your theory, is it?" Markham spoke without any show of aggressiveness or antagonism.

"Exactly," nodded Vance. "Far too many leadin' clues. Really, the culprit overdid it. An *embarras de richesses*. Whole structure does a bit of topplin' of its own weight. Very thorough. Too dashed thorough. Nothing left to the imagination."

Markham took a few steps up the room, turned, and then walked back.

"You think it's a real kidnapping then?"

"It could be," murmured Vance. "But that doesn't strike me as wholly consistent either. Too many counter-indications. But I'm only advancin' a theory. For instance, if Kaspar was allowed time to change his suit and shoes—as we know he did—he had time to call out, or to make a disturbance of some kind which would have upset all the kind-hearted villain's plans. Hanging up his dinner jacket so carefully, transferring things from his pockets, and putting away his oxfords in the closet, all indicate leisure in the process—a leisure which the kidnappers would hardly have permitted. Kidnappers are not benevolent persons, Markham."

"Well, what *do* you think happened?" Markham asked in a subdued, worried tone.

"Really, I don't know." Vance studied the tip of his cigarette with concern. "We do know, however, that Kaspar had an engagement last night which kept him out until three this morning; and that upon his return here he telephoned to some one and then changed to street clothes. It might therefore be assumed that he made some appointment to be kept between three and six and saw no necessity of going to bed in the interval. This would also account for the leisurely changing of his attire; and it is highly possible he went quietly out through the front door when he fared forth to keep his early-morning rendezvous. Assumin' that this theory is correct, I'd say further that he expected to return anon, for he left all the lights on. And one more thing: I think it safe to assume that the door from his bedroom into the hall was unlocked this morning—otherwise, Mrs. Kenting would have remembered unlocking it when she ordered coffee and went downstairs."

"And even if everything you say is true," argued Markham, "what could have happened to him?"

Vance sighed deeply.

"All we actually know at the moment, my dear Markham," he answered, "is that the johnnie did not come back. He seems to have disappeared. At any rate, he isn't here."

"Even so,"—Markham drew himself up with a slight show of annoyance—"why do you take it for granted that Kaspar Kenting is already dead?"

"I don't take it for granted." Vance, too, drew himself up and spoke somewhat vigorously. "I said merely that I *feared* the johnnie is already dead. If he did not, as it were, kidnap himself, d' ye see, and if he wasn't actually kidnapped as the term is commonly understood, then the chances are he was murdered when he went forth to keep his appointment. His disappearance and the elaborate clues arranged hereabouts to make it appear like a deliberate self-abduction, imply a connection between his appointment and the evidence we observed in his room. Therefore, it's more than likely, don't y' know, that if he were held alive and later released, he could relate enough—whom he had the appointment with, for instance—to lead us to the guilty person or persons. His immediate death would have been the only safe course."

As Vance spoke Heath had come forward and stood close to Markham.

"Your theory, Mr. Vance, sounds reasonable enough the way you tell it," the Sergeant commented doggedly. "But still and all——"

Vance had risen and was breaking his cigarette in an ash tray.

"Why argue about the case, Sergeant," he interrupted, "when, as yet, there is so little evidence to go on? . . . Let's dawdle about a bit longer and learn more about things."

"Learn what, and about what things?" Markham almost barked.

Vance was in one of his most dulcet moods.

"Really, if we knew, Markham, we wouldn't have to learn, would we? But Kenyon Kenting, I ween, harbors a number of fruitful items:—I'm sure a bit of social intercourse with the gentleman would be most illuminatin'. And then there's your friend, Mr. Fleel, the trusted Justinian of the Kenting household: I've a feelin' he might be prevailed upon to suggest a few details here and there and elsewhere. And Mrs. Kenting herself might cast a few more rays of light into the darkness. And let's not overlook old Mrs. Falloway—Mrs. Kenting's mother, y' know—who I think lives here. Exceptional old dowager. I met her once or twice before she became an invalid. Fascinatin' creature, Markham; bulgin' with original ideas, and shrewd no end. And it could be that even the butler Weem would be willin' to spin a yarn or two—he appears displeased and restive enough to give vent to some unflatterin' family confidences. . . . Really, y' know, I think all these seemingly trivial matters should be attended to ere we depart."

"Don't worry about such things, Vance," Markham advised him gravely. "They are all routine matters, and they'll be taken care of at the proper time."

"Oh, Markham—my dear Markham!" Vance was

lighting another cigarette. "The present time is always the proper time." He took a few inhalations and blew the smoke forth indolently. "Really, I'm rather interested in the case, don't y' know. It has most amazin' possibilities. And as long as you've deprived me of attendin' the dog show today, I think I'll do a bit of snoopin' here and about."

"All right," Markham acquiesced. "What is it you wish to focus your prodigious powers on first?"

"My word, such flattery!" exclaimed Vance. "I haven't a single prodigious power—I'm a mere broken reed. But I simply can't bear not to inspect that ladder."

Heath chuckled.

"Well, that's easy, Mr. Vance. Come on round to the yard. No trouble getting in from the street."

And he started energetically toward the front door.

CHAPTER V

ON THE RUNGS OF THE LADDER

(*Wednesday, July 20; 12:30 p.m.*)

We followed the Sergeant through the ponderous front door, down the stone steps, and across the flagstones. The sun was still shining brightly, and there was hardly a cloud in the sky. The light was so brilliant that for a moment it almost blinded me after the dimness of the Kenting interior. The Sergeant led the way thirty or forty feet east, along the sidewalk, until he came to the small gate in the low iron fence which divided the attractively sodded court of the Kenting house from the street. The gate was not on the latch, but stood slightly ajar, and the Sergeant pushed it wide open with his foot.

Heath was first to enter the enclosure, and he walked ahead with arms outstretched, holding us back from a too precipitate intrusion, like a prudent brood-hen guiding her recalcitrant and over-ambitious chicks.

"Don't come too close," he admonished us with a

solemn air. "There are footprints at the bottom of the ladder and we gotta save 'em for Cap Jerym's * plaster casts."

"Well, well," smiled Vance. "Maybe you'll permit me to come as near as Captain Jerym will have to go to perform his sculpture?"

"Sure." Heath grinned. "But I don't want them footprints interfered with. They may be the best clue we'll get."

"Dear me!" sighed Vance. "As important as all that, Sergeant?"

Heath leaned forward and scowled as Vance stood beside him.

"Look at this one, Mr. Vance,"—and the Sergeant pointed to an impression in the border of the hedge within a foot of where the ladder stood.

"My word!" exclaimed Vance. "I'm abominably flattered by even such consideration as letting me come within viewing distance of the bally footprints." Again taking out his monocle he adjusted it carefully and, kneeling down on the lawn, inspected the imprint. He took several moments doing so, and a puzzled frown slowly spread over his face as he carefully scrutinized the mark in the neatly raked soil of the hedge.

"You know, sir, we was lucky," Heath asserted.

* Captain Anthony P. Jerym, Bertillon expert of the New York Police Department.

"It drizzled most of yesterday afternoon, and around about eight o'clock last night it got to raining pretty hard, though it did clear up before midnight."

"Really, Sergeant! I knew it only too well!" Vance did not look up. "I planned to go to the tennis matches at Forest Hills yesterday afternoon, to see young Henshaw * play, but I simply couldn't bear the inclement weather." He said nothing more for several moments—his entire interest seemed to be centred on the footprint he was inspecting. At length he murmured without turning: "Rather small footprint here—eh, what?"

"I'll say it is," agreed Heath. "Mighta been a dame. And it looks like it was made with flat slippers of some kind. There's no heel mark."

"No, no heel mark," agreed Vance abstractedly. "As you say, no heel mark. Quite right. Obvious, in fact. Curious. I wonder. . . ."

He leaned closer to the impression in the sod of the hedge, and went on:

"But really, y' know, I shouldn't say the print was made by a slipper—unless, of course, you wish to call a sandal a slipper."

"Is that it, Mr. Vance?" The Sergeant was half contemptuous and half interested.

"Yes, yes; rather plain," Vance returned in a low

* The sensational Davis cup winner and America's first seeded player at the time.

voice. "Not an ordin'ry sandal, either. A Chinese sandal I'd say. Slightly turned-up tip."

"A Chinese sandal?" Heath's tone was almost one of ridicule now.

"More than likely, don't y' know." Vance rose and brushed the soil from his trousers.

"I suppose you'll be telling us next that this whole case is just another Tong war." Heath evidently did not deem Vance's conclusion worthy of serious consideration.

Vance was still leaning forward, rubbing vigorously at a spot on one knee. He stopped suddenly and, ignoring the Sergeant's raillery, leaned still farther forward.

"And, by Jove! here's another imprint." He pointed with his cigarette to a slight depression in the lawn just at the foot of the ladder.

The Sergeant leaned over curiously.

"So it is, sir!" he exclaimed, and his tone had become respectful. "I didn't see that one before."

"It really doesn't matter, y' know. Similar to the other one." Vance stepped past Heath and grasped the ladder with both hands.

"Look out, sir!" cautioned Heath angrily. "You'll make finger-prints on that ladder."

Vance relaxed his hold on the ladder momentarily, and turned to Heath with an amused smile.

"I'll at least give Dubois and Bellamy something

to work on," he said lightly. "I fear there won't be any other finger-prints on this irrelevant exhibit. And it will be rather difficult to pin the crime on me. I've an unimpeachable alibi. Sittin' at home with Van Dine here, and readin' a bedtime story from Boccaccio."

Heath was spluttering. Before he could answer, Vance turned, grasped the ladder again, and lifted it so that its base was clear of the ground. Then he set it down several inches to the right.

"Really, Sergeant, you have nothing whatever to be squeamish about. Cheer up, and be more trustin'. Consider the lilies, and don't forget that the snail's on the thorn."

"What's lilies and snails gotta do with it?" demanded Heath irritably. "I'm tryin' to tell you——"

Before the Sergeant could protest Vance had thrown his cigarette carelessly away and was moving quickly up the ladder, rung by rung. When he was about three-quarters of the way up he stopped and made his way down. When he had descended and stood again on the lawn, he carefully and deliberately lighted another cigarette.

"I'm rather afraid to look and see just what happened. It would be most humiliatin' if I were wrong. However. . . ."

Again he lifted the ladder and moved it still farther to the right. Then he went a second time on his knees and inspected the new imprints which the two uprights of the ladder had made in the ground. After a moment he looked studiously at the original imprints of the ladder; and I could see that he was comparing the two sets.

"Very interestin'," he murmured as he rose and turned to Heath.

"What's interesting?" demanded the Sergeant. He again seemed to be nettled by Vance's complete disregard of the risk of making finger-prints on the ladder.

"Sergeant," Vance told him seriously, "the imprints I just made when I mounted the ladder are of practically the same depth as the imprints made by the ladder last night." Vance took a deep puff on his cigarette. "Do you see the significance of the results of that little test of mine?"

Heath corrugated his forehead, pursed his lips, and looked at Vance questioningly.

"Well, Mr. Vance, to tell you the truth——" He hesitated. "I can't say as I do see what it means—except that you've maybe spoiled a lot of good finger-prints."

"It means several other things. And don't stew so horribly about your beloved hypothetical finger-prints." Vance broke the ashes from his cigarette against the ladder, and sat down lazily on the second rung. "*Imprimis*, it means that two men were not on the ladder at the same time last night—or, rather, this morning. Secondly, it means that whoever was on that ladder was a very slight person who could not have weighed over 120 or 130 pounds. Thirdly, it means that Mr. Kaspar Kenting was not kidnapped via yon open window at all. . . . Does any of that help?"

"I still can't see it." Heath was holding his cigar meditatively between thumb and forefinger.

"My dear Sergeant!" sighed Vance. "Let us reflect and analyze for a moment. When the ladder was placed against this window between dawn and six o'clock, before the sun had come up, the ground was much softer than it is now, and any weight or pressure on the ladder would have created imprints of a certain depth in the moist sod. At the present time the soil is obviously drier and harder, for the sun has been shining on it for several hours. However, you noted—did you not?—that the ladder sank into the ground—or, rather, made impressions in the ground—when I mounted it, of equal depth with that of the earlier imprints. I have a feelin' that if I had mounted the ladder when the ground was considerably damper the ladder would have gone in deeper—eh, what?"

"I getcha now," blurted Heath. "The guy who went up that ladder early this morning musta been a damn sight lighter than you, Mr. Vance."

"Right-o, Sergeant." Vance smiled musingly. "It was a very small person. And if *two* persons had been on that ladder—that is, Mr. Kaspar Kenting and his supposed abductor—I rather think the original impressions made by the ladder would have been far deeper."

"Sure they would." Heath was gazing down at the two sets of impressions as if hypnotized.

"Therefore," Vance went on casually, "aren't we justified in assuming that only one person stepped on this ladder early this morning, and that that person was a very slight and fragile human being?"

Heath looked up at Vance with puzzled admiration.

"Yes, sir. But where does that get us?"

"The findings, as it were," continued Vance, "taken in connection with the footprints, seem to tell us that a Chinese gentleman of small stature was the only person who used this ladder. Pure supposition, of course, Sergeant; but I rather opine that——"

"Yes, yes," Markham interrupted. He had been drawing vigorously on his cigar, giving his earnest attention to the demonstration and Vance's subsequent conversation with Heath. He now nodded comprehendingly. "Yes," he repeated. "You see some connection between these footprints and the more-or-less Chinese signature on that ransom note."

"Oh, quite—quite," agreed Vance. "You show

amazin' perspicacity. That's precisely what I was thinkin'."

Markham was silent for a moment.

"Any other ideas, Vance?" he demanded somewhat peevishly.

"Oh, no—not a thing, old dear." Vance blew a ribbon of smoke into the air, and rose lackadaisically.

He cast a meditative glance back at the ladder and at the trimmed privet hedge behind it, which ran the full length of the house. He stood motionless for a moment and squinted.

"I say, Markham," he commented in a low voice; "there's something shining there in the hedge. I don't think it's a leaf that's reflecting the light at that one spot."

As he spoke he moved quickly to a point just at the left of where the ladder now stood. He looked down at the small green leaves of the privet for a moment, and then, reaching forward with both hands, he separated the dense foliage and leaned over, as if seeking something.

"Ah! . . . My word!"

As Vance separated the foliage still farther, I saw a silver-backed dressing comb wedged between two closely forked branches of the privet.

Markham, who was standing at an angle to Vance, started forward.

"What is it, Vance?" he demanded.

Vance, without answering him, reached down and retrieving the comb, turned and held it out in the palm of his hand.

"It's just a comb, as you see, old dear," he said. "An ordin'ry comb from a gentleman's dressing set. Ordin'ry, except for the somewhat elaborate scroll-work of the silver back." He glanced at the astonished Heath. "Oh, no need to be upset, Sergeant. The scrolled silver wouldn't take any clear finger-prints, anyway. And I'm quite certain you wouldn't find any, in any event."

"You think that's Kaspar Kenting's missing comb?" asked Markham quickly.

"It could be, of course," nodded Vance. "I rather surmise as much. It was just beneath the open window of the chappie's boudoir."

Heath was shaking his head somewhat shame-facedly.

"How the hell did Snitkin and I miss that?" His tone carried a tinge of regret and self-criticism.

"Oh, cheer up, Sergeant," Vance encouraged him good-naturedly. "You see, it was caught in the hedge before reaching the ground, and was jolly well hidden by the density of the leaves. I happened to be standing at just the right angle to get a glimpse of it through the leaves with the sun on it. . . . I imagine that whoever dropped it couldn't find it either, and, as time was pressin', the curs'ry search was abandoned. Interestin' item—what?" He tucked the comb into his upper waistcoat pocket.

Markham was still scowling, his eyes fixed inquiringly on Vance.

"What do you think about it?" he asked.

"Oh, I'm not thinkin', Markham." Vance started toward the gate. "I'm utterly exhausted. Let's stagger back into the Kenting domicile."

As we entered the front door, Mrs. Kenting, Kenyon Kenting, and Fleel were just descending the stairs.

Vance approached them and asked, "Do any of you happen to know anything about that ladder in the yard?"

"I never saw it before this morning," Mrs. Kenting answered slowly, in a deadened voice.

"Nor I," added her brother-in-law. "I can't imagine where it came from, unless it was brought here last night by the kidnappers."

"And I, of course," said Fleel, "would have no way of knowing anything about any ladders here. I haven't been here for a long time, and I never remember seeing a ladder around the premises before."

"You're quite sure, Mrs. Kenting," pursued Vance, "the ladder doesn't belong here? Might it, perhaps, have been kept somewhere at the rear of the house without your having seen it?" He looked at the woman with a slight frown.

"I'm quite sure it doesn't belong here," she said in the same muffled tone of voice. "Had it ever been here, I should have known about it. And, anyway, we have no need of such a ladder."

"Most curious," murmured Vance. "The ladder was resting against the maple tree in your courtyard early this morning when Officer McLaughlin passed the house."

"The maple tree?" Kenyon Kenting spoke with noticeable astonishment. "Then it was moved from the maple tree to the side of the house later?"

"Exactly. Obviously the people concerned in this affair made two trips here last night. Very confusin' —what?"

Vance dismissed the subject, and, reaching in his pocket, brought out the comb he had found in the privet hedge, and held it out to the woman.

"By the by, Mrs. Kenting, is this, by any chance, your husband's comb?"

The woman stared at it with frightened eyes.

"Yes, yes!" she exclaimed almost inaudibly. "That's Kaspar's comb. Where did you find it, Mr. Vance,—and what does it mean?"

"I found it in the privet hedge just beneath his window," Vance told her. "But I don't know yet what it means, Mrs. Kenting."

Before the woman could ask further questions Vance turned quickly to Kenyon Kenting and said:

"We should like to have a little chat with you, Mr. Kenting. Where can we go?"

The man looked around as if slightly dazed and undecided.

"I think the den might be the best place," he said. He walked down the hall to a room just beyond the still open entrance to the gem-room, and, throwing the door wide, stepped to one side for us to enter. Mrs. Kenting and Fleel proceeded through the sliding doors into the drawing-room on the opposite side of the hall.

CHAPTER VI

$50,000

(*Wednesday, July 20; 12:45 p.m.*)

Kenyon Kenting followed us into the den and, closing the door, stepped to a large leather armchair, and sat down uneasily on the edge of it.

"I will be very glad to tell you anything I know," he assured us. Then he added, "But I'm afraid I can be of little help."

"That, of course, remains to be seen," murmured Vance. He had gone to the small bay window and stood looking out with his hands deep in his coat pockets. "First of all, we wish to know just what the financial arrangement is between you and your brother. I understand that when your father died the estate was all left at your disposal, and that whatever money Kaspar Kenting should receive would be subject to your discretion."

Kenting nodded his head repeatedly, as if agreeing; but it was evident that he was thinking the matter over. Finally he said:

"That is quite right. Fleel, however, was appointed the custodian, so to speak, of the estate. And

I wish to assure you that not only have I maintained this house for Kaspar, but have given him even more money than I thought was good for him."

"Your brother is a bit of a spendthrift—eh, what?"

"He is very wasteful—and very fond of gambling." Kenting spoke in a guarded semi-resentful tone. "He is constantly making demands on me for his gambling debts. I've paid a great many of them, but I had to draw the line somewhere. He has a remarkable facility for getting into trouble. He drinks far too much. He has always been a very difficult problem—especially in view of the fact that Madelaine, his wife, has to be considered."

"Did you always decide these monet'ry matters entirely by yourself?" Vance asked the man casually. "Or did you confer with Mr. Fleel about them?"

Kenting shot Vance a quick look and then glanced down again.

"I naturally consulted Mr. Fleel on any matters of importance regarding the estate. He is co-executor, appointed by my father. In minor matters this is not necessary, of course; but I do not have a free hand, as the distribution of the money is a matter of joint responsibility; and, as I say, Mr. Fleel has, in a way, complete legal charge of it. But I can assure you that there were never any clashes of opinion on the subject,—Fleel is wholly reasonable and understands the situation thoroughly. I find it an ideal arrangement."

Vance smoked for several moments in silence, while the other man looked vaguely before him. Then Vance turned from the window and sat down in the swivel chair before the old-fashioned roll-top desk of oak at one side of the window.

"When was the last time you saw your brother?" he asked, busying himself with his cigarette.

"The day before yesterday," the man answered promptly. "I generally see him at least three times a week—either here or at my office downtown—there are always minor matters of one kind or another to decide on, and he naturally depends a great deal on my judgment. In fact, the situation is such that even the ordinary household expenses have always been referred to me."

Vance nodded without looking up.

"And did your brother bring up the subject of finances on Monday?"

Kenyon Kenting fidgeted a bit and shifted his position in the chair. He did not answer at once. But at length he said, in a half-hearted tone, "I would prefer not to go into that, inasmuch as I regard it as a personal matter, and I cannot see that it has any bearing on the present situation."

Vance studied the man for a moment.

"That is a point for us to decide, I believe," he

said in a peculiarly hard voice. "We should like you to answer the question."

Kenting looked again at Vance and then fixed his eyes on the wall ahead of him.

"If you deem it necessary, of course——" he began. "But I would much prefer to say nothing about it."

"I'm afraid, sir," put in Markham, in his most aggressive official manner, "we must insist that you answer the question."

Kenting shrugged reluctantly and settled back in his chair, joining the tips of his fingers.

"Very well," he said resignedly. "If you insist. On Monday my brother asked me for a large sum of money—in fact, he was persistent about it, and became somewhat hysterical when I refused him."

"Did he state what he required this money for?" asked Vance.

"Oh, yes," the man said angrily. "The usual thing —gambling and unwarranted debts connected with some woman."

"Would you be more specific as to the gambling debts?" pursued Vance.

"Well, you know the sort of thing." Kenting again shifted in his chair. "Roulette, black-jack, the bird-cage, cards—but principally horses. He owed several book-makers some preposterous amount."

"Do you happen to know the names of any of these book-makers?"

"No, I don't." Once more the man glanced momentarily at Vance then lowered his eyes. "Wait—I think one of them had a name something like Hannix." *

"Ah! Hannix, eh?" Vance contemplated his cigarette for a few moments. "What was so urgent about this as to produce hysterics?"

"The fact is," the other went on, "Kaspar told me the men were unscrupulous and dangerous, and that he feared for himself if he did not pay them off immediately. He said he had already been threatened."

"That doesn't sound like Hannix," mused Vance. "Hannix looks pretty hard, I know, but he's really a babe at heart. He's a shrewd gentleman, but hardly a vicious one. . . . And I say, Mr. Kenting, what was the nature of your brother's debts in connection with the mysterious lady you mentioned? Jewelry, perhaps?"

The man nodded vigorously.

"Yes, that's just it," he said emphatically.

"Well, well. Everything seems to be running true to form. Your brother's position was not in the least

* This was the same Mr. Hannix whom Vance had already met both at Bowie and at Empire, and who had acted as Floyd Garden's book-maker before that young man lost his interest in racing as a result of the tragic events related in "The Garden Murder Case."

original—what? Gamblin' debts, liquor, and ladies cravin' precious gems. Most conventional, don't y' know." A faint smile played over Vance's lips. "And you denied your brother the money?"

"I had to," asserted Kenting. "The amount would almost have beggared the estate, what with so much tied up in what we've come to call 'frozen assets.' It was far more than I could readily get together at the time, and anyway, I would have had to take the matter up with Fleel, even if I had been inclined to comply with Kaspar's demands. And I knew perfectly well that Fleel would not approve my doing so. He has a moral as well as legal responsibility, you understand."

Vance took several deep inhalations on his *Régie* and sent a succession of ribbons of blue smoke toward the old discolored Queen-Anne ceiling.

"Did your brother approach Mr. Fleel about the matter?"

"Yes, he did," the other returned. "Whenever I refuse him anything he goes immediately to Fleel. As a matter of fact, Fleel has always been more sympathetic with Kaspar than I have. But Kaspar's demand this time was too utterly outrageous, and Fleel turned him down as definitely as I did. And— although I don't like to say so—I really think Kaspar was grossly exaggerating his needs. Fleel got the same impression, and mentioned to me over the phone the next morning that he was very angry with Kaspar. He told me, too, that legally he was quite helpless in the matter and could not accommodate Kaspar, even if he had personally wanted to."

"Has Mrs. Kenting any money of her own?" Vance asked unexpectedly.

"Nothing—absolutely nothing!" the man assured him. "She is entirely dependent upon what Kaspar gives her—which, of course, means some part of what I allow him from the estate. Often I think that he does not do the right thing by her and deprives her of many of the things she should have, so that he himself can fritter the money away." A scowl came over the man's face. "But there's nothing I can do about it. I have tried to remonstrate with him, but it's worse than useless."

"In view of this morning's occurrence," suggested Vance, "it may be that your brother was not unduly exaggerating about the necessity for this money."

Kenting became suddenly serious, and his eyes wandered unhappily about the room.

"That is a horrible thought, sir," he said, half under his breath. "But it is one that occurred to me immediately when I arrived here early this morning. And you can be sure it left me uncomfortable."

Vance regarded the man dubiously as he addressed him again.

"When you receive further instructions regarding

the ransom money, what do you intend to do about it—that is to say, just what is your feeling in the matter?"

Kenting rose from his chair and stood looking down at the floor. He appeared deeply troubled.

"As a brother," he said slowly, "what can I do? I suppose I must manage somehow to get the money and pay it. I can't let Kaspar be murdered. . . . It's a frightful situation."

"Yes—quite," agreed Vance.

"And then there's Madelaine. I could never forgive myself. . . . I say again, it's a frightful situation."

"Nasty mess. Rather. Still, I have a groggy notion," Vance went on, "that you won't be called upon to pay the ransom money at all. . . . And, by the by, Mr. Kenting, you didn't mention the amount that your brother asked for when you last saw him. Tell me: how much did he want to get him out of his imagin'ry difficulties?"

Kenting raised his head sharply and looked at Vance with a shrewdness he had not hitherto displayed during the interview. Withal, he seemed ill at ease and took a few nervous steps back and forth before replying.

"I was hoping you wouldn't ask me that question," he said regretfully. "I avoided it purposely, for I am afraid it might create an erroneous impression."

"How much was it?" snapped Markham. "We must get on with this."

"Well, the truth is," Kenting stammered with evident reluctance, "Kaspar wanted fifty thousand dollars. Sounds incredible, doesn't it?" he added apologetically.

Vance leaned back in the swivel chair and looked unseeingly at one of the old etchings over the desk.

"I imagined that was the figure," he murmured. "Thanks awfully, Mr. Kenting. We sha'n't bother you any more just now, except that I should like to know whether Mrs. Kenting's mother, Mrs. Falloway, still lives here in the Purple House."

Kenting seemed surprised at the question.

"Oh, yes," he said with disgruntled emphasis. "She still occupies the front suite on the third floor with her son, Mrs. Kenting's brother. But the woman is crippled now and can get about only with a cane. She rarely is able to come downstairs, and she almost never goes outdoors."

"What about the son?" asked Vance.

"He's the most incompetent young whippersnapper I've ever known. He always seems to be sickly and has never earned so much as a penny. He's perfectly content to live here with his mother at the expense of the Kenting estate." The man's manner now had something of resentment and venom in it.

"Most unpleasant and annoyin' situation—what?"

Vance rose and put out his cigarette. "Does Mrs. Falloway or her son know about what happened here last night?"

"Oh, yes," the man told him. "Both Madelaine and I spoke to them about it this morning, as we saw no point in keeping the matter a secret."

"And we, too, should like to speak to them," said Vance. "Would you be so good as to take us upstairs?"

Kenting seemed greatly relieved.

"I'll be glad to," he said, and started for the door. We followed him upstairs.

Mrs. Falloway was a woman between sixty and sixty-five years old. She was of heavy build and seemed to possess a corresponding aggressiveness. Her skin was somewhat wrinkled, but her thick hair was almost black, despite her years. There was an unmistakable masculinity about her, and her hands were large and bony, like those of a man. She had an intelligent and canny expression, and her features were large and striking. Withal, there was a wistful feminine look in her eyes. She impressed me as a woman with an iron will, but also with an innate sense of loyalty and sympathy.

When we entered her room that morning Mrs. Falloway was sitting placidly in a wicker armchair in front of the large bay window. She wore an antiquated black alpaca dress which fell in voluminous folds about her and completely hid her feet. An old-fashioned hand-crocheted afghan was thrown over her shoulders. On the floor beside her chair lay a long heavy Malakka cane with a shepherd's-crook gold handle.

At an old and somewhat dilapidated walnut secretary sat a thin, sickly youth, with straight dark hair which fell forward over his forehead, and large, prominent features. There was no mistaking mother and son. The pale youth held a magnifying glass in one hand and was moving it back and forth over a page of exhibits in a stamp album which was propped up at an angle facing the light.

"These gentlemen wish to speak to you, Mrs. Falloway," Kenyon Kenting said in an unfriendly tone. (It was obvious that an antagonism of some kind existed between the woman and this man on whose bounty she depended.) "I won't remain," Kenting added. "I think I'd better join Madelaine." He went to the door and opened it. "I'll be downstairs if you should need me." This last remark was addressed to Vance.

When he had gone, Vance took a few steps toward the woman with an air of solicitation.

"Perhaps you remember me, Mrs. Falloway——" he began.

"Oh, very well, Mr. Vance. It is very pleasant to see you again. Do sit down in that armchair there, and try to imagine that this meager room is a Louis-Seize salon." There was a note of apology in her voice, accompanied by an unmistakable undertone of rancor.

Vance bowed formally.

"Any room you grace, Mrs. Falloway," he said, "becomes the most charming of salons." He did not accept her invitation to sit down, however, but remained standing deferentially.

"What do you make of this situation?" she went on. "And do you really think anything has happened to my son-in-law?" Her voice was hard and low-pitched.

"I really cannot say just yet," Vance answered. "We were hopin' you might be able to help us." He casually presented the others of us, and the woman acknowledged the introductions with dignified graciousness.

"This is my son, Fraim," she said, waving with a bony hand toward the anæmic young man at the secretary.

Fraim Falloway rose awkwardly and inclined his head without a word; then he sank back listlessly into his chair.

"Philatelist?" asked Vance, studying the youth.

"I collect American stamps." There was no enthusiasm in the lethargic voice, and Vance did not pursue the subject.

"Did you hear anything in the house early this morning?" Vance went on. "That is, did you hear Mr. Kaspar Kenting come in—or any kind of a noise between three and six o'clock?"

Fraim Falloway shook his head without any show of interest.

"I didn't hear anything," he said. "I was asleep."

Vance turned to the mother.

"Did you hear anything, Mrs. Falloway?"

"I heard Kaspar come in—he woke me up banging the front door shut." She spoke with bitterness. "But that's nothing new. I went to sleep again, however, and didn't know anything had happened until Madelaine and Mr. Kenyon Kenting informed me of it this morning, after my breakfast."

"Could you suggest any reason," asked Vance, "why any one should wish to kidnap Kaspar Kenting?"

The woman uttered a harsh, mirthless chuckle.

"No. But I can give you many reasons why any one should *not* wish to kidnap him," she returned with a hard, intolerant look. "He is not an admirable character," she went on, "nor a pleasant person to have around. And I regret the day my daughter married him. However," she added—and it seemed to me grudgingly—"I wouldn't wish to see any harm come to the scamp."

"And why not, mater?" asked Fraim Falloway

with a whine. "You know perfectly well he has made us all miserable, including Sis. Personally, I think it's good riddance." The last words were barely audible.

"Don't be vindictive, son," the woman reproved him with a sudden softening in her tone, as the youth turned back to his stamps.

Vance sighed as if this interchange between mother and son bored him.

"Then you are not able, Mrs. Falloway, to suggest any reason for Mr. Kenting's sudden disappearance, or tell us anything that might be at all helpful?"

"No. I know nothing, and have nothing to tell you." Mrs. Falloway closed her lips with an audible sound.

"In that case," Vance returned politely, "I think we had better be going downstairs."

The woman picked up her cane and struggled to her feet, despite Vance's protestations.

"I wish I could help you," she said with sudden kindliness. "But I am so well isolated these days with my infirmity. Walking, you know, is quite a painful process for me. I'm afraid I'm growing old."

She limped beside us slowly to the door, her son, who had risen, holding her tightly by one arm and casting reproachful glances at us.

In the hall Vance waited till the door was shut.

"An amusing old girl," he remarked. "Her mind

is as young and shrewd as it ever was. . . . Unpleasant young citizen, Fraim. He's as ill as the old lady, but he doesn't know it. Endocrine imbalance," Vance continued as we went downstairs. "Needs medical attention. I wonder when he had a basal metabolism taken last. I'd say his chart would read in the minus thirties. May be thyroid. But it's more than possible, y' know, he needs the suprarenal hormone."

Markham snorted.

"He simply looks like a weakling to me."

"Oh, yes. Doubtless. As you say, devoid of stamina. And full of resentment against his fellowmen and especially against his brother-in-law. At any rate, an unpleasant character, Markham."

"A queer and unwholesome case," Markham commented, half to himself, and then lapsed into thoughtful silence as he descended the stairs with Vance. When we had reached the lower hall Vance went immediately toward the drawing-room and stepped inside.

Mrs. Kenting, who seemed perturbed and ill at ease, sat rigidly upright on the small sofa where we had first seen her. Her brother-in-law sat beside her, looking at her with a solicitous, comforting air. Fleel was leaning back in an easy chair near the desk, smoking a cigar and endeavoring to maintain a judicious and unconcerned mien.

Vance glanced about him casually and, drawing up a small, straight-backed chair beside the sofa, sat down and addressed himself to the obviously unhappy woman.

"I know you told us, Mrs. Kenting," he began, "that you could not describe the men who called on your husband several nights ago. I wish, however, you would make an effort to give us at least a general description of them."

"It's strange that you should ask me that," the woman said. "I was just speaking to Kenyon about them and trying to recall what they looked like. The fact is, Mr. Vance, I paid little attention to them, but I know that one of them was a large man and seemed to me to have a very thick neck. And, as I recall, there was a lot of grey in his hair; and he may have had a clipped mustache—I really don't remember: it's all very vague. That was the man who came twice. . . ."

"Your description, madam," remarked Vance, nodding his head, "corresponds to the appearance of a certain gentleman I have in mind; and if it is the same person, your impression regarding the clipped mustache is quite correct——"

"Oh, who was he, Mr. Vance?" The woman leaned forward eagerly with a show of nervous animation. "Do you think you know who is responsible for this terrible thing?"

Vance shook his head and smiled sadly.

"No," he said, "I'm deuced sorry I cannot offer any hope in that particular quarter. If this man who called on your husband is the one I think it is, he is merely a good-natured book-maker who is at times aroused to futile anger when his clients fail to pay their debts. I'm quite sure, don't y' know, that if he should pop in here again at the present moment, you would find him inclined to exert his efforts in your behalf. I fear that we must dismiss him as a possibility. . . . But, by the by, Mrs. Kenting," Vance continued quickly, "can you tell me anything definite about the second man that called on your husband?"

The woman shook her head vaguely.

"Almost nothing, Mr. Vance," she returned. "I'm very sorry, but I caught only a glimpse of him. However, I recall that he was much shorter than the first man, and very dark. And my impression is that he was very well dressed. I remember thinking at the time that he seemed far less dangerous than his companion. But I do know that, in the fleeting glimpses I had of both the men, they struck me as being undesirable and untrustworthy characters. And I admit I worried about them on Kaspar's account. . . . Oh, I do wish I could tell you more, but I can't."

Vance thanked her with a slight bow.

"I can understand just how you felt, and how you feel now," he said in a kindly tone. "But I hardly

think that either of these two objectionable visitors
are in any way connected with your husband's disappearance. If they had really contemplated anything,
I seriously doubt that they would have come here to
their proposed victim's home and run the risk of
being identified later. The second man—whom you
describe as short, dark, and dapper—was probably
a gambling-house keeper who had an account against
your husband for overenthusiastic wagering. I can
easily understand how he might be acquainted with
the book-making gentleman who makes his livelihood
through the cupidity of persons who persist in the
belief that past-performance figures are an indication of how any horse will run at a given time."

As Vance spoke he rose from his chair and turned
to Fleel, who had been listening intently to Vance's
brief interchange with Mrs. Kenting.

"Before we go, sir," Vance said, "we wish to speak
with you for a moment in the den. There are one or
two points with which I feel you may be able to help
us. . . . Do you mind?"

The lawyer rose with alacrity.

"I'll be very glad to do whatever I can to be of
assistance," he said. "But I'm of the opinion I can
tell you nothing more than you already know."

CHAPTER VII

THE BLACK OPALS

(*Wednesday, July 20; 1:15 p.m.*)

In the den Fleel seated himself with an easy, confident air and waited for Vance or Markham to speak. His manner was businesslike and competent, despite a certain lack of energy. I had a feeling he could, if he wished, supply us with more accurate and reasoned information than any of the members of the family. But Vance did not question him to any great extent. He seemed uninterested in any phase of the case on which the lawyer might have had information or suggestions to offer.

"Mr. Kenting tells us," Vance began, "that his brother demanded a large sum of money recently, to meet his debts, and that, when the demand was refused, Kaspar went to you as one of the executors of the estate."

"That is quite correct," Fleel responded, taking the cigar from his mouth and smoothing the wrapper with a moistened forefinger. "I, too, refused the demand; for, to begin with, I did not entirely believe

the story Mr. Kaspar Kenting told me. He has cried
'wolf' so often that I have become skeptical, and did
nothing about it. Moreover, Mr. Kenyon Kenting
and I had consented to give him a large sum of
money—ten thousand dollars, to be exact—only a
few weeks ago. There were similar difficulties in
which he said he had become involved at the time.
We did it then, of course, for his wife's sake more
than for his own—as, indeed, we had often done it
before; but, unfortunately, no benefit ever accrued
to her from these advances on her husband's patri-
mony."

"Did Mr. Kaspar see you personally?" asked
Vance.

"No, he did not. He called me on the telephone,"
Fleel replied. "Frankly, I didn't ask him for any
details other than those he volunteered, and I was
rather brusque with him. . . . I might say that
Kaspar has been a trying problem to the executors
of the estate."

"Despite which," continued Vance, "I imagine his
brother, as well as you yourself, will do everything
possible to get him back, even to meeting the terms
of the ransom note. Am I right?"

"I see nothing else to be done," the lawyer said
without enthusiasm. "Unless, of course, the situation
can be satisfactorily adjusted without payment of
the ransom money. Of course we don't know for cer-

tain whether or not this is a *bona fide* kidnapping. Kidnapping is a damnable crime. . . ."

"Quite," agreed Vance with a sigh. "It places every one in a most irksome predicament. But, of course, there is nothing to be done until we have some further word from the supposed abductors. . . ."

Vance looked up and added quickly:

"By the by, Mrs. Kenting has informed us that Kaspar spoke to some one on the telephone when he came home in the early hours of this morning, and that he became angry. I wonder if it could have been you he called again?"

"Yes, damn it!" the lawyer returned with stern bitterness. "It was I. He woke me up some time after three, and became very vituperative when I refused to alter my previous decision. In fact, he said that both Kenyon and I would regret our penuriousness in refusing to help him, as he was certain it would result in some mischief, but did not say just what guise it might take. As a matter of fact, he sounded very much upset, and flew off the handle. But, I frankly admit, I didn't take him too seriously, for I had been through the same sort of thing with him before. . . . It seems now," the lawyer added a little uncomfortably, "that he was telling the truth for once—that it wasn't just an idle conjecture; and I am wondering if Kenyon and I shouldn't have investigated the situation before taking a definite stand."

"No, no; I think not," murmured Vance. "I doubt that it would have done any good. I have an idea the situation was not a new development—although there are, to be sure, few enough facts in hand at present on which to base an opinion. I don't like the outlook at all. It has too many conflictin' elements. . . . By the by, Mr. Fleel,"—Vance looked frankly at the man—"just how large a sum did Kaspar Kenting ask you for?"

"Too large an amount even to have been considered," returned the lawyer. "He asked for thirty thousand dollars."

"Thirty thousand," Vance repeated. "That's very interestin'." He rose lazily to his feet and straightened his clothes. "That will be all, I think, for the moment, Mr. Fleel," he said. "And many thanks for the trouble you've taken. There's little left to be done at the moment, aside from the usual routine. We will, of course, guard the matter as best we can. And we will get in touch with you if there is any new development."

Fleel stood up and bowed stiffly.

"You can always reach me through my office during the day, or through my home in the evening." He took an engraved card from his pocket and handed it to Vance. "There are my phone numbers, sir. . . . I think I shall remain a while with Mrs. Kenting and Kenyon." And he went from the den.

Markham, looking serious and puzzled, held Vance back.

"What do you make of that discrepancy in the amount, Vance?" he asked in a gruff, lowered tone.

"My dear Markham!" Vance shook his head solemnly. "There are many things we cannot make anything of at the present moment. One never knows —does one?—at this stage of the game. Perhaps young Kaspar, having failed with his brother, reduced the ante, as it were, in approaching Fleel, thinking he might get better results at the lower figure. Curious though; the amount demanded in the ransom note corresponds to what he told Kenyon he needed. On the other hand—— I wonder. . . . However, let's commune with the butler before we toddle on."

Vance went to the door and opened it. Just outside stood Weem, bending slightly forward, as if he had been eavesdropping. Instead of showing any signs of embarrassment, the man looked up truculently and turned away.

"See here, Weem," Vance halted him. "Step inside a moment," he said with an amused smile. "You can hear better; and, anyway, there are one or two questions we'd like to put to you."

The man turned back without a word and entered the den with an air of sulkiness. He looked past us all with his watery eyes and waited.

"Weem, how long have you been the Kenting butler?" asked Vance.

"Going on three years," was the surly response.

"Three years," repeated Vance thoughtfully. "Good. . . . Have you any ideas, Weem, as to what happened here last night?" Vance reached in his pocket for his cigarette case.

"No, sir; none whatever," the butler returned, without looking at any of us. "But nothing would surprise me in this house. There are too many people who'd like to get rid of Mr. Kaspar."

"Are you, by any chance, one of them?" asked Vance lightly, watching the other with faint amusement.

"I'd just as soon never see him again." The answer came readily, in a disgruntled, morose tone.

"And who else do you think feels the same way about Mr. Kaspar Kenting?" Vance went on.

"Mrs. Falloway and young Mr. Falloway have no love for him, sir." There was no change in the man's tone. "And even Mrs. Kenting herself has had more than enough of him, I think. She and Mr. Kenyon are very good friends—and there was never any great love between the two brothers. . . . Mr. Kaspar is a very difficult man to get along with—he is very unreasonable. Other people have some rights, sir; but he doesn't think so. He's the kind of man that strikes his wife when he has too much to drink——"

"I think that will be all," Vance broke in sharply. "You're an unspeakable gossip, Weem." He turned away with a look of keen distaste, and the butler shuffled from the room without any sign of displeasure or offense.

"Come, Markham," said Vance. "Let's get out into the air. I don't like it in this house—I don't at all like it."

"But it strikes me——" began Markham.

"Oh, don't let your conscience bother you," interrupted Vance. "The only course we can possibly take is to wait for the next step on the part of our dire plotters." Although Vance spoke in a bantering tone, it was obvious from the deliberate way he lighted a cigarette that he was deeply troubled. "Something will happen soon, Markham. The next move will be expertly engineered, I'll wager. The case is by no means ended with this concocted kidnappin'. Too many loose ends—oh, far too many." He moved across the room. "Patience, my dear chap." He threw the admonition lightly over his shoulder to Markham. "We're supposed to be bustlin' with various anticipated activities. Some one is hopin' we'll take just the route indicated for us and thus be led entirely off the track. But, I say, let's not be gullible. Patience is our watchword.

Patience and placidity. Nonchalance. Let the other johnnies make the next move. Live patiently and learn. Imitate the mountain—Mohammed is trudgin' your way."

Markham stood still in the centre of the room, looking down at the worn early-American art square. — He seemed to be pondering something that bothered him.

"See here, Vance," he said after a brief silence, lifting his head and looking squarely at the other. "You speak of 'plotters' and 'johnnies'—both plural. You really think, then, that this damnable situation is the doing of more than one person?"

"Oh, yes—undoubtedly," Vance returned readily. "Far too many diverse activities for just one. A certain co-ordination was needed—and one person cannot be in two different places at the same time, don't y' know. Oh, undoubtedly more than one person. One lured the gentleman away from the house; another—possibly two—took care of the chappie at the place appointed by the first; and I rather think it more than likely there was at least another who arranged the elaborate setting in Kaspar's room—but this is not necess'rily correct, as any one of the three might have returned for the stage setting and been the person that Mrs. Kenting heard in the bedroom."

"I see what you mean." Markham nodded laboriously. "You're thinking of the two men whom Mc-Laughlin saw in the car in the street here this morning."

"Oh, yes. Quite." Vance's response was spoken casually. "They fit into the picture nicely. But neither of them was a small man, and I doubt if either of them was the ladder-climber in the smallish Chinese sandals. Considerable evidence against that conclusion. That is why I say I'm inclined to think that there may have been still another helper who attended to the details of the boudoir setting—makin' four in all."

"But, good heavens!" argued Markham; "if there were several persons involved in the affair, it may be just another gang kidnapping, after all."

"It's always possible, of course, despite the contr'ry indications," Vance returned. "However, Markham, although I have said that there were undoubtedly several persons taking part in the execution of the plot, I am thoroughly convinced there is only a single mind at work on the case—the main organizing culprit, so to speak—some one who merely secured the necess'ry help—what the newspapers amusingly designate as a master-mind. And the person who planned and manipulated this whole distressin' affair is some one who is quite intimately *au courant* with the conditions in the Kenting house here. The various episodes have dovetailed together far too neatly to have been managed by an outsider. And really, y' know, I hardly think that the Purple House harbors, or is in any way related to, a professional kidnapper."

Markham shook his head skeptically.

"Granting," he said, "for the sake of hypothesis, that you are correct so far, what could have been the motive for such a dastardly act by any one who was close to Kaspar?"

"Money—unquestionably money," Vance ventured. "The exact amount named in the pretty little kindergarten paste-and-paper note attached to the window-sill. . . . Oh, yes; that was a very significant item. Some one wishes the money immediately. It is urgently needed. I rather think a genuine kidnapper—and especially a gang of kidnappers operating for themselves—would not have been so hasty in stating the exact sum, but would have let that little detail wait until a satisfact'ry contact was established and negotiations were definitely under way. And of course, if it had really been Kaspar who had abducted himself for the sake of the gain, the note could be easily understood; but once we eliminate Kaspar as the author of this crime, then we are confronted with the necessity of evolving an entirely new interpretation of the facts. The crime then becomes one of desperation and immediacy, with the money as an imperative desideratum."

"I am not so sure you are right this time, Vance," said Markham seriously.

Vance sighed.

"Neither am I, Markham old dear." He went to the door and opened it. "Let's move along." And he walked up the hall.

Vance stopped at the drawing-room door, bade the occupants a brief farewell; and a minute later we were descending the outside steps of the house into the noonday sunshine of the street.

We entered the District Attorney's car and drove toward Central Park. When we had almost reached the corner of Central Park West, Vance leaned forward suddenly and, tapping the chauffeur on the shoulder, requested him to stop at the entrance to the Nottingham Hotel which we were just passing.

"Really, y' know, Markham," he said as he stepped out of the car, "I think it might be just as well if we paid a little visit to the as-yet-unknown Mr. Quaggy. Queer name—what? He was the last person known to have been with young Kaspar. He's a gentleman of means and a gentleman of leisure, as well as a gentleman of nocturnal habits. He may be at home, don't y' know. . . . But I think we'd better go directly to his apartment without apprising him of the visit by being announced." He turned to Heath. "I am sure you can manage that, Sergeant,

—unless you forgot to bring your pretty gilt badge with you this morning."

Heath snorted.

"Sure, we'll go right to his rooms, if that's what you want, Mr. Vance. Don't you worry about that. This ain't the first time I've had to handle these babies in a hotel."

Heath was as good as his word. We had no difficulty in obtaining the number of Quaggy's apartment and being taken up in the elevator without an announcement.

In answer to our ringing, the door was opened by a generously proportioned colored woman, in a Hoover apron and an old stocking tied round her head.

"We want to see Mr. Quaggy." Heath's manner was as intimidating as it was curt.

The negress looked frightened.

"I don't think Mr. Quaggy——" she began in a tremulous voice.

"Never mind what you think, Aunt Jemima." Heath cut her short. "Is your boss here, or isn't he?" He flashed his badge. "We're from the police."

"Yes, sir; yes, sir. He's here." The woman was completely cowed by this time. "He's in the sittin'-room, over yonder."

The Sergeant brushed past her to the archway at

the end of the foyer, toward which she waved her arm. Markham, Vance and I followed him.

The room into which we stepped was comfortably and expensively furnished, differing little from the conventional exclusive hotel-apartment living-room. There was a mahogany cellarette near a built-in modern fireplace, comfortable overstuffed chairs covered with brocaded satin that was almost colorless, a baby grand piano in one corner, two parchment-shaded table-lamps with green pottery bases, and a small glass-doored Tudor bookcase filled with colorful assorted volumes. At the front end of the room were two windows facing on the street, hung with heavy velour drapes and topped with scrolled-metal cornices.

As we entered, a haggard, dissipated-looking man of about forty rose from a low lounging chair in one corner of the room. He seemed both surprised and resentful at our intrusion. He was an attractive man, with finely chiseled features, but not a man whom one could call handsome. He was unmistakably the gambler type—that is, the type one sees habitually at gaming houses and the race-track. There was weariness and pallor in his face that morning, and his eyelids were œdematous and drawn down at the corners, like those of a man suffering with Bright's disease. He was still in evening clothes, and his linen was the worse for wear. He wore patent leather pumps which showed distinct traces of dried mud.

Before he could speak Vance addressed him courteously.

"Forgive our unceremonious entry. You're Mr. Porter Quaggy, I believe?"

The man's eyes became cold.

"What if I am?" he demanded. "I don't understand why you——"

"You will in a moment, sir," Vance broke in ingratiatingly. And he introduced himself, as well as Markham and Heath and me. "We have just come from the Kentings' down the street," he went on. "A calamity took place there early this morning, and we understand from Mrs. Kaspar Kenting that Mr. Kenting was with you last night."

Quaggy's eyes narrowed to mere slits.

"Has anything happened to Kaspar?" he asked. He turned to the cellarette and poured himself a generous drink of whiskey. He gulped it down and repeated his question.

"We'll get to that later," Vance replied. "Tell me, what time did you and Mr. Kenting get home last night?"

"Who said I was with him when he came home?" The man was obviously on his guard.

"Mrs. Kenting informed us that you and her husband went together to the opening of a casino in Jersey last night, and that Mr. Kenting returned

somewhere around three o'clock in the morning. Is
that correct?"

The man hesitated.

"Even if it is true, what of it?" he asked after a
moment.

"Nothing—really nothing of any importance,"
murmured Vance. "Just lookin' for information. I
note you're still bedecked in your evenin' togs. And
your pumps are a bit muddy. It hasn't rained since
yesterday, don't y' know. Offhand, I'd say you'd
been sittin' up all night."

"Isn't that my privilege?" grumbled the other.

"I think you'd better do some straight talking,
Mr. Quaggy," put in Markham angrily. "We're in-
vestigating a crime, and we haven't time to waste.
You'll save yourself a lot of trouble, too. Unless, of
course, you're afraid of implicating yourself. In that
event, I'll allow you time to communicate with your
attorney."

"Attorney hell!" snapped Quaggy. "I don't need
any lawyers. I've nothing to be afraid of, and I'll
speak for myself. . . . Yes, I went with Kaspar last
night to the new casino in Paterson, and we got back,
as Mrs. Kenting says, around three o'clock——"

"Did you go to the Kenting house with Mr. Kenting?" asked Vance.

"No; our cab came down Central Park West, and
I got out here. I wish now I had gone with him. He

asked me to—said he was worried as the devil about
something, and wanted to put me up for the night.
I thought he was stewed, and didn't pay any attention to him. But after he had gone on, I got to thinking about what he'd said—he's always getting into
trouble of one kind or another—and I walked down
there about an hour later. But everything seemed
all right. There was a light in Kaspar's room, and
I merely figured he hadn't gone to bed yet. So I
decided not to disturb him."

Vance nodded understandingly.

"Did you, by any chance, step into the side yard?"

"Just inside the gate," the other admitted.

"Was the side window of his room open? And was
the blind up?"

"The window might have been open or shut, but
the blind was down. I'm sure of that because the
light was coming from around the edges."

"Did you see a ladder anywhere in the court?"

"A ladder? No, there was no ladder. What would
a ladder be doing there?"

"Did you remain there long, Mr. Quaggy?"

"No. I came back here and had a drink."

"But you didn't go to bed, I notice."

"It's every man's privilege to sit up if he wants
to, isn't it?" Quaggy asked coldly. "The truth is, I
began to worry about Kaspar. He was in a hell of
a mood last night—all steamed up. I never saw him

just that way before. To tell you the truth, I half expected something to happen to him. That's why I went down to the house."

"Was it only Mr. Kaspar Kenting that you were thinking about?" Vance inquired with a shrewd, fixed look. "I understand you're a close friend of the family and are very highly regarded by Mrs. Kenting."

"Glad to know it," muttered the man, meeting Vance's gaze squarely. "Madelaine is a very fine woman, and I should hate to see anything happen to her."

"Thanks awfully for the information," murmured Vance. "I think I see your point of view perfectly. Well, your premonitions were quite accurate. Something did happen to the young gentleman, and Mrs. Kenting is frightfully distressed."

"Is he all right?" asked Quaggy quickly.

"We're not sure yet. The fact is, Mr. Quaggy, your companion of yestereve has disappeared— superficial indications pointin' to abduction."

"The hell you say!" The man showed remarkable control and spoke without change of expression.

"Oh, yes—quite," Vance said disinterestedly.

Quaggy went to the cellarette again and poured himself another drink of whiskey. He offered the bottle to us all in general, and getting no response from us, replaced it on the stand.

"When did this happen?" he asked between swallows of the whiskey.

"Oh, early this morning some time," Vance informed him. "That's why we're here. Thought maybe you could give us an idea or two."

Quaggy finished the remainder of his glass of whiskey.

"Sorry, I can't help you," he said as he put down the glass. "I've told you everything I know."

"That's frightfully good of you," said Vance indifferently. "We may want to talk to you later, however."

"That's all right with me." The man turned, without looking up from the liquor stand. "Ask me whatever you want whenever you damn please. But it won't get you anywhere, for I've already told you all I know."

"Perhaps you'll recall an additional item or two when you are rested."

"If you mean when I'm sober, why don't you say so?" Quaggy asked with annoyance.

"No, no, Mr. Quaggy. Oh, no. I think you're far too shrewd and cautious a man to permit yourself the questionable luxury of inebriety. Clear head always essential, don't y' know. Helps no end in figuring percentages quickly."

Vance was at the archway now, and I was just behind him. Markham and Heath had already preceded us. Vance paused for a moment and looked down at a small conventional desk which stood near the entrance. Quickly he adjusted his monocle and scrutinized the desk. On it lay a crumpled piece of tissue paper in the centre of which reposed two perfectly matched dark stones, with a remarkable play of color in them—a pair of black opals!

When we were back in the car and headed downtown, Markham, after a minute or two spent in getting his cigar going, said:

"Too many factors seem to counteract your original theory, Vance. If this affair was plotted so carefully to be carried out at a certain time, how do you account for the fact that Kaspar seemed to have a definite premonition of something dire and unforeseen happening to him?"

"Premonition?" Vance smiled slightly. "I'm afraid you're waxing esoteric, old dear. After Hannix's threat and after, perhaps, a bit of pressure thrown in by the other gentleman to whom he owed money, Kaspar was naturally in a sensitive and worried state of mind. He took their blustering, but harmless, talk too seriously. Suffered from fright and craved the comfort of company. Probably why he went to the casino—trying to put his despondency out of mind. With the threats of the two creditors uppermost in his consciousness, he used them as an argument with both his brother and Fleel. And his invitin' Quaggy home with him was merely part of this perturbation. Simple. Very simple."

"You're still stubborn enough to believe it had nothing to do with the facts of the case?" asked Markham irritably.

"Oh, yes, yes—quite," Vance replied cheerfully. "I can't see that his psychic warnings had anything whatsoever to do with what actually befell him later. . . . By the by, Markham,"—Vance changed the subject—"there were two rather amazin' black opals on the desk in Quaggy's apartment. Noticed them as I was going out."

"What's that!" Markham turned in surprise. Then a look of understanding came into his eyes. "You think they came from the Kenting collection?"

"It's possible." Vance nodded slowly. "The collection was quite deficient in black opals when I gazed upon it. The few remainin' specimens were quite inferior. No self-respectin' connoisseur would have admitted them to his collection unless he already had more valuable ones to offset them. Those that Quaggy had were undoubtedly a pair of the finest specimens from New South Wales."

"That puts a different complexion on things," said Markham grudgingly. "How do you think Quaggy got hold of them?"

Vance shrugged.

"Ah! Who knows? Pertinent question. We might ask the gentleman sometime. . . ."

We continued downtown in silence.

CHAPTER VIII

ULTIMATUM

(*Thursday, July 21; 10 a.m.*)

The next morning, shortly before ten o'clock, Markham telephoned Vance at his apartment, and I answered.

"Tell Vance," came the District Attorney's peremptory voice, "I think he'd better come down to my office at once. Fleel is here, and I'll keep him engaged till Vance arrives."

I repeated the message to Vance while I still held the receiver to my ear, and he nodded his head in agreement.

A few minutes later, as we were about to leave the house, he became unduly serious.

"Van, it may have happened already," he murmured, "though I really didn't expect it so soon. Thought we'd have at least a day or two before the next move was made. However, we shall soon know."

We arrived at Markham's office a half-hour later. Vance did not go to the secretary in the reception-room of the District Attorney's suite in the old Criminal Courts Building, but through the private side door which led from the corridor into Markham's spacious sanctum.

Markham was seated at his desk, looking decidedly troubled; and in a large upholstered chair before him sat Fleel.

After casual greetings Markham announced:

"The instructions promised in the ransom note have been received. A note came in Mr. Fleel's mail this morning, and he brought it directly to me. I hardly know what to make of it, or how to advise him. But you seemed to have ideas about the case which you would not divulge. And I think, therefore, you ought to see this note immediately, as it is obvious something must be done about it at once."

He picked up the small sheet of paper before him and held it out to Vance. It was a piece of ruled note-paper, folded twice. The quality was of a very cheap, coarse nature, such as comes in thick tablets which can be bought for a trifle at any stationer's. The writing on it was in pencil, in an obviously disguised handwriting. Half of the letters were printed, and whether it was the composition of an illiterate person, or purposely designed to give the impression of ignorance on the writer's part, I could not tell as I looked at it over Vance's shoulder.

"I say, let's see the envelope," Vance requested. "That's rather important, don't y' know."

Markham shot him a shrewd look and handed him

a stamped envelope, of no better quality than the paper, which had been slit neatly across the top. The postmark showed that the note had passed through the post-office the previous afternoon at five o'clock from the Westchester Station.

"And where might the Westchester Station be?" asked Vance, sinking lazily into a chair and taking out a cigarette.

"I had it looked up as soon as Mr. Fleel showed me the note," responded Markham. "It's in the upper Bronx."

"Interestin'," murmured Vance. " 'East Side, West Side, All Around the Town,' so to speak. . . . And what are the bound'ries of the district it serves?"

Markham glanced down at the yellow pad on his desk.

"It takes in a section of nine or ten square miles on the upper east side of the Bronx, between the Hutchinson and Bronx Rivers and a zigzag line on the west boundary.* A lot of it is pretty desolate

---

* The Westchester Station of the Post-Office Department, situated at 1436 Williamsbridge Road, at the intersection of East Tremont Avenue, collects and delivers mail in the following territory, starting from Paulding Avenue and Pelham Parkway: South side of Pelham Parkway to Kingsland Avenue; to Mace Avenue; to Wickham Avenue; to Gunhill Road; to Bushnell Avenue; to Hutchinson River; west side of Hutchinson River to Givans Creek; to Eastchester Bay; to Long Island Sound; to Bronx River; to Ludlow Avenue (now known as Eastern Boulevard); to Pugsley Avenue; to McGraw Avenue; to Storrow Street; to Unionport Road; to East Tremont Avenue; to Bronxdale Avenue; to Van Nest Avenue; to Paulding Avenue; to Pelham Parkway.

territory, and can probably be eliminated without consideration. As a matter of fact, it's the toughest district in New York in which to trace any one by a postmark."

Vance nodded casually and, opening the note, adjusted his monocle and read the pencil-scrawled communication carefully. It ran:

> Sir: I no you and famly have money and unless 50 thousand $ is placed in hole of oke tree 200 foot west of Southeast corner of old resivore in central park thursday at leven oclock at nite we will kill Casper Kenton. This is finel. If you tell police deel is off and we will no it. We are watching every move you make.

The ominous message was signed with interlocking squares made with brush strokes, like those we had already seen on the ransom note found pinned to the window-sill of the Kenting house.

"No more original than the first communication," commented Vance dryly. "And it strikes me, offhand, that the person who worded this threatening epistle is not as unschooled as he would have us believe. . . ."

He looked up at the lawyer, who was watching him intently.

"Just what are your ideas on the situation, Mr. Fleel?" he asked.

"Personally," the man said, "I am willing to leave the whole matter to Mr. Markham here, and his advisors. I—I don't know exactly what to say—I'd rather not offer any suggestions. The ransom demands can't possibly be met out of the estate, as what funds were entrusted to me are largely in long-term bonds. However, I feel sure that Mr. Kenyon Kenting will be able to get the necessary amount together and take care of the situation—if that is his wish. The decision, naturally, must be left entirely up to him."

"Does he know of this note?" asked Vance.

Fleel shook his head in negation.

"Not yet," he said, "unless he, too, received a copy. I brought this one immediately to Mr. Markham. But my opinion is that Kenyon should know about it, and it was my intention to go to the Kenting house from here and inform Kenyon of this new development. He is not at his office this morning, and I imagine he is spending the day with Mrs. Kenting. I'll do nothing, however, without the consent of Mr. Markham." He looked toward the District Attorney as if he expected an answer to his remark.

Markham had risen, and now moved toward one of the windows which looked out into Franklin Street and over the grey walls of the Tombs. His hands were clasped behind him, and an unlighted cigar hung listlessly from his lips. It was Markham's characteristic attitude when he was making an important decision. After a while he turned, came back to the desk, and reseated himself.

"Mr. Fleel," he said slowly, "I think you should go to Kenyon Kenting at once, and tell him the exact circumstances." There was a hesitant note in his words, as if he had reached a decision but was uncertain as to the feasibility of its logical application.

"I'm glad you feel that way, Mr. Markham," the lawyer said, "for I certainly believe that he is entitled to know. After all, if a decision is to be made regarding the money, he must be the one to make it." He rose as he spoke, taking his hat from the floor beside him. With ponderous steps he moved toward the door.

"I quite agree with you both," murmured Vance, who was drawing vigorously on his cigarette and looking straight before him into space. "Only, I would ask you, Mr. Fleel, to remain at the Kenting house until Mr. Markham and I arrive there. We will be joining you very soon."

"I'll wait," mumbled Fleel as he passed through the swinging leather door out to the reception-room.

Vance settled back in his chair, stretched out his long legs, and gazed dreamily through the window. Markham watched him expectantly for some time without speaking. At last it seemed that he could bear the silence no longer, and he asked anxiously:

"Well, Vance, what do you think?"

"So many things," Vance told him, "that I couldn't begin to enumerate them. All probably frivolous and worthless."

"Well, to be more specific," Markham went on, endeavoring to control his rising anger, "what do you think of that note you have there?"

"Quite authentic—oh, quite," Vance returned without hesitation. "As I said, the money is passionately desired. Hasty business is afoot. A bit too precipitate for my liking, however. But there's no overlooking the earnestness of the request. I've a feelin' something must be done without loss of time."

"The instructions seem somewhat vague."

"No. Oh, no, Markham. On the contr'ry. Quite explicit. I know the tree well. Romantic lovers leave *billets-doux* there. No difficulties in that quarter. Quiet spot. All approaches visible. As good a crossroads as any for the transaction of dirty work. However, it could be adequately covered by the police. I wonder. . . ."

Markham was silent for a long time, smoking intently, his brow deeply corrugated.

"This situation upsets me," he rumbled at length. "The newspapers were full of it this morning, as you may have noticed. The police are being condemned for refusing information to the federal boys. Maybe it would have been best if I had washed my hands of it all in the first place. I don't like it—it's poison. And there's nothing to go on. I was trusting, as usual, to your impressions."

"Let us not repine, Markham old dear," Vance encouraged him. "It was only yesterday the bally thing happened."

"But I must get some action," Markham asserted, striking his clenched fist on the desk. "This new note changes the whole complexion of things."

"Tut, tut." Vance's admonition was almost frivolous. "Really, y' know, it changes nothing. *It was precisely what I was waitin' for.*"

"Well," snapped Markham, "now that you have it, what do you intend to do?"

Vance looked at the District Attorney in mock surprise.

"Why, I intend to go to the Purple House," he said calmly. "I'm not psychic, but something tells me we shall find a hand pointin' to our future activities when we arrive there."

"Well, if that's your idea," demanded Markham, "why didn't you go with Fleel?"

"Merely wished to give him sufficient time to break the news to the others and to discuss the matter with brother Kenyon." Vance expelled a series of smoke rings toward the chandelier. "Nothing like letting every one know the details of the case. We'll get forrader that way."

Markham half closed his eyes and regarded Vance appraisingly.

"You think, perhaps," he asked, "that Kenyon Kenting is going to try to raise the money and meet the demands of that outrageous note?"

"It's quite possible, don't y' know. And I rather think he'll want the police to give him a free hand. Anyway, it's time we were toddlin' out and ascertainin'." Vance struggled to his feet and adjusted his Bangkok hat carefully. "Could you bear to come along, Markham?"

Markham pressed a buzzer under the ledge of his desk and gave various instructions to the secretary who answered his call.

"This thing is too important," he said as he turned back to Vance. "I'm joining you." He glanced at his watch. "My car is downstairs."

And we went out through the private office and judges' chambers and descended in the special elevator.

CHAPTER IX

DECISIONS ARE REACHED

(Thursday, July 21; 11:15 a.m.)

At the Kenting residence we found Kenyon Kenting, Fleel, young Falloway, and Porter Quaggy assembled in the drawing-room. They all seemed solemn and tense, and greeted us with grave restraint that suited the occasion.

"Did you bring the note with you, gentlemen?" Kenting asked immediately, with frightened eagerness. "Fleel told me just what's in it, but I'd like to see the message itself."

Vance nodded and took the note from his pocket, placing it on the small desk near him.

"It's the usual thing," he said. "I doubt if you'll find any more in it than Mr. Fleel has reported to you."

Kenting, without a word, bustled across the room, took the folded piece of paper from its envelope, and read it carefully as he smoothed it out on the green blotting pad.

137

"What do you think should be done about it?" Markham asked him. "Personally, I'm not inclined to have you meet that demand just yet."

Kenting shook his head in perturbed silence. At last he said:

"I'd always feel guilty and selfish if I did anything else. If I didn't comply with this request and anything should really happen to Kaspar———"

He left the sentence unfinished as he turned and rested against the edge of the desk, looking dolefully down at the floor.

"But I've no idea exactly how I'm going to raise that much money—and at such short notice. It'll pretty well break me, even if I can manage to get it together."

"I can help contribute to the fund," offered Quaggy, in a hard tone, looking up from his chair in the shadows of the room.

"And I'd like to do something, too," put in Fleel, "but, as you know, my personal funds are pretty well depleted at this time. As a trustee of the Kenting estate I couldn't use that money for such a purpose without a court order. And I couldn't get one in such a limited time."

Fraim Falloway stood back against the wall, listening intently. A half-smoked cigarette drooped limply between his thick, colorless lips.

"Why don't you let it go?" he suggested, with

malicious querulousness. "Kaspar's not worth that much money to any one, if you ask me. And how do you know you're going to save his life, anyway?"

"Shut up, Fraim!" snapped Kenting. "Your opinion hasn't been asked for."

Young Falloway shrugged indifferently and said nothing. The ashes from his cigarette fell over his shiny black suit, but he did not take the trouble to brush them off.

"I say, Mr. Fleel," put in Vance, "just what would be the financial standing of Mrs. Kenting in the hypothetical case that Kaspar Kenting should die? Would she benefit by his demise—that is, to whom would Kaspar Kenting's share in the estate go?"

"To his wife," answered Fleel. "It was so stipulated in Karl Kenting's will, although he did not know Mrs. Kenting at the time, as Kaspar was not yet married. But the will clearly states that his share of the inheritance should go to his wife if he were married and she survived him."

"Sure," said Fraim Falloway sulkily, "my sister gets everything, and there are no strings attached to it. Kaspar has never done the right thing by Sis, anyway, and it's about time she was coming in for something. That's why I say it's rank nonsense to give up all this money to get Kaspar back. Nobody here thinks he's worth fifty cents, if they'll be frank."

"A sweet and lovable point of view," murmured Vance. "I suppose your sister is very lenient with you whenever possible?"

It was Kenyon Kenting who answered.

"That's it exactly, Mr. Vance. She's the kind that would sacrifice everything for her brother and her mother. That's natural, perhaps. But, after all, Kaspar is my brother, and *I* think something ought to be done about it, even on the mere chance it may save him, if it *does* take practically every cent I've got in the world. But I'm willing to go through with it, if you gentlemen and the police will agree to keep entirely out of it, until I have found out what I can do without any official assistance which might frighten off the kidnappers."

He looked at Markham apologetically and then added:

"You see, I discussed the point with Mr. Fleel just before you gentlemen arrived. We are agreed that the police should allow me a clear field in handling this matter in exact accordance with the instructions in the note; for if it is true, don't you see, that the kidnappers are watching my moves, and if they so much as suspect that the police are waiting for them, they may not act at all, and Kaspar would still remain in jeopardy."

Markham nodded thoughtfully.

"I can understand your attitude in the matter,

Mr. Kenting," he said reassuringly. "And there-fore,"—he made a suave gesture—"the decision on that point must rest solely with you. The police will turn their backs, as it were, for the time being, if that is what you wish."

Fleel nodded his approval of Markham's words.

"If Kenyon is financially able to go through with it," he said, "I feel that that course is the wisest one to follow. Even if it means shutting our eyes momentarily to the legal issues of the situation, he may have a better chance of having his brother safely returned. And that, after all, I am sure you will all agree, is the prime consideration in the present instance."

Vance had, to all appearances, been ignoring this brief discussion, but I knew, from the slow and deliberate movement of his hand as he smoked, that he was absorbing with interest every word spoken. At this point he rose to his feet and entered the conversation with a curious finality.

"I think," he began, "both of you gentlemen are in error, and I am definitely opposed to the withdrawal of the authorities, even temporarily, at this time in such a vital situation. It would amount to the compounding of a felony. Moreover, the reference in the note regarding the police is, I believe, merely an attempt at intimidation. I can see no valid reason why the police should not be permitted a certain discreet activity in the matter." His voice was firm and bitter and carried a stinging rebuke to both Kenting and Fleel.

Markham remained silent when Vance had finished, for I am convinced he felt, as I did, that Vance's remarks were based on a subtle and definite motivation. They had their effect on Kenting as well, for it was obvious that he was definitely wavering. And even Fleel seemed to be considering the point anew.

"You may be right, Mr. Vance," Kenting admitted finally in a hesitant tone. "On second thought, I am inclined to follow your suggestion."

"You're all stupid," mumbled Falloway. Then he leaned forward. His eyes opened wide, his jowls sagged and he burst forth hysterically: "It's Kaspar, Kaspar, *Kaspar!* He's no good anyway, and he's the only one that gets a break around here. Nobody thinks of any one else but Kaspar. . . ." His voice was high-pitched and ended in a scream.

"Shut up, you ninny," ordered Kenting. "What are you doing down here, anyway? Go on up to your room."

Falloway sneered without replying, walked across the room, and threw himself into a large upholstered chair by the window.

"Well, what's the decision, gentlemen?" asked Markham, in a calm, quiet tone. "Are we to go ahead on the basis of your paying the ransom alone, or shall I turn the case over to the Police Department to handle as they see fit?"

Kenting stood up and took a deep breath.

"I think I'll go down to my office now," he said wearily, "and try to raise the cash." Then he added to Markham, "And I think the police had better go ahead with the case." He turned quickly to Fleel with an interrogative look.

"I'm sorry I can't advise you, Kenyon," the lawyer said in answer to Kenting's unstated question. "It's a damned difficult problem on which to offer positive advice. But if you decide to take this step, I think I should leave the details in the hands of Mr. Markham. If I can be of any help——"

"Oh, don't worry, Fleel, I'll get in touch with you." Kenting turned to the dark corner of the room. "And thank you, Quaggy, for your kindness; but I think I can handle the situation without your assistance, though we all appreciate your generous offer."

Markham was evidently becoming impatient.

"I will be at my office," he said, "until five o'clock this afternoon. I'll expect you to communicate with me before that time, Mr. Kenting."

"Oh, I will—without fail," returned Kenting, with a mirthless laugh. "I'll be there in person, if I can possibly manage it." With a listless wave of the hand, he went from the room and out the front door.

Fleel followed a few moments later, but Fraim

Falloway still sat brooding sneeringly by the window.

Quaggy rose from his chair and confronted Markham.

"I think I'll remain a while," he said, "and speak to Mrs. Kenting."

"Oh, by all means," agreed Vance. "I'm sure the young woman needs cheering up." He went to the desk, refolded the note carefully, and, placing it in its envelope, slipped it into an inside pocket. Then he motioned to Markham, and we went out into the sultry summer noon.

When we were back at the District Attorney's office, Markham sent immediately for Heath. As soon as the Sergeant arrived from Centre Street, a short time later, the situation was outlined to him, and he was shown the letter which Fleel had received. He read the note hastily and looked up.

"If you ask me, I wouldn't give those babies a nickel," he commented gruffly. "But if this fellow Kenyon Kenting insists, I suppose we'll have to let him do it. Too much responsibility in tryin' to stop him."

"Exactly," assented Markham emphatically. "Do you know where this particular tree is in Central Park, Sergeant?"

"Hah!" Heath said explosively. "I've seen it so often, I'm sick of lookin' at it. But it's not a bad location, at that. It's near the traffic lanes, and you can see in all directions from there."

"Could you and the boys cover it," asked Markham, "in case Mr. Kenting does go through with this and we decide it would be best to have the spot under surveillance?"

"Leave that to me, Chief," the Sergeant returned confidently. "There's lots of ways of doing it. Searchlights from the houses along Fifth Avenue could light up the place like daytime when we're ready. And some of the boys hiding in taxicabs, or even up the tree itself, could catch the baby who takes the money and tie him up in bow-knots."

"On the other hand, Sergeant," Markham demurred, "it might be better to let the ransom money go, so we can get young Kenting back—that is, if the abductors are playing straight."

"Playing straight!" Heath repeated with contempt. "Say, Chief, did you ever know any of these palookas to be on the level? I says, let's catch the guy who comes after the money, and we'll give him the works at Headquarters and turn him inside out. There won't be nothing we won't know when the boys get through shellackin' him. Then we can save the money and get this no-good Kaspar back for 'em, and round up the sweet little darlings who done it— all at the same time."

Vance was smiling musingly during this optimistic

prophecy of future events. In the pause that followed Heath's last words he spoke.

"Really, y' know, Sergeant, I think you're going to be disappointed. This case isn't as simple as you and Mr. Markham think. . . ." The Sergeant started to protest, but Vance continued. "Oh, yes. Quite. You may round up somebody, but I doubt if you will ever be able to connect your victim with the kidnapping. Somehow, don't y' know, I can't take this illiterate note too seriously. I have an idea it is designed to throw us off the track. Still, the experiment may be interestin'. Fact is, I'd be overjoyed to participate in it myself."

Heath looked at Vance humorously.

"You like to climb trees, maybe, Mr. Vance?" he asked.

"I adore it, Sergeant," Vance told him. "But I simply must change my clothes."

Heath chuckled and then became more serious.

"That's all right with me, Mr. Vance," he said. "There'll be plenty of time for that."

(I knew that the Sergeant wished Vance to take this strategic position in the tree, for despite Vance's constant good-natured spoofing and his undisguised contempt for Heath's routine procedure, the Sergeant had a great admiration and fondness for, not to say a profound faith in, the debonair man before him.)

"That's bully, Sergeant," commented Vance. "What would you suggest as an appropriate costume?"

"Try rompers!" retorted Heath. "But make 'em a dark color." With a snort he turned to Markham. "When will we know about the final decision, Chief?"

"Kenting is going to communicate with me sometime before I leave the office today."

"Swell," said Heath heartily. "That'll give us plenty of time to make our arrangements."

It was four o'clock that afternoon when Kenyon Kenting arrived. Vance, eager to be on hand for anything new that might develop, had waited in Markham's office, and I stayed with him. Kenting had a large bundle of $100 bills with him, and threw it down on Markham's desk with a disgruntled air of finality.

"There's the money, Mr. Markham," he said. "Fifty thousand good American dollars. It has completely impoverished me. It took everything I owned. . . . How do you suggest we go about it?"

Markham took the money and placed it in one of the drawers of his steel filing cabinet.

"I'll give the matter careful consideration," he answered. "And I'll get in touch with you later."

"I'm willing to leave everything to you," Kenting said with relief.

There was little more talk of any importance, and

finally Kenting left the office with Markham's promise to communicate with him within two or three hours.

Heath, who had gone out earlier in the afternoon, came in shortly, and the matter was discussed pro and con. The plan eventually agreed on was that Heath should have his searchlights focused on the tree and ready to be flashed on at a given signal; and that three or four men of the Homicide Bureau should be on the ground and available at a moment's notice. Vance and I, fully armed, were to perch in the upper branches of the tree.

Vance remained silent during the discussion, but at length he said in his lazy drawl:

"I think your plans are admirable, Sergeant, but I really see no necessity of actually plantin' the money. Any package of the same size would answer the purpose just as well, don't y' know. And notify Fleel: I think he would be the best man to place the package in the tree for us."

Heath nodded.

"That's the idea, sir. Exactly what I was thinking. . . . And now I think I'd better be running along—or toddlin', as you would say—and get busy."

CHAPTER X

(Thursday, July 21; 9:45 p.m.)

Vance and Markham and I had dinner at the Stuyvesant Club that night. I had accompanied Vance home where he changed to a rough tweed suit. He had had little to say after we had left Markham's office at five o'clock. All the details for the night's project had been arranged.

Vance was in a peculiar mood. I felt he ought to be taking the matter more seriously, but he appeared only a little puzzled, as if the situation was not clear in his mind. He did not exhibit the slightest apprehension, however, although as we were about to leave the apartment he handed me a .45-automatic. When I put it in my outside coat pocket, where it would be handy, he shook his head whimsically and smiled.

"No call for so much precaution, Van. Put it in your trousers pocket and forget it. As a matter of fact, I'm not even sure it's loaded. I'm taking one myself, but only to humor the Sergeant. I haven't the groggiest notion what's goin' to happen, but I can assure you there will be no necessity for a display

149

of fireworks. The doughty Sergeant's pre-arranged
melodrama is bally nonsense."

I protested that kidnappers were dangerous
people, and that ransom notes with orders of the
kind that Fleel had brought to the District Attorney's office were not to be taken too lightly.

Vance smiled cryptically.

"Oh, I'm not takin' it lightly," he said. "But I'm
quite sure that note need not be taken at its face
value. And sittin' on the limb of a tree indefinitely
is not what I should call a jolly evening's sport. . . .
However," he added, "we may learn something enlightenin', even if we don't have the opportunity to
embrace the person accountable for Kaspar's disappearance."

He slipped the gun in his pocket, buttoned the
flap, and arranged his clothes more comfortably.
Then he donned a soft, black Homburg hat and went
to the door.

"*Allons-y!*"

At eight o'clock we found Markham waiting at the
Stuyvesant Club. He seemed perturbed and nervous,
and Vance attempted to cheer him. In the dining-
room Vance had some difficulties with his order. He
asked for the most exotic dishes, none of which was
available, and finally compromised on *tournedos de
bœuf* and *pommes de terre soufflées*. He had a long
discussion with the *sommelier* regarding the wine,

and he lingered over his *crêpes suzettes* after having explained elaborately to the waiter just how he wished them made. During the meal he was in a gay humor and refused to react to Markham's sombre mood. As a matter of fact, his conversation was limited almost entirely to the types and qualities of the two-year-old horses that year had produced and of their chances in the Hopeful Stakes.

We had finished our dinner and were having our coffee in the lounge, shortly before ten o'clock, when Sergeant Heath joined us and reported the arrangements he had made.

"Well, everything's been fixed, Chief," he announced proudly. "I got four powerful searchlights in the apartment house on Fifth Avenue, just opposite the tree. They'll all go on when I give the signal."

"What signal, Sergeant?" asked Markham anxiously.

"That was easy, Chief," Heath explained with satisfaction. "I had a red electric flood-light put on a traffic-light post on the north-bound road near the tree, and when I switch that on, with a traveling switch I'll have in my pocket, that will be the signal."

"What else, Sergeant?"

"Well, sir, I got three guys in taxicabs stationed along Fifth Avenue, all dressed up like chauffeurs, and they'll swing into the park at the same time the searchlights go on. I got a couple of taxicabs at every entrance on the east side of the park that'll plug up the place good and tight; and I also got a bunch of innocent-looking family cars running along the east and west roads every two or three minutes. On top of that, you can't stop people strolling in the park—there's always a bunch of lovers moving around in the evening—but this time it ain't gonna be only lovers on the path by that tree—there's gonna be some tough babies too. We'll stroll back and forth down the east lane ourselves where we can see the tree; and Mr. Vance and Mr. Van Dine will be up in the branches—which are pretty thick at this time of year, and will make good cover. . . . I don't see how the guys can get away from us, unless they're mighty slick." He chuckled and turned to Vance. "I don't think there'll be much for you two to do, sir, except lookin' on from a ringside seat."

"I'm sure we won't be annoyed," answered Vance good-naturedly. "You're so thorough, Sergeant—and so trustin'."

"What about the package?" Markham asked of Heath.

"Don't worry about that, sir. I got that all fixed too." The Sergeant's voice, though serious and earnest, exuded pride. "I had a talk with Fleel, like Mr. Vance suggested, and he's gonna put it in the tree a little while before eleven. And it's a swell package.

Exactly the size and weight of that bunch of green-backs Kenting brought to your office this afternoon."

"What about Kenting himself?"

"He's meeting us at half-past ten, and so is Fleel, in the superintendent's room at the new yellow brick apartment house on Fifth Avenue. I gave 'em both the number, and you can bet your sweet life they'll be there. . . . Don't you think Mr. Vance and Mr. Van Dine had better be gettin' themselves fixed in the tree pretty *pronto?*"

"Oh, quite, Sergeant. Bully idea. I think we'll be staggerin' along now." Vance rose and stretched himself in mock weariness. "Good luck, and cheerio."

It seemed to me that he was still treating the matter like an unnecessary farce.

Vance dismissed our taxicab at the corner of 83rd Street and Fifth Avenue, and we continued north-ward on foot to the pedestrians' entrance to the park. As we walked along without undue haste, a chauffeur from a near-by taxi jumped to the sidewalk with alacrity and, overtaking us, stepped leisurely in front of us across our path. I immediately recog-nized Snitkin in the old tan duster and chauffeur's cap. He apparently took no notice of us but must have recognized Vance, for he turned back, and when I looked over my shoulder a moment later, he had returned to the cab and taken his place again at the wheel.

It was a warm, sultry night, and I confess I felt a certain tinge of excitement as we walked slowly down the winding flagged pathway southward. There were several couples seated in the dark benches along the pathway, and an occasional shambling pedestrian. I looked at all of them closely, trying to determine their status, and wondering if they were sinister figures who might have some connection with the kidnapping. Vance paid no attention to them. His eyebrows were lifted cynically, and his surroundings seemed not to interest him at all.

"What a silly adventure," he murmured as he took my arm and led me due west into a narrow footpath toward a clump of oak trees, silhouetted against the silvered waters of the reservoir beyond. "Still, who can prophesy? One can never tell what may happen in this fickle world. One never knows, y' know. Maybe when you get atop your favorite limb in the tree you'd better shift your automatic. And I think I'll unbutton the flap on my hip pocket."

This was the first indication Vance had given that he attached any importance to the matter.

Far across the park the gaunt structures on Central Park West loomed against the dark blue western sky, and the lights in the windows suddenly seemed unusually friendly to me.

Vance led the way across a wide stretch of lawn to a large oak tree whose size set it apart from the others. It stood in comparative darkness, at least fifty feet from the nearest dimly flickering electric light.

"Well, here we are, Van," he announced in a low voice. "Now for the fun—if you regard emulating the sparrow as fun. . . . I'll go up first. Find yourself a limb where you won't be exposed, but where you can see pretty well all around you through the leaves."

He paused a moment, and then reaching upward to one of the lower branches of the tree, he pulled himself up easily. I saw him stand up on the branch, reach over his head to the next one, and draw himself up again. In a moment he had disappeared among the black foliage.

I followed at once, although I had not the skill he displayed—in fact, I had to sit down astride the lower limb for a moment or two before I could work myself upward into the outspreading branches. It was very dark, and I had difficulty keeping a sure foothold while I gave my attention to climbing higher. At last I found a fork-shaped limb on which I could establish myself with more or less comfort, and from which I could see, through various narrow openings in the leaves, in nearly all directions. After a few moments I heard Vance's voice at my left—he was evidently on the other side of the broad trunk.

"Well, well," he drawled. "What an experience!

I thought my boyhood days were over. And there's not an apple on the tree. No, not so much as a cherry. A pillow would be most comfortin'.'"

We had been sitting in silence in our precarious seclusion for about ten minutes when a corpulent figure, which I recognized as Fleel, came into sight on the pathway to the left. He stood irresolutely opposite the tree for several moments and looked about him. Then he strolled along the footpath, across the greensward, and approached the tree. If any one had been watching, Fleel must certainly have been observed, for he chose a moment when there was no other person visible within a considerable radius of him.

He paused beneath where I sat twelve or fourteen feet above him, and ran his hand around the trunk of the tree until he found the large irregular hole on the east side; then he took a package from under his coat. The package was about ten inches long and four inches square, and he inserted it slowly and carefully into the hole. Backing away, he ostentatiously relighted his cigar, tossed the burnt match-end aside, and walked slowly toward the west, to another pathway at least a hundred yards away.

At that moment I happened to glance toward the narrow path by which we had entered the park and, by the light from a passing car, I suddenly noticed a shabbily dressed man leaning lazily against a bench in the shadows and evidently watching Fleel as he moved away in the distance. After a few moments I saw the same man step out from the darkness, stretch his arms, and move along the pathway to the north.

"My word!" muttered Vance in the darkness, in a low, guarded tone, "the assiduous Fleel has been observed—which is probably what the Sergeant wished. If everything moves according to schedule we shouldn't have to cling here precariously for more than fifteen minutes longer. I do hope the abductor or his agent is a prompt chappie. I'm gettin' jolly well worn out."

It was, in fact, less than ten minutes later that I saw a figure moving toward us from the north. No one had passed along that little-known, illy-lighted pathway since we had taken our places in the tree. At each succeeding light I picked out an additional detail of the approaching figure: a long dark cape which seemed to trail on the ground; a curious toque-shaped, dark hat, with a turned-down visor extending far over the eyes; and a slim walking-stick.

I felt an involuntary tightening of my muscles: I was not only expectant, but half frightened. Holding tightly with my left hand to the branch on which I was sitting, I reached into my coat pocket and fingered the butt of the automatic, to make sure that it was handy.

"How positively thrillin'!" I heard Vance whisper, though his voice did not sound in the least excited. "This may be the culprit we're waitin' for. But what in the world will we do with him when we catch him? If only he wouldn't walk so deuced slowly."

As a matter of fact, the dark-caped figure was moving at a most deliberate gait, pausing frequently to look right and left, as if sizing up the situation in all directions. It was impossible to tell whether the figure was stout or thin, because of the flowing cape. It was a sinister-looking form, moving along in the semidarkness, and cast a grotesque shadow on the path as it proceeded toward us. Its gait was so dilatory and cautious that a chill ran over me as I watched—it was like a mysterious nemesis, imperceptibly but inevitably creeping up on us.

"A purely fictional character," murmured Vance. "Only Eugène Sue could have thought of it. I do hope this tree is its destination. That would be most fittin'—eh, what?"

The shapeless form was now opposite us and, halting ominously, looked in our direction. Then it peered forward up the narrow winding path and backward along the route it had come. After a few moments the black form turned and approached the cluster of oak trees. Its progress over the lawn was even slower than on the cement walk. It seemed an interminable time before the dim shape reached the tree in which Vance and I were perched, and I could feel cold chills running up and down my spine. The figure was there beneath the branches, and stood several feet from the trunk, turning and gazing in all directions.

Then, as if with a burst of vigor, the cloaked form stepped toward the natural cache on the east side of the trunk and, fumbling round a moment or two, withdrew the package that Fleel had placed there a quarter of an hour earlier.

I glanced apprehensively at the red flood-light on the lamppost Heath had described to us, and saw it flash on and off like a grotesquely winking monster. Suddenly there were wide shafts of white light from the direction of Fifth Avenue splitting the gloom; and the whole tree and its immediate environs were flooded with brilliant illumination. For a moment I was blinded by the glare, but I could hear a bustle of activity all about us. Then came Vance's startled and awestruck voice somewhere at my left.

"Oh, my word!" he exclaimed over and over again; and there was the sound of his scrambling down the tree. At length I saw him swing from the lower limb and drop gracefully to the ground, like a well balanced pole-vaulter.

Everything seemed to happen simultaneously. Markham and Fleel and Kenyon Kenting came rushing across the eastern lawn, preceded by Heath and

Sullivan.* The two detectives were the first to reach the spot, and they grasped the black-clad figure just as it straightened up to move away from the tree. Each man had an arm tight in his clasp, and escape was impossible.

"Pretty nice work," Heath sang out with satisfaction, just as I reached the ground and took a tighter hold on my automatic. Vance brushed by me from around the tree and stood directly in front of Heath.

"My dear fellow—oh, my dear fellow!" he said with quick sternness. "Don't be too precipitate."

As he spoke, two taxicabs swung crazily along the pedestrian walk on the left with a continuous shrill blowing of horns. They came to a jerky stop with a tremendous clatter and squeaking of brakes. Then the two chauffeurs leaped out of the cabs and came rushing to the scene with sub-machine guns poised ominously before them.

Heath and Sullivan looked at Vance in angry amazement.

"Step back, Sergeant," Vance commanded. "You're far too rough. I'll handle this situation." Something in his voice overrode Heath's zeal—there was no ignoring the authority his words carried. Both Heath and Sullivan released their hold on the

---

* A detective of the Homicide Bureau who participated in nearly all of Vance's criminal investigations.

silent figure between them and took a backward step, bumping unseeingly into the startled group formed by Markham, Fleel and Kenting behind them.

The apprehended culprit did not move, except to reach up and push back the visor of the toque cap, revealing the face in the glare of the searchlights.

There before us, leaning weakly and shakily on a straight snakewood stick, the package of false bank notes still clutched tightly in the left hand, was the benign, yet cynical, Mrs. Andrews Falloway. Her face showed no trace of fear or of agitation. In fact, there was an air of calm satisfaction in her somewhat triumphant gaze.

In her deep, cultured voice she said, as if exchanging pleasantries with some one at an afternoon tea:

"How are you, Mr. Vance?" A slight smile played over her features.

"I am quite well, thank you, Mrs. Falloway," Vance returned suavely, with a courteous bow; "although I must admit the rough limb which I chose in the dark was a bit sharp and uncomfortable."

"Truly I am desolated, Mr. Vance." The woman was still smiling.

Just then a slender form skulked swiftly across the lawn from the near-by path and, without a word, joined the group directly behind the woman. It was Fraim Falloway. His expression was both puzzled and downcast. Vance threw him a quick glance, but took no more notice of him. His mother must have seen him out of the corner of her eye, but she showed no indication that she was aware of her son's presence.

"You're out late tonight, Mrs. Falloway," Vance was saying graciously. "Did you enjoy your evening stroll?"

"I at least found it very profitable," the woman answered with a hardening voice. As she spoke she held out the package. "Here's the bundle—containing money, I believe—which I found in the hole of the tree. You know," she added lightly, "I'm getting rather old for lovers' trysts. Don't you think so?"

Vance took the package and threw it to Heath who caught it with automatic dexterity. The Sergeant, as well as the rest of the group, was looking on in stupefied astonishment at the strange and unexpected little drama.

"I am sure you will never be too old for lovers' trysts," murmured Vance gallantly.

"You're an outrageous flatterer, Mr. Vance," smiled the woman. "Tell me, what do you really think of me after this little—what shall we call it? —escapade tonight?"

Vance looked at her, and his light cynical expression quickly changed to one of solemnity.

"I think you're a very loyal mother," he said in a low voice, his eyes fixed on the woman. Quickly his mood changed again. "But, really, y' know, it's dampish, and far too late for you to walk home." Then he looked at the gaping Heath. "Sergeant, can either of your pseudo-chauffeurs drive his taxi with a modicum of safety?"

"Sure they can," stammered Heath. "Snitkin was a private chauffeur for years before he took up police work." (I now noticed that one of the two men who had dashed across the lawn with the sub-machine guns, which they had now lowered in utter astonishment, was the same driver who had crossed in front of us as we entered the park.)

"That's bully—what?" said Vance. He moved to Mrs. Falloway's side and offered her his arm. "May I have the pleasure of taking you home?"

The woman took his arm without hesitation.

"You're very chivalrous, Mr. Vance, and I would appreciate the courtesy."

Vance started across the lawn with the woman.

"Come, Snitkin," he called peremptorily, and the detective walked swiftly to his cab and opened the door. A moment later they were headed toward the main traffic artery which leads to Central Park West.

CHAPTER XI

(*Thursday, July 21; 11:10 p.m.*)

It was but a short time before the rest of us started for the Kenting house. As soon as Snitkin had driven off with Vance and Mrs. Falloway, Heath began to dash around excitedly, giving innumerable brusque orders to Burke,* who came ambling toward us across the narrow path from the east. When he had made all his arrangements, he walked to the wide lane where the second taxicab still stood. This cab, I noticed, was manned by the diminutive Guilfoyle,† one of the two "chauffeurs" who came to the tree with sub-machine guns, ready for action.

"I guess we'd better follow Mr. Vance," Heath growled. "There's something mighty phony about this whole business."

Markham, Fleel and young Falloway got into the back seat of the cab; Kenting and I took our places on the two small folding seats forward in the ton-

---

* Burke was a detective from the Homicide Bureau, who, as a rule, acted as Sergeant Heath's right-hand man.

† Guilfoyle was another detective from the Homicide Bureau, and had helped with the investigation of the "Canary" murder case.

neau; and the Sergeant crowded into the front of
the cab with Guilfoyle. When the doors were shut
Guilfoyle drove off rapidly toward the main roadway
on the west side of the park. Nothing was said on
that short ride. Every one, it seemed, was too dumbfounded to make any comment on the unexpected
outcome of the night's adventure.

Markham sat stiffly upright, looking out of the
window, a dark frown on his face. Fleel leaned back
more comfortably against the cushions in silence,
staring straight ahead but apparently seeing nothing. Fraim Falloway crouched morosely in the
corner of the seat, with his hat pulled far down over
his eyes, his face a puzzled mask; and when I offered
him a cigarette he seemed utterly oblivious to my
gesture. Once or twice on the way to his home he
uttered a cackling, breathless chuckle, as if at some
thought that had flashed through his mind. Kenyon
Kenting, sitting at my left, seemed weary and distressed, and bent forward with his elbows on his
knees, his head bowed in his hands.

Through the plate-glass panel in front of me, I
could see the Sergeant bobbing up and down with
the motion of the cab, and shifting his cigar angrily
from one side of his mouth to the other. Occasionally
he turned to Guilfoyle, and I could see his lips move,
but I could hear nothing over the hum of the motor;
then he would resume his dour and bitter silence. It

was obvious he was deeply disappointed and believed all his plans had gone awry for some reason he could not figure out.

After all, the whole incident that night had been unexpected and amazing. I tried to reason out what had happened, but could not fit any of the known factors together, and finally gave the matter up. The climax of the episode was the last thing I could possibly have dreamed of, and I am sure the others felt the same way about it. If no one had come to the tree for the package of supposed bank notes, it would have been easily understandable, but the fact that a crippled old woman had turned out to be the collector of the money was as astonishing as it was incredible. And, to add to every one's perplexity, there was Vance's attitude toward her—which was perhaps the most astounding thing of all.

Where had been the person who sent the note? And then I suddenly remembered the shabby man who had been leaning against the bench on the pathway, watching Fleel. Could this have been the person?—had he seen us at the tree and known that the spot was under observation?—had he lost his courage and gone off without attempting to secure the package of bills?—or was my imagination keyed up to a pitch where I was ready to suspect every stray figure? The problem was far too confusing, and I could not arrive at even a tentative solution.

When we pulled up in front of the Kenting house, which suddenly seemed black and sinister in the semi-dark, we all quickly jumped to the sidewalk and hastened in a body to the front door. Only Guilfoyle did not move; he relaxed a little in his narrow seat and remained there, his hands still at the wheel.

Weem, in a dark pongee dressing-robe, opened the door for us and made a superfluous gesture toward the drawing-room. Through the wide-open sliding doors we could see Vance and Mrs. Falloway seated. Vance, without rising, greeted us whimsically as we entered.

"Mrs. Falloway," he explained to us, "wished to remain here a short while to rest before going upstairs. Beastly ascent, y' know."

"I really feel exhausted," the woman supplemented in her low, cultured voice, looking at Markham and ignoring the rest of us. "I simply had to rest a while before climbing those long flights of stairs. I do wish old Karl Kenting hadn't put such unnecessarily high ceilings in this old house, or else that he had added a lift. It's very tiring, you know, to walk from one floor to another. And I'm so fatigued just now, after my long walk in the park." She smiled cryptically and adjusted the pillow behind her back.

At that moment there was a ring at the front door, and Heath went out quickly to answer it. As he swung the ponderous door back, I could easily see, from where I stood, the figure of Porter Quaggy outside.

"What do you want?" Heath demanded bluntly, barring the way with his thick body.

"I don't want anything," Quaggy returned in a cold, unfriendly voice; "—if that answer will benefit you in any way—except to ask how Mrs. Kenting is and if you know anything more about Kaspar. I saw you drive past my hotel just now and get off here. . . . Do you want to tell me, or don't you?"

"Let the johnnie come in, Sergeant," Vance called out in a low, commanding voice. "I'll tell him what he wants to know. And I also desire to ask him a question or two."

"All right," Heath grumbled in a modified tone to the man waiting on the threshold. "Come on in and get an earful."

Quaggy stepped inside briskly and joined us in the drawing-room. He glanced round the room with narrowed eyes and then asked of no one in particular:

"Well, what happened tonight?"

"Nothing—really nothing," Vance answered casually, without looking up. "Positively nothing. Quite a fizzle, don't y' know. Very sad. . . . But I am rather glad you decided to pay us this impromptu visit, Mr. Quaggy. Would you mind telling us where you were tonight?"

The man's eyelids drooped still lower, till they were almost entirely shut, and he looked down at Vance for several moments with a passive and expressionless face.

"I was at home," he said finally, in an arctic, aggressive tone, "fretting about Kaspar." Then he suddenly shot forth, "Where were *you?*"

Vance smiled and sighed.

"Not that it should concern you in the slightest, sir," he said in his most dulcet voice, "but—since you ask—I was climbing a tree. Silly pastime— what?"

Quaggy swung about to Kenting.

"You raised the money, Kenyon, and complied with the instructions in the follow-up note?" he asked.

Kenting inclined his head: he was still solemn and perturbed.

"Yes," he said in a low voice, "but it did no good."

"A swell bunch of cheap dicks," Quaggy sneered, flashing Heath a contemptuous glance. "Didn't any one show up to collect?"

"Oh, yes, Mr. Quaggy." It was Vance who answered. "Some one called for the money at the appointed hour, and actually took it."

"And I suppose he got away from the police—as usual. Is that it?" Quaggy had turned again and was contemplating Vance's bland features.

"Oh, no. No. We saw to that." Vance took a long puff on his cigarette. "The culprit is here with us in this room."

Quaggy straightened with a start.

"The fact is," went on Vance, "I escorted the guilty person home myself. It was Mrs. Falloway."

Quaggy's expression did not change—he was as unemotional and noncommittal as a veteran poker player; but I had a feeling the news had shocked him considerably. Before the man had time to say anything Vance continued lackadaisically.

"By the by, Mr. Quaggy, are you particularly interested in black opals? I noticed a jolly good pair of them on your desk yesterday."

Quaggy hesitated for several moments.

"And if I am, what then?" His lips barely moved as he spoke, and there was no change in the intonation of his voice.

"Queer, don't y' know," Vance went on, "that there are no representative black opals in Karl Kenting's collection. Blank spaces in the case where they should be. I can't imagine, really, how an expert collector of semiprecious stones should have overlooked so important an item as the rarer black opal."

"I get the implication. Anything else?" Quaggy was standing relaxed but motionless in front of Vance. Slowly he moved one foot forward, as if shifting the burden of his weight from an overtired leg.

By an almost imperceptible movement his foot came to within a few inches of Vance's shoe.

"Really, y' know," Vance said with a cold smile, lifting his eyes to the man, "I shouldn't try that if I were you—unless, of course, you wish to have me break your leg and dislocate your hip. I'm quite familiar with the trick. Picked it up in Japan."

Quaggy abruptly withdrew his foot, but said nothing.

"I found a balas-ruby in Kaspar Kenting's dinner jacket yesterday morning," Vance proceeded calmly. "A balas-ruby is also missing from the collection across the hall. Interestin' mathematical item —eh?"

"What the hell's interesting about it?" retorted the other with a sneer.

Vance looked at him mildly.

"I was only wonderin'," he said, "if there might be some connection between that imitation ruby and the black opals in your apartment. . . . By the by, do you care to mention where you obtained such valuable gem specimens?"

Quaggy made a noise in his throat which sounded to me like a contemptuous laugh, but the expression on his face did not change. He did not answer, and Vance turned to the District Attorney.

"I think, in view of the gentleman's attitude, Markham, and the fact that he is the last person known to have been with the missing Kaspar, it would be advisable to hold him as a material witness."

Quaggy drew himself erect with a jerk.

"I came by those opals legitimately," he said quickly. "I bought them from Kaspar last night, as he said he needed some immediate cash for the evening."

"You knew, perhaps, that the stones were part of the Kenting collection?" asked Vance coldly.

"I didn't inquire where they came from," the man returned sullenly. "I naturally trusted him."

" 'Naturally,' " murmured Vance.

Mrs. Falloway struggled to her feet, leaning heavily on her stick.

"I've suspected for a long time," she said, "that Kaspar had been resorting to that collection of gems for gambling money. I've come down occasionally and gone over the exhibits, and it seemed to me each time there were a few more missing. . . . But I'm very tired, and I'm sufficiently rested now to return to my room. . . ."

"But, Mrs. Falloway," blurted Kenting—I had noticed that he had been staring at the woman incredulously ever since we had returned to the house, and he could not, apparently, restrain his curiosity any longer; "I—I don't understand your being in the park tonight. Why—why——?"

The woman gave him a withering look.

"Mr. Vance understands," she answered curtly. "That, I think, is quite sufficient." Her gaze shifted from Kenting and she seemed to take us all in with a gracious glance. "Good night, gentlemen. . . ."

She started unsteadily toward the door, and Vance sprang to her side.

"Permit me, madam, to accompany you. It's a long climb to your room."

The woman bowed a courteous acknowledgment and, for the second time that evening, took his arm. Fraim Falloway did not rise to assist his mother; he seemed oblivious to everything that was going on. Markham, with a significant look at the Sergeant, left his chair and took the woman's free arm. Heath moved closer to Quaggy who remained standing. Mrs. Falloway, with her two escorts, went slowly from the drawing-room, and I followed them.

It was with considerable effort that the woman mounted the stairs. She found it necessary to pause momentarily at each step, and when we reached her room she sank into the large wicker armchair with the air of a person wholly exhausted.

Vance took her stick and placed it on the floor beside the chair. Then he said in a kindly voice:

"I should like to ask one or two questions, if you are not too weary."

The woman nodded and smiled faintly.

"A question or two won't do any harm, Mr. Vance," she said. "Please go ahead."

"Why did you make the tremendous effort," Vance began, "of walking in the park tonight?"

"Why, to get all that money, of course," the old woman answered in mock surprise. "Anyway, I didn't attempt to walk all the way: I took a cab to within a few hundred feet of the tree. Think how rich I would have been had I not been caught in the disgraceful act. And," she added with a sigh, "you have spoiled everything for me."

"I'm frightfully sorry," said Vance in a bantering manner. "But really, there wasn't a dollar in that package." He paused and looked down earnestly at the woman. "Tell me, Mrs. Falloway, how you knew your son intended to go to the tree for that ransom package."

For a moment Mrs. Falloway's face was a mask. Then she said in a deep, clear voice:

"It is very difficult to fool a mother, Mr. Vance. Fraim knew of the ransom note and the instructions in it. He knew also that Kenyon would raise the money somehow. The boy came upstairs and told me about it after you had left the house this afternoon. Then, when he came to my room a little before ten o'clock tonight, after having spent the evening with his sister and Kenyon, and said he was going out, I knew what was in his mind—although he very often does go out late of an evening. He invented an important engagement—I always know when Fraim isn't telling the truth, although he doesn't realize that I do. I knew well enough where he was going and what he was going for. I could read it in his eyes. And I—I wished to save him from that infamy." *

Vance was silent for a moment as he regarded the weary old woman with pity and admiration, and Markham nodded sympathetically.

"But Fraim is a good boy at heart—please believe that," the woman added. "He merely lacks something—strength of body and spirit, perhaps."

Vance bowed.

"Quite. He's not well, Mrs. Falloway. He needs medical attention. Have you ever had a basal metabolism test made on him?"

The woman shook her head.

"A blood sugar?" proceeded Vance.

"No." Mrs. Falloway's voice was barely audible.

"A blood count?"

Again the woman shook her head.

---

* Vance's immediate knowledge regarding the exact truth of the situation, when he recognized Mrs. Falloway beneath the tree that night, was another instance of his uncanny ability to read human nature. I myself was startled by the simplicity and accuracy of his logic as the woman confessed the facts; for Vance had reasoned, almost in a flash, that the crippled old woman, who obviously was not guilty of the crime of kidnapping, could not have summoned sufficient strength for so heroic an act, unless it was on behalf of some one very dear to her and whose welfare and protection were foremost in her mind.

"A Wassermann?"

"The truth is, Mr. Vance," the woman said, "he has never been examined." Then she asked quickly: "What do you think it is?"

"I wouldn't dare to venture an opinion, don't y' know," Vance returned, "though I'd say there was an endocrine insufficiency somewhere—an inadequacy of some internal secretion, a definite and prolonged hormone disturbance. It may be thyroid, parathyroid, or pituitary, or adrenal. Or maybe neurocirculatory asthenia. It is deplorable how little science knows as yet about the ductless glands. A great work, however, is being done along those lines, and progress is constantly being made. I think you should have your son checked up. It may be something that can be remedied."

He scribbled something on a page from a small note-book and, tearing it out, handed it to Mrs. Falloway.

"Here is the name and address of one of the country's greatest endocrinologists. Look him up, for your son's sake."

The woman took the slip of paper, folded it, and put it in one of the large pockets of her skirt.

"You are very good—and very understanding, Mr. Vance," she said. "The moment I saw you in the park tonight, I knew you would understand. A mother's love——"

"Yes, yes—of course," murmured Vance. "And now I think we'll return to the drawing-room. And may you have a well-earned night's rest."

The woman looked at him gratefully and held out her hand. He took it and, bowing, raised it to his lips.

"My eternal admiration, madam," he said.

When we re-entered the drawing-room we found the group just as we had left it. Fleel and Kenyon Kenting still sat stiffly in their chairs near the front window, like awed wooden figures. Quaggy stood smoking thoughtfully before the chair where Vance had sat; and Heath, his sturdy legs spread, was at his side, glowering at him morosely. On the sofa, his head drooping forward, his mouth slightly open, and his arms hanging listlessly, lounged Fraim Falloway. He did not even look up as we entered; and the thought flashed through my mind that he might not be a glandular case at all, but that he was merely suffering from the early stages of encephalitis lethargica.

Vance glanced about him sharply and then strolled to his chair. Reseating himself with unconcern, he lighted a fresh cigarette. Markham and I remained standing in the doorway.

"There are one or two matters——" drawled Vance and stopped abruptly. Then he said: "But I think Mrs. Kenting should be here with us for this discussion. After all, it is her husband who has disappeared, and her suggestions might be dashed helpful."

Kenyon Kenting stood up, nodding his head vigorously in approval.

"I think you're right, Mr. Vance," he said, going toward the door. "I'll get Madelaine myself."

"I trust it is not too late to disturb her," said Vance.

"Oh, no, no," Kenting assured him. "She almost never retires so early. She has not been able to sleep well for a long time, and reads far into the night. And tonight I was with her till after half-past nine, and she was terribly keyed up; I know she wouldn't think of retiring till she heard the outcome of our plans tonight."

He bustled from the room as he finished speaking, and we heard him going up the stairs. A few moments later we could hear his sharp, repeated knocking on a door. Then there was a long silence, and the sound of a door being opened hurriedly. Vance leaned forward in his chair and seemed to be waiting expectantly.

A few minutes later Kenting came rushing down the stairs. He stopped in the doorway, glaring at us with wide-open eyes. He looked breathless and horror-stricken as he leaned for support against the door-frame.

"She's not there!" he exclaimed in an awed voice. He took a deep breath. "I knocked on her door several times, but I got no answer—and a chill went through me. I tried the door, but it was locked. So I went through Kaspar's room, into Madelaine's. The lights are all on, but she isn't there. . . ."

He sucked in his breath again excitedly and stammered as if with tremendous effort:

"The window—over the yard—is wide open, and —and the ladder is standing against it!"

CHAPTER XII

(Thursday, July 21; 11:30 p.m.)

Kenyon Kenting's announcement that his sister-in-law was gone from her room and that the portentous ladder was standing below the open window had an instantaneous effect upon the gathering in the drawing-room. Markham and I had stepped into the room, and instinctively both of us turned to Heath who was, after all, technically in charge of the routine end of the Kenting kidnapping case. The wordless feud which had been going on between Heath and Porter Quaggy was immediately forgotten, and Heath was now directing his fierce glance to Kenting as he stood dejectedly in the doorway.

Quaggy's cigarette fell from his lips to the rug, where he stepped on it with automatic quickness, without even looking down.

"Good God, Kenyon!" he exclaimed, half under his breath. The man seemed deeply moved.

Fleel rose to his feet and, as he jerked down his waistcoat with both hands, appeared dazed and inarticulate. Even Fraim Falloway raised himself suddenly out of his stupor and, glowering at Kenting, began babbling hysterically.

"The hell you say! The hell you say!" he cried out in a high-pitched voice. "That's some more of Kaspar's dirty work. He's playing a game to get money, I tell you. I don't believe he was kidnapped at all——"

The Sergeant swung about and grabbed the youth roughly by the shoulder.

"Pipe down, young fella," he ordered. "Makin' fool statements like that ain't gonna help anything."

Falloway subsided and made a nervous search through his pockets till he found a crumpled cigarette.

I myself was shocked and dumbfounded by this startling turn of events. As a matter of fact, I hadn't yet recovered from the strange adventure in the park, and I was totally unprepared for this new blow.

Only Vance seemed unruffled and composed. He always had astounding control of his nerves, and it was difficult to judge just what was his reaction to the news of Mrs. Kenting's disappearance.

Markham, I noticed, was watching Vance closely, and as Vance slowly crushed out his cigarette and got indolently to his feet, Markham blurted out angrily:

"This doesn't seem to surprise you, Vance. You're

taking it too damned calmly to suit me. Had you any idea of this—this new outrage when you suggested that Mrs. Kenting be called?"

"Oh, I rather expected something of the kind, but, frankly, I didn't think it would happen so soon."

"If you expected this thing," Markham snapped, "why didn't you let me know, so that we could do something about it?"

"My dear Markham!" Vance spoke with pacifying coolness. "There was nothing any one could do. The predicament was far from simple; and it's still a difficult one."

Heath had gone to the telephone, and I could hear him, with one ear, as it were, calling the Homicide Bureau and giving officious instructions. Then he slammed down the receiver and stalked toward the stairs.

"I want to look at that room," he announced. "Two of the boys from the Bureau are coming up right away. This is a hell of a night. . . ." His voice trailed off as he went up the steps two at a time. Vance and Markham and I had left the drawing-room and were immediately behind him.

Heath first tried the door-knob of Mrs. Kenting's room, but, as Kenting had informed us, the door was locked. He went up the hall to Kaspar Kenting's room. The door here was standing ajar, and at the far end of the room we could see into Mrs. Kenting's

brightly lighted boudoir. Stepping through the first
chamber, we entered the lighted bedroom. As Kenting had said, the window facing on the court was
wide open, and not only was the Venetian blind raised
to the top, but the heavy drapes were drawn apart.
Cautiously avoiding any contact with the window-sill,
Heath leaned out at the window, and then turned
quickly back.

"The ladder's there, all right," he asserted. "The
same like it was at the other window yesterday."

Vance was apparently not listening. He had adjusted his monocle and was looking round the room
without any apparent show of interest. Leisurely he
walked to the dressing-table opposite the window and
looked down at it for a moment. A round cut-glass
powder jar stood uncovered at one side; the tinted
glass top was resting on its side several inches away.
A large powder puff lay on the floor beneath the
table. Vance reached down, picked it up, fitted it
back into the jar, and replaced the cover.

Then he lifted up a small perfume atomizer which
was resting perilously near the edge of the dressing-
table, and pressed the bulb slightly. He sniffed at
the spray, and set the bottle down at the rear of the
table, on the crystal tray where it evidently belonged.

"Courtet's emerald," he murmured. "I'm sure this
was not the lady's personal preference in perfumes.
Blondes know better, don't y' know. Emerald is suit-

able only for brunettes, especially those with olive complexions and abundant hair. . . . Very interestin'."

Heath was eyeing Vance with obvious annoyance. He could not understand Vance's actions. But he said nothing and merely watched impatiently.

Vance then went to the door and inspected it briefly.

"The night latch isn't on," he murmured, as if to himself. "And the turn-bolt hasn't been thrown. Door locked with a key. And no key in the keyhole."

"What are you getting at, Vance?" demanded Markham. "What if there is no key there? The door could have been locked and the key removed."

"Quite so—theoretically," returned Vance. "But rather an unusual procedure just the same—eh, what? When one locks oneself in a bedroom with a key, one usually leaves the key in the lock. Just what would be the object in removing it? Dashed if I know. . . . It could be, however. . . ."

He went across the room and into the bathroom. This room too was brightly lit. He glanced at the long metal cord hanging from the electric fixture, and with his hand tested the weight of the painted glass cylindrical ornament attached to the end of the chain. He released it and watched it swing back and forth. He looked into the tumbler which stood on the wide rim of the washbowl and, setting it down again, examined the washbowl itself, and around the edges. He then bent over the soap dish. Markham, standing in the bathroom doorway, followed his movements with a puzzled frown.

"What in the name of God——" he began irritably.

"Tut, tut, my dear fellow," Vance interrupted, turning to him with a contemplative look. "I was merely attemptin' to ascertain at just what time the lady departed. . . . I would surmise, don't y' know, that it was round ten o'clock this evening."

Markham still looked perplexed.

"How do you figure that out?" he asked skeptically.

"Indications may be entirely misleadin'." Vance sighed slightly. "Nothing certain, nothing accurate in this world. One may only venture an opinion. I'm no oracle, Delphic or otherwise. Merely strugglin' toward the light." He pointed with his cigarette to the pull-chain of the electric fixture overhead. It was still swinging back and forth like a pendulum, but with a slight rotary motion, and its to-and-fro movement had not perceptibly abated.

"When I came into the bathroom," Vance explained, "yon polished brass chain was at rest—oh, quite—and I opined that its movement, with that heavy and abominable solid glass cylinder to control it, would discernibly continue, once it was pulled and released, for at least an hour. And it's just half-past eleven now. . . . Moreover, the glass here is quite dry, showing that it has not been used for an hour or two. Also, there's not a drop of water, either in the washbowl or on the edge; and a certain number of drops and a little dampness always remain after the washbowl has been used. And, by the by, the rubber stopper is dry. That process, I believe, would take in the neighborhood of an hour and a half. Even the small amount of lather left on the cake of soap is dry and crumbly, which would point to the fact that it had not been used for at least an hour or so."

He took several puffs on his cigarette.

"And I cannot imagine Mrs. Kenting, with her habit of remaining up late, performing her nightly toilet as early as these matters would indicate. And yet the light was on in the bathroom, and there is a certain amount of evidence that she had been powdering her nose and spraying herself with perfume some time during the evening. Moreover, my dear Markham, there are indications of haste in the performance of these feminine rites, for she did not put the perfume atomizer back where it belongs, nor did she stop to retrieve the powder puff from where it had fallen on the floor."

Markham nodded glumly.

"I begin to see what you are trying to get at, Vance," he mumbled.

"And all these little details, taken in connection with the open latch and the unthrown bolt and the missing key in the hall door, lead me—rather vaguely and shakily, I admit—to the theory that she had a rendezvous elsewhere, for which she was a wee bit late, at some time around the far-from-witching hour of ten o'clock."

Markham thought a moment. Then he said slowly:

"But that's only a theory, Vance. It might have been at any time earlier in the evening after the dusk was sufficiently advanced to make artificial light necessary."

"Quite true," agreed Vance, "on the mere visible evidence hereabouts. But don't you recall that Kenting informed us only a few minutes ago that he was here at the house with Mrs. Kaspar Kenting until half-past nine this evening? And have you forgot already, my dear Markham, that Mrs. Falloway mentioned that young Fraim had been with his sister until a short time before he had his important engagement at ten o'clock?—which may have accounted for the lady's flustered state in preparing herself for the rendezvous, provided the assignation was made for ten o'clock. You see how nicely it all dovetails."

Markham nodded comprehendingly.

"All right," he said. "But what follows from all that?"

Without answering the question, Vance turned to Heath.

"What time, Sergeant," he asked, "did you notify Fleel and Kenyon Kenting about the arrangements for tonight?"

"Oh,—I should say——" Heath thought a moment. "Round six o'clock. Maybe a little after."

"And where did you find these gentlemen?"

"Well, I called Fleel at his home and he wasn't there yet. But I left word for him and he called me back in a little while. But I didn't think to ask him where he was. And Kenting was here."

Vance smoked a moment and said nothing, but he seemed satisfied with the answer. He glanced about him and again addressed Heath.

"I'm afraid, Sergeant, your finger-print men and your photographers and your busy boys from the Homicide Bureau are going to draw a blank here. But I'm sure you'd be horribly disappointed if they didn't clutter this room up with insufflators and tripods and what not."

"I still want to know," persisted Markham, "what all this time-table hocus-pocus means."

Vance looked at him with unwonted seriousness.

"It means deviltry, Markham." His voice was unusually low and resonant. "It means something damnable. I don't like this case.—I don't at all like it. It infuriates me because it leaves us so helpless. Again, I fear, we must wait."

"But we can't just sit back," said Markham in a dispirited voice. "Isn't there some step you can suggest?"

"Well, yes. But it won't help much. I propose that first we ask one or two questions of the gentlemen downstairs. And then I propose that we go into the yard and take a look at the ladder." Vance turned to Heath. "Have you your flashlight, Sergeant?"

"Sure I have," the other answered.

"And after that," Vance went on, resuming his reply to Markham, "I propose that we go home and bide our time. The Sergeant will carry on with his prescribed but futile activities while we slumber."

Heath grunted and started toward Kaspar Kenting's room, headed for the hallway.

When we reached the drawing-room we found all four of its occupants anxious and alert. Even Fraim Falloway seemed excited and expectant. They were all standing in a small group, talking to each other in short jerky sentences the gist of which I did not catch, for the conversation stopped abruptly, and they turned to us eagerly the moment we entered the room.

"Have you learned anything?" asked Fraim Falloway, in a semi-hysterical falsetto.

"We're not through looking round yet," Vance returned placatingly. "We hope to know something definite very soon. Just now, however, I wish to ask each of you gentlemen a question."

He did not seem particularly concerned and sat down as he spoke, crossing his knees leisurely. When he had selected a cigarette from his platinum-and-jet case he turned suddenly to the lawyer.

"What is your favorite perfume, Mr. Fleel?" he asked unexpectedly.

The man stared at him in blank astonishment, and I am sure that had he been in a courtroom, he would have appealed instantly to the judge with the usual incompetent - irrelevant - and - immaterial objection. However, he managed a condescending smile and replied:

"I have no favorite perfume—I know nothing about such things. It's true, I send bottles of perfume to my women clients at Christmas, instead of the conventional flower-baskets, but I always leave the selection to my secretary."

"Do you regard Mrs. Kenting as one of your women clients?" Vance continued.

"Naturally," answered the lawyer.

"By the by, Mr. Fleel, is your secret'ry blond or brunette?"

The man seemed more disconcerted than ever, but answered immediately.

"I don't know. I suppose you'd call her brunette. Her hair certainly doesn't look anything like Jean Harlow's or like Peggy Hopkins Joyce's—if that's what you mean."

"Many thanks," said Vance curtly, and shifted his gaze to Fraim Falloway who stood a few feet away, gaping before him with unseeing eyes.

"What is *your* favorite scent, Mr. Falloway?" Vance asked, watching the youth closely and appraisingly.

"I—I don't know," Falloway stammered. "I'm not familiar with such feminine matters. But I think emerald is wonderful—so mysterious—so exotic—so subtle." He raised his eyes almost rapturously, like a young poet reciting his own verses.

"You're quite right," murmured Vance; and then he focused his gaze on Kenyon Kenting.

"All perfumes smell alike to me," was the man's annoyed assertion before Vance could frame the question again. "I can't tell one from another—except gardenia. Whenever I give any woman perfume, I give her gardenia."

A faint smile appeared at the corners of Vance's mouth.

"Really, y' know," he said, "I shouldn't do it, if I were you."

As he spoke he turned his head to Porter Quaggy.

"And how about you, Mr. Quaggy?" he asked

lightly. "If you were giving a lady perfume, what scent would you select?"

Quaggy gave a mirthless chuckle.

"I haven't yet been guilty of such foolishness," he replied. "I stick to flowers. They're easier. But if I were compelled to present a fair creature with perfume, I'd first find out what she liked."

"Quite a sensible point of view," murmured Vance, rising as if with great effort and turning. "And now, I say, Sergeant, let's have a curs'ry look at that ladder."

As we walked down the front steps I saw Guilfoyle still sitting at the wheel of his cab, with the motor humming gently.

Heath flashed on his powerful pocket light, and for the second time we went through the street gate leading into the yard, and approached the ladder leaning against the side of the house.

The short grass was entirely dry, and the ground had completely hardened since the rain two nights ago. Vance again bent over at the foot of the ladder while Heath held the flashlight.

"There's no need to fear my spoiling your adored footprints tonight, Sergeant,—the ground is much too hard. Not even Sweet Alice Cherry * could have made an impression on this sod." Vance straightened up after a moment and moved the ladder slightly to

* A famous side-show "fat woman" of the time.

the right, as he had done the previous morning. "And don't get jittery about finger-prints, Sergeant," he went on. "I'm quite convinced you'll find none. This ladder, I opine, is merely a stage-prop, as it were; and the person who set it here was clever enough to have used gloves."

He bent over again and inspected the lawn, but rose almost immediately.

"Not the slightest depression—only a few blades of grass crushed. . . . I say, *sergente mio*, it's your turn to step on the ladder—I'm frightfully tired."

Heath immediately clambered up five or six rungs and then descended; and Vance again moved the ladder a few inches. Both he and Heath now knelt down and scrutinized the ground.

"Observe," said Vance as he rose to his feet, "that the uprights make a slight depression in the soil, even with the weight of only one person pressing upon the ladder. . . . Let's go inside again and dispense our adieux."

On re-entering the house Vance immediately joined Kenting at the entrance to the drawing-room and announced to him, as well as to the others inside, that we were going, and that the house would be taken over very shortly by the police. There was a general silent acquiescence to his announcement.

"I might as well be going along myself," said Kenting despondently. "There is obviously nothing

I can do here. But I hope you gentlemen will let me know the moment you learn anything. I'll be at home all night, and in my office tomorrow."

"Oh, quite," returned Vance, without looking at the man. "Go home, by all means. This has been a trying night, and you can help us better tomorrow if you are able to get any rest now."

The man seemed grateful: it was obvious he was much discouraged by the shock he had just received. Taking his hat from the hall bench, he hurried out the front door.

Quaggy's eyes followed the departing man. Then he rose and began pacing up and down the drawing-room.

"I guess I'll be getting along too," he said finally, with a note of interrogation in his voice. "I may go, I suppose?" There was a suggestion of sneering belligerence in his tone.

"That's quite all right," Vance told him pleasantly. "You probably need a bit of extra sleep, don't y' know, after your recent all-night vigil."

"Thanks," muttered Quaggy sarcastically, keeping his eyes down. And he too left the house.

When the front door had closed after him, Fleel looked up rather apologetically.

"I trust you gentlemen will not misunderstand my seeming right-about-face this morning regarding the assistance of the Police Department. The fact is, I

was entirely sincere in telling you in the District
Attorney's office that I was inclined to leave everything in your hands regarding the payment of the
fifty thousand dollars. But on my way to the house
here to see Kenting, I weighed the matter more carefully, and when I saw how eager Kenting was to
follow the thing through alone, I decided it might
be better, after all, to agree with him regarding the
elimination of the police tonight. I see now that I
was mistaken, and that my first instinct was correct.
I feel, after what happened in the park tonight——"

"Pray don't worry on that score, Mr. Fleel,"
Vance returned negligently. "We quite understand
your advis'ry attitude in the matter. Difficult position—eh, what? After all, one can only make guesses,
subject to change."

Fleel was now on his feet, looking down meditatively at his half-smoked cigar.

"Yes," he muttered; "it is, as you say, a most
difficult situation. . . ." He glanced up swiftly.
"What do you make of this second terrible episode
tonight?"

"Really, y' know,"—Vance was covertly watching
the man—"it is far too early to arrive at any definite
conclusions. Perhaps tomorrow. . . ." His voice
faded away.

Fleel shook himself slightly, as with an involuntary
tremor.

"I feel that we have not reached the end of this atrocious business yet. There appears to be a malicious desperation back of these happenings. . . . I wish I had never been brought into the case—I'm actually beginning to harbor fears for my own safety."

"We appreciate just how you feel," Vance returned.

Fleel straightened up with an effort and moved forward resolutely.

"I think I too will be going." He spoke in a weary tone, and I noticed that his hand trembled slightly as he picked up his hat and adjusted it.

"Cheerio," said Vance as the lawyer turned at the front door and bowed stiffly to us.

Meanwhile Fraim Falloway had risen from his place on the davenport. He now moved silently past us, with a drawn look on his face, and trudged heavily up the stairs.

Falloway had barely time to reach the first landing when the telephone resting on a small wobbly stand in the hall began ringing. Weem suddenly appeared from the dimness of the rear hall and picked up the receiver with a blunt "hello." He listened for a moment; then laying down the receiver, turned sullenly in our direction.

"It's a call for Sergeant Heath," he announced, as if his privacy had been needlessly invaded.

The Sergeant went quickly to the telephone and put the receiver to his ear.

"Well, what is it?" he started belligerently. ". . . . Sure it's the Sarge—shoot! . . . Well, for the love of—— Hold it a minute." He clapped his hand over the mouthpiece and swung about quickly.

"Where'll we be in half an hour, Chief?"

"We'll be at Mr. Vance's apartment," Markham answered after one glance at Heath's expression.

"Oh, my word!" sighed Vance. "I had hoped to be reposing. . . ."

The Sergeant turned back to the instrument.

"Listen, you," he fairly bawled; "we'll be at Mr. Vance's apartment in East 38th Street. Know where it is? . . . That's right—and make it snappy." He banged down the receiver.

"Important, is it, Sergeant?" asked Markham.

"I'll say it is." Heath stepped quickly away from the telephone table. "Let's get going, sir. I'll tell you about it on the way down. Snitkin's meeting us at Mr. Vance's apartment. And Sullivan and Hennessey will be here any minute to take over."

The butler was still in the hall, half standing and half leaning against one of the large newel posts at the foot of the stairs, and Heath now addressed him peremptorily.

"Some of my men will be here pretty soon, Weem. And then you can go to bed. This house is in the hands of the police from now on—understand?"

The butler nodded his head dourly, and shuffled away toward the rear of the house.

"Just a moment, Weem," called Vance.

The man turned and approached us again, sulky and antagonistic.

"Weem, did you or your wife hear any one go out or enter this house around ten o'clock tonight?" Vance asked.

"No, I didn't hear anything. Neither did Gertrude. Mrs. Kenting told both of us that we wouldn't be needed and could do as we pleased after dinner. We had a long day and were tired, and we were both asleep from nine o'clock till you and Mrs. Falloway rang and I had to let you in. After the others came I got dressed and came down to see if there was anything I could do."

"Most admirable of you, Weem," Vance commended him, turning to the front door. "That's all I wanted to ask just now."

CHAPTER XIII

THE GREEN COUPÉ

(Thursday, July 21; midnight.)

Just as Markham and Heath and I turned to follow Vance, there came, from somewhere outside, a startling and ominous rattle that sounded like the staccato and rapid sputtering of a machine-gun. So keyed up were my nerves that the reports went through me with a sickening horror, almost as if it had been the bullets themselves.

"God Almighty!" came the explosive exclamation of the Sergeant, who was at my side; and he stopped abruptly, as if he, too, had been struck by a bombardment of bullets. Then he suddenly sprang forward past Vance and, jerking the front door open, hurried out into the warm summer night without a word to any one. The rest of us followed close behind him. The Sergeant had halted at the edge of the stone pathway to the sidewalk and was looking confusedly up and down the street, uncertain which way to turn. Guilfoyle had jumped down from his seat in the cab as we came out of the vestibule, and was gesticulating excitedly in front of Heath.

199

"The shots came from up that way," he told Heath, waving his arm toward Central Park West. "What do you want me to do, Sarge?"

"Stay here and keep your eyes open," Heath ordered in clipped accents, "until Sullivan and Hennessey arrive. . . . And," he added as he started off toward the park, "stick around after that, in case of any emergency."

"I'm wise," Guilfoyle called after him.

Guilfoyle saluted half-heartedly, as Markham and Vance appeared on the sidewalk, and again he waved his arm to indicate, I presume, which way Heath had gone. He leaned reluctantly against his cab as we followed the Sergeant up the street.

"No," murmured Vance as we hurried along, "not a pleasant case. . . . And if my intuition is correct, these shots are another manifestation of its complexity."

Heath was now breaking into a run ahead of us; and Markham and I had difficulty keeping pace with Vance as he, too, lengthened his stride.

Just this side of the Nottingham Hotel at the corner, a small group of excited men were gathered under the bright light of the lamppost set between two trees along the curb. As Heath came abreast of the cluster of onlookers we could hear his gruff voice ordering them to disperse, and one by one they reluctantly moved off. Some continued on whatever business they had been about, while others remained to look on from the opposite side of the street. In the few moments it took us to reach the lamppost, the Sergeant had succeeded in clearing the scene.

There, leaning in a crouching attitude against the iron lamppost, was Fleel. His face was deathly pale. I have yet to see so unmistakable a picture of collapse from fright as he presented. His nerves were completely shattered. He was as pitiful a figure as I have ever looked at, huddled beneath the unflattering glare of the large electric light overhead, as he leaned weakly for support against the lamppost. In front of the lawyer stood Quaggy, looking at him with a curious hard-faced serenity.

Heath was staring at Fleel with a startled, inquisitive look in his eyes; but before he could speak to Fleel, Vance took the man under the arms and, knocking his feet from under him, set him down gently on the narrow strip of lawn which bordered the sidewalk, with his back against the lamppost.

"Breathe deeply," Vance advised the lawyer, when he had settled him on the ground. "And pull yourself together. Then see if you can tell us what happened."

Fleel looked up, his chest rising and falling as he sucked in the stagnant air of that humid July night. Slowly he struggled to his feet again and leaned heavily against the post, his eyes fixed before him.

Quaggy put a hand on the man's shoulder, as if to steady him, and shook him gently as he did so.

Fleel managed a sickly grimace intended for a smile, and turned his head weakly back and forth, blinking his eyes as if to clear his vision.

"That was a close call," he muttered. "They almost got me."

"Who almost got you, Mr. Fleel?" asked Vance.

"Why—why——" the man stammered, and paused for breath. "The men in the car, of course. I—didn't see—who they were——"

"Try to tell us, Mr. Fleel," came Vance's steadying voice, "just what happened."

Fleel took another deep breath and, with an obvious effort, straightened up a little more.

"Didn't you see it all?" he asked, his voice high and unnatural. "I was on my way to the corner, to get a taxicab, when a car drove up from behind me. I naturally paid no attention to it until it suddenly swerved toward the curb and stopped with a screeching of brakes, just as I reached this street light. As I turned round to see what it was, a small machine-gun was thrust over the ledge of the open window of the car and the firing began. I instinctively grasped this iron post and crouched down. After a number of shots the car jerked forward. I admit I was too frightened to notice which way it turned."

"But at least you were not hit, Mr. Fleel."

The man moved his hands over his body.

"No, thank Heaven for that," he muttered.

"And," Vance continued, "the car couldn't have been over ten feet away from you. A very poor shot, I should say. You were lucky, sir, this time." He spun round quickly to Quaggy, who had taken a step or two backward from the frightened man. "I don't quite understand your being here, Mr. Quaggy. Surely, you've had more than ample time to ensconce yourself safely in your boudoir."

Quaggy stepped forward resentfully.

"I *was* in my apartment. As you can see,"—he pointed indignantly to his two open front windows in the near-by hotel—"my lights are on. When I got to my rooms I didn't go directly to bed—I hope it wasn't a crime. I went to the front window and stood there for a few minutes, trying to get a breath of fresh air. Then I caught sight of Mr. Fleel coming up the street—he had apparently just left the Kenting house—and behind him came a car. Not that I paid any particular attention to it, but I did notice it. Only, when it turned in to the curb and stopped directly opposite Mr. Fleel as he reached the light post my curiosity was naturally aroused. And when I heard the machine-gun and saw the spits of fire coming through the window, and also saw Mr. Fleel grasp the lamppost and sink down, I thought he had been shot. I naturally dashed down—so here I am. . . . Anything illegal in that procedure?" he asked with cold sarcasm.

"No—oh, no," smiled Vance. "Quite normal. Far more normal, in fact, than if you had gone immediately to bed without a bit of airin' by the open window." He glanced at Quaggy with an enigmatical smile. "By the by," he went on, "did you, by any chance, note what type of car it was that attacked Mr. Fleel?"

"No, I didn't get a very good look at it," Quaggy returned in a chilly tone. "At first I didn't pay much attention to it, as I said; and when the shooting began I was too excited to get any vivid impression. But I think it was a coupé of some kind—not a very large car, and certainly not a new model."

"And the color?" prompted Vance.

"It was a dingy, nondescript color." Quaggy narrowed his eyes, as if trying to recall a definite picture. "It might have been a faded green—it was hard to be certain from the window. In fact, I think it *was* green."

Heath was watching Quaggy shrewdly.

"Yeah?" he said skeptically. "Which way did it go?"

Quaggy turned to the Sergeant.

"I really didn't notice," he replied none too cordially. "I caught only a glimpse of it as it started toward the park."

"A fine bunch of spectators," Heath snorted. "I'll see about that car myself." And he started running toward Central Park West.

As he neared the corner, a burly figure in uniform turned suddenly into 86th Street from the south, and almost collided with the Sergeant. By the bright corner light I could see that the newcomer was McLaughlin, the night officer on duty in that section, who had reported to us the morning of Kaspar Kenting's disappearance. He drew up quickly and saluted with a jerk.

"What was it, Sergeant?" His breathless, excited query carried down to us. "I heard the shots, and been trying to locate 'em. Did they come outa this street?"

"You're damn tootin', McLaughlin," replied Heath, and, grasping the officer by the arm, he swung him about, and the two started off again.

"Did you see any car come out of this street, into Central Park West?" demanded Heath.

I could not now hear what the officer answered, but when the two had reached the curb at the corner McLaughlin was waving his arm uptown, and I assumed that he was pointing in the direction that the green coupé had taken.

Heath looked up and down the avenue for a moment, no doubt trying to find a car he could requisition for the chase; but there was apparently none in sight, and he started diagonally across the street uptown, with McLaughlin at his heels. In the middle of the crossing the Sergeant turned his head and called out over his shoulder to us:

"Wait here at the corner for me." Then he and McLaughlin disappeared past the building on the north corner of Central Park West.

"My word, such energy!" sighed Vance when Heath and the officer were out of sight. "The coupé could be at 110th Street by this time—and thus the mad search would end. Heath is all action and no mentation. Sad, sad. . . . Vital ingredient of the police routine, I imagine—eh, what, Markham?"

Markham was in a solemn mood, and took no offense at Vance's levity.

"There's a taxicab stand just a block up on Central Park West," he explained patiently. "The Sergeant is probably headed for that in order to commandeer a cab for the chase."

"Marvellous," murmured Vance. "But I imagine even the green coupé could outrun a nocturnal taxicab if they both started from scratch."

"Not if the Sergeant were to puncture one of its rear tires with a bullet or two," retorted Markham angrily.

"I doubt if the Sergeant will have the opportunity, by this time." Vance smiled despondently. Then he turned to Fleel. "Feeling better?" he asked pleasantly.

"I'm all right now," the lawyer returned, taking a wobbly step or two forward and biting the end from a cigar he took from his pocket.

"That's bully," Vance said consolingly. "Do you want an escort home?"

"No, thanks," said Fleel, in a voice that was still dazed. "I'll make it all right." And when he had his cigar going he turned shakily toward Central Park West. "I'll pick up a taxicab." He held out his hand to Quaggy, who took it with surprising cordiality. "Many thanks, Mr. Quaggy," he said weakly and, I thought, a little shamefacedly. Then he bowed somewhat stiffly and haughtily to us and moved away out of the ring of light.

"Queer episode," commented Vance, as if to himself. "Fits in rather nicely, though. Lucky for your lawyer friend, Markham, that the gentleman in the green coupé wasn't a better shot. . . . Ah, well, we might as well toddle to the corner and await the energetic Sergeant. Really, y' know, Markham, there's no use gazing at the lamppost any longer."

Markham silently followed Vance toward the park.

Quaggy turned too and walked with us the short distance to the entrance of his apartment-hotel, where he took leave of us. At the great iron-grilled door he turned and said tauntingly: "Many thanks for not arresting me."

"Oh, that's quite all right, Mr. Quaggy," Vance

returned, halting momentarily and smiling. "The case isn't over yet, don't y' know. . . . Cheerio."

At the corner Vance very deliberately lighted a cigarette and seated himself indolently on the wide stone balustrade extending along the east wall of the Nottingham Hotel.

"I'm not bloodthirsty at all, Markham," he said, looking quizzically at the District Attorney; "but I rather wish the gentleman with the machine-gun had potted Mr. Fleel. And he was at such short range. I've never wielded a machine-gun myself, but I'm quite sure I could have done better than that. . . . And the poor Sergeant, dashing madly around at this hour. My heart goes out to him. The whole explanation of this evening's little *contretemps* lies elsewhere than with the mysterious green coupé."

Markham was annoyed. He was standing at the curb, straining his eyes up the avenue to the north.

"Sometimes, Vance," he said, without taking his eyes from the wide macadamized roadway, "you infuriate me with your babble. A lot of good it would have done us to have Fleel shot a few feet away from myself and the police."

Vance joined Markham at the edge of the sidewalk and followed his intense gaze northward to the quiet blocks in the distance.

"Lovely night," murmured Vance tantalizingly. "So quiet and lonely. But much too warm."

"I'll warrant the Sergeant and McLaughlin over-
haul that car somewhere." Markham was apparently
following his own trend of thought.

"Oh, I dare say," sighed Vance. "But I doubt if it
will get us forrader. One can't send a green coupé
to the electric chair. Silly notion—what?"

There were several moments of silence, and then a
taxicab came at a perilous rate out of the transverse
in the park, swung south, and drew up directly in
front of us.

Simultaneously with the car's abrupt stop the
door swung open, and Heath and McLaughlin
stepped down.

"We got the car all right," announced Heath
triumphantly. "The same dirty-green coupé Mc-
Laughlin here saw outside the Kenting house
Wednesday morning."

The officer nodded his head enthusiastically.

"It's the same, all right," he asserted. "I'd swear
to it. Jeez, what a break!"

"Where did you find it, Sergeant?" asked Markham. (Vance was unimpressed and was blowing
smoke-rings playfully into the still summer air.)

"Right up there in the transverse leading through
the park." The Sergeant waved his arm with an impatient backward flourish, and barely missed striking
McLaughlin who stood beside him. "It was half-way
up on the curb. Abandoned. After the guys in it

ditched the car they musta come out and hopped a taxicab up the street, because shortly after the green coupé turned into the transverse two guys walked out and, according to the driver here, took the cab in front of his."

Without waiting for a reply from either Markham or Vance, Heath swung about and beckoned imperiously to the chauffeur of the cab from which he had just alighted. A short rotund man of perhaps thirty, with a flat cap and a duster too long for him, struggled out of the front seat and joined us.

"Look here, you," bawled Heath, "do you know the name of the man who was running the cab ahead of you on the stand tonight who took the two guys what come out of the transverse?"

"Sure I know him," returned the chauffeur. "He's a buddy of mine."

"Know where he lives?"

"Sure I know where he lives. Up on Kelly Street, in the Bronx. He's got a wife and three kids."

"The hell with his family!" snapped Heath. "Get hold of that baby as soon as you can, and tell him to beat it down to the Homicide Bureau *pronto*. I wanta know where he took those two guys that came out of the transverse."

"I can tell ya that right now, officer," came the chauffeur's respectful answer. "I was standin' talkin' to Abe when the fares came over from the park. I

opened the door for 'em myself. An' they told Abe
to drive like hell to the uptown station of the Lexington Avenue subway at 86th Street."

"Ah!" It was Vance who spoke. "That's very
interestin'. Uptown—eh, what?"

"Anyway, I wanta see this buddy of yours,"
Heath went on to the chauffeur, ignoring Vance's
interpolated comment. "Get me, fella?"

"Sure I getcha, officer," the chauffeur returned
subserviently. "Abe ought to be back on the stand
in half an hour."

"That's O.-K.," growled Heath, turning to Markham. "Gosh, Chief, I gotta get to a telephone quick
and get the boys lookin' for these guys."

"Why rush the matter, Sergeant?" Vance spoke
casually. "We really ought not to keep Snitkin waiting too long at the apartment, don't y' know. I say,
let's take this taxi and we'll be home in a few minutes.
You can then use my phone to your heart's content.
And this gentleman here"—indicating the chauffeur
—"can return at once to his stand and await the
arrival of his friend, Mr. Abraham."

Heath hesitated, and Markham nodded after a
quick look at Vance.

"I think that will be the best course, Sergeant,"
the District Attorney said, and opened the door of
the taxicab.

We all got inside, leaving McLaughlin standing

on the curb, and Heath gave Vance's address to the driver. As we pulled away, Heath put his head out of the window.

"Report that empty car," he called out to McLaughlin. "And then keep your eye on it till the boys come up for it. Also watch for Abie till this fellow gets back—then get to the Kenting house and stand by with Guilfoyle."

CHAPTER XIV

KASPAR IS FOUND

(*Friday, July 22; 12:30 a.m.*)

As we drove rapidly down Central Park West, Markham nervously lighted a cigar and asked Heath, who was sitting on the seat in front of him:

"Well, what about that telephone call you got at the Kenting house, Sergeant?"

Heath turned his head and spoke out of the corner of his mouth.

"Kaspar Kenting's body has been found in the East River, around 150th Street. The report came in right after Snitkin got back to Headquarters. He's got all the details. . . . I thought I'd better not say anything about it up at the Kentings' place with that snoopy butler hanging around."

Markham did not speak for a few seconds. Then he asked:

"Is that all you know, Sergeant?"

"My God, Chief!" Heath exclaimed. "Ain't that enough?" And he settled down in the narrow, cramped quarters of his seat.

Again there was silence in the cab. Though I could not see Markham's face, I could well imagine his mixed reactions to this disturbing piece of news.

"Then you were right, Vance," he commented at length, in a strained, barely audible tone.

"The East River—eh?" Vance spoke quietly and without emotion. "Yes, it could easily be. Very distressin'. . . ." He said no more; nor was there any further talk until we reached Vance's apartment.

Snitkin was already waiting in the upper hallway, just outside the library. Heath merely grunted to him as he brushed by and picked up the telephone. He talked for five minutes or more, making innumerable reports relating to the night's happenings and giving various instructions. When he had the routine police ball rolling he beckoned to Snitkin, and entered the library where Vance, Markham, and I were waiting.

"Go ahead, Snitkin," ordered Heath, before the man was barely in the room. "Tell us what you know."

"Oh, I say, Sergeant," put in Vance, "let Snitkin have a bit of this brandy first." And he poured a copious drink of his rare *Napoléon* into a whiskey glass on the end of the library table. "The gruesome particulars will keep a moment."

Snitkin hesitated and glanced sheepishly at the District Attorney. Markham merely nodded his head, and the detective gulped down the cognac.

"Much obliged, Mr. Vance," he said. "And here's all I know about it:"—It is interesting to note that Snitkin addressed himself to Vance and not to either Markham or Heath, although Vance had no official standing in the Police Department.—"There's a small inlet up there in the river, which isn't over three feet deep, and the fellow on the beat—Nelson, I think it was—saw this baby lying on the bank, with his legs sticking out of the water, along about nine o'clock tonight. So he called in and reported it right away, and they sent over a buggy from the local station. The Medical Examiner of the Bronx gave the body the once-over, and it seems the fellow didn't even die from drowning. He was already dead when he was dumped into the water. His head was bashed in with——"

"With the usual blunt instrument," broke in Vance, finishing the sentence. "That's what the medicos always call it when they are not sure just how a johnnie was laid low by violence."

"That's right, Mr. Vance," resumed Snitkin with a grin. "The fellow's head was bashed in with a blunt instrument—that's just what the report said. . . . Well, the doc guessed the guy had been dead twelve hours maybe. There's no telling how long he'd been lying there in the inlet. It's not a place that's likely to be seen by anybody, and it was only by accident that Nelson ran across the body."

"What about identification?" asked Heath officiously.

"Oh, there was plenty identification, Sarge," Snitkin answered. "The guy not only fit the description like a glove, but his clothes and his pockets was full of identification. Looked almost like whoever threw him there wanted him to be identified quick. He had his name on a label on the inside of his coat pocket, and another one under the strap of his vest, and still another one sewed into the watch pocket of his pants. And that ain't all: his name was written on the inside of his shoes—though I don't get that exactly. . . ."

"That's quite correct, Snitkin," remarked Vance. "It's the practice of all custom boot-makers. And the three labels in his clothes merely mean that they were made to order by a custom tailor. Quite custom'ry and understandable."

"Anyhow," Snitkin went on, "I'm simply tellin' you how we know the body is Kenting's. There was a wallet with initials in his inside coat pocket, with a couple of letters addressed to him, and a bunch of callin' cards. . . ."

"I do wish you'd call them visitin' cards," murmured Vance.

"Hell, I'll call 'em anything you want," grinned

Snitkin. "Anyhow, they was there. And there was a fancy pocket comb with his initials on it——"

"A pocket comb—eh?" Vance nodded with satisfaction. "Very interestin', Markham. When a gentleman carries a pocket comb—not a particularly popular practice these days, since beards went out of fashion—he would certainly not add a toilet comb to his equipment. . . . Forgive the interruption, Snitkin. Go ahead."

"Well, there was monograms on damn-near everything else he had in his pockets, like his cigarette case and lighter and knife and key-ring and handkerchiefs; and there was even monograms on his underwear. According to the boys at the local station, he was either the Kaspar Kenting we're looking for, or he wasn't nobody. And that was a pretty complete description of him we sent out this morning to all the local precincts."

"No pajamas and no toothbrush in his pocket, Snitkin?" Vance asked.

"Pajamas—a toothbrush?" Snitkin was as much surprised as he was puzzled. "Nothing was said about 'em, Mr. Vance, so I guess they wasn't there. Are they needed for identification?"

"Oh, no—no," Vance returned quickly. "Just a bit of curiosity on my part. Oh, I don't question the identification for a moment, Snitkin. It needs far less proof than you've given us."

"Who gave you all this dope, Snitkin?" asked the Sergeant in a somewhat mollified tone.

"The desk sergeant uptown," Snitkin told him. "He telephoned the Bureau as soon as he got the report from the doc. I had just come in, and took the call myself. Then I phoned you."

Heath nodded as if satisfied.

"That's all right, Snitkin. You'd better go home now and hit the hay,—you been wearin' out your dogs all day. But get down to the Bureau early tomorrow—I'll be needin' you. I'll see about getting some members of the family for official indentification of the body in the morning—probably the fellow's brother will be enough. This is a hell of a case."

"But ain't you gonna tear off some rest yourself, Sergeant?" Snitkin asked solicitously.

"I'm a *young* fellow," retorted Heath with good-natured contempt. "I can take it. You old guys need a lot of beauty sleep."

Snitkin grinned again and looked at the Sergeant admiringly.

"Have another little spot, Snitkin, before you go," suggested Vance. And, without waiting for a response, he refilled the whiskey glass.

As before, Snitkin hesitated.

"You know, I'm not officially on duty now, Chief," he said, looking toward Markham almost coyly.

Markham did not glance up—he seemed depressed and worried.

"Go ahead," he barked, but not without a certain kindliness. "And don't talk so much. We all need a little support right now."

Snitkin picked up the whiskey glass and emptied it with alacrity. As he set the glass down he drew his coat sleeve across his mouth.

"Chief, you're a swell——" he began. But Heath cut him short.

"Get the hell out of here," he bawled at his subordinate. The Sergeant knew only too well Markham's aversion for any compliments and the curious reticence of the District Attorney's nature.*

Snitkin went out—somewhat meekly and wonderingly, but, withal, gratefully—and ten minutes later Heath followed. When we were alone Markham asked:

"What do you think of it, Vance?"

"Thinkin' is an awful bore, Markham," Vance answered with irritating nonchalance. "And it's growing frightfully late, especially considerin' how early I dragged myself into consciousness this morning."

* It is interesting to note that in the entire association between Markham and Vance I had never heard either of them pay the other a compliment of any kind. When one of them so much as bordered on a compliment, the other always broke in sharply with a remark which made any further outward display of sentiment impossible. To me it seemed as if both of them had a deep-rooted instinct to keep the intimate and personal side of their affection for each other disguised and unspoken.

"Never mind all that." Markham spoke with exasperation. "How did you know Kaspar Kenting was dead when I spoke to you on the stairway yesterday morning?"

"You flatter me," said Vance. "I didn't really know. I merely surmised it—basin' my conclusion on the indications."

"So that's your mood," snorted Markham hopelessly. "I'm telling you, you outrageous fop, that this is a damned serious situation—what happened to Fleel tonight ought to prove that."

Vance smoked a moment in silence, and his brow clouded: his whole expression, in fact, changed.

"I know only too well, Markham, how serious the situation is," he said in a grave and curiously subdued voice. "But there's really nothing we can do. We must wait—please believe me. Our hands and feet are tied." He looked at Markham and continued with unwonted earnestness. "The most serious part of the whole affair is that this is not a kidnapping case at all, in the conventional sense. It goes deeper than that. It's cold-blooded, diabolical murder. But I can't quite see my way yet to proving it. I'm far more worried than you, Markham. The whole thing is unspeakably horrible. There are subtle and abnormal elements mixed up in the situation. It's an abominable affair, but as we sit here tonight, I want to tell you that I don't know—I don't know. . . .

I'm afraid to make a move until we learn more."

I had rarely heard Vance speak in this tone, and a curious sensation of fear, so potent as to be almost a physical reaction, ran through me.

I am certain that Vance's words had a similar effect on Markham, who made no comment: he sat silent for several minutes. Then he took his leave, without again referring to the case. Vance bade him good night absent-mindedly and remained in his chair, gazing before him into the empty grate.

I myself went immediately to bed and—I am a little loath to admit it—slept fairly well: I was somewhat exhausted, and a physical relaxation had come over me, despite my mental tension. But had I known what terrible and heart-paralyzing events the following day held in store, I doubt if I could have slept a wink that night.

CHAPTER XV

ALEXANDRITE AND AMETHYST

(Friday, July 22; 8:40 a.m.)

I shall never forget the following day. It will ever remain in my memory as one of the great horrors of my life. It was the day when Vance and Heath and I came nearer to death than ever before or since. I still remember the scene in the private office of the now closed Kinkaid Casino; * and the report of Vance's hideous death in the course of the Garden murder case will never be erased from my mind. But as I look back upon these and other frightful episodes which froze my blood and filled my heart with cold fear, not one of them looms as appalling as do the events of that memorable Friday in the blistering heat of this particular summer.

It was, in a way, the outcome of Vance's own decision. He deliberately sought it as the result of some strange and unusual emotional reaction. He staked his own life in the attempt to prevent something which he considered diabolical. Vance was a man whose cold mental processes generally governed

* "The Casino Murder Case" (Scribners, 1934).

his every action; but in this emergency he impulsively followed his instincts. I frankly admit that it was, to me, a new phase of the man's many-sided character—a phase with which I was unfamiliar, and which I would not have believed was actually part of his make-up.

The day began conventionally enough, except that Vance rose at eight. I did not know how much sleep he actually got after Markham departed the night before. I know only that I myself woke up for a brief interval, hours after I had retired, and could hear his footsteps as if he were pacing up and down in the library. But when I joined him for breakfast at half-past eight that morning, there was no indication either in his eyes or in his manner—which was as nonchalant and disinterested as ever—that he had been deprived of his rest.

He was dressed in a dark grey herring-bone suit, a pair of soft black leather oxfords, and a dark green cravat with white polka-dots. He greeted me with his customarily cynical but pleasant ease. But he made no comment to explain his early (for him) rising. He seemed altogether natural and unconcerned about the happenings of the day before. When he had finished his Turkish coffee and lighted a second *Régie* he settled back in his chair and spoke, quite casually, about the Kenting case.

"An amazin' and complicated affair—eh, what,

Van? There are far too many facets to it—same like those stones in old Karl Kenting's collection—to leave one entirely comfortable. Dashed elusive—and deuced tangled. I naturally have certain suspicions, but I am by no means sure of my ground. I don't like those missin' gems—they tie up too consistently with the rest of the incidents. I don't like that unused ladder—so subtly and uselessly moved from one window to another. I don't like that abortive attempt on Fleel's life last night, or Quaggy's fortuitous appearance on the scene—Fleel was undoubtedly in a jittery state when we found him and actually incredulous at finding himself still alive. And I don't at all like the general situation in that old high-ceilinged purple house—it's not a wholesome place and has too many sinister possibilities. . . . There has already been one murder that we know of, and there may be another which we haven't yet heard about."

He looked up with a troubled glance and drew in a deep breath.

"No—oh, no; it's not a nice case," he went on as if to himself. "But what are we to do about it? To-day may bring an answer. Haste on our part might spoil everything. But haste—oh, tremendous haste —is now of the utmost importance to the killer. That is why I think something will happen before very long. I'm hopin', Van. I'm also countin' on the anxiety of the person who has plotted and carried out this beastly affair to this point. . . ."

He smoked a while in silence. I offered no comment or opinion, for I knew he had been thinking aloud rather than addressing me personally. When the lighted tip of his cigarette had almost reached the platinum rim of his slender ivory holder he got up slowly, moved to the front window, and stood gazing out at the sunlit street. Despite the sunshine, a humid mist fell over the city and presaged a stagnant, airless day. When Vance turned back to me he seemed to have made a decision.

"I think we'll take a spin down to Markham's office, Van," he said. "There's nothing to do here, and there may be some news which Markham naively regards as too trivial to telephone me about. But it's the little obscure things that are goin' to solve this case." *

Vance walked energetically across the room and, ringing for Currie, ordered his car.

Vance drove swiftly down Madison Avenue in a curiously abstracted mood. We arrived at Markham's office a few minutes before ten o'clock.

"Glad you came, Vance," was Markham's greeting. "I was about to call you on the phone."

---

* Vance was greatly mistaken on this point, as I now have reason to know. It turned out to be no less than a matter of life and death.

"Ah!" Vance sat down lazily. "Any tidin's, glad or otherwise?"

"I'm afraid not," Markham returned dispiritedly, "although things have been going ahead. A great deal of the necessary police work has been done, but we haven't come upon any promising lead as yet."

"Oh, yes. Of course." Vance smiled mildly. "Jolly old Police Department simply must imitate the whirling dervish before they feel entitled to settle down to the serious business in hand. I suppose you mean finger-prints, photographs, and the futile search for possible lookers-on, and the grilling—as you call it—of perfectly innocent and harmless people, and a careful search of the spot where Kaspar was found, as well as a thorough overhauling of the abandoned car."

Markham responded with a contemptuous snort.

"Those things simply have to be done. Very often they lead us to vital facts in the case. All criminals are not super-geniuses—they make mistakes occasionally."

"Oh, to be sure," Vance sighed. "Concatenation of circumstances impossible of duplication. Reconstruction from two points of view—and so on *ad infinitum*. I think I know all the catch phrases by this time. . . . However, proceed to unburden thyself."

"Well," said Markham in a hard, practical voice,

ignoring Vance's frivolous interlude, "Kenyon Kenting was taken to the uptown morgue this morning and he identified his brother's body beyond a doubt. And I saw no need to put any other members of the family through the harrowing experience."

"Most considerate of you," murmured Vance—and it was difficult to know whether his remark was intended to convey a tinge of sarcasm or was merely a conventional retort. In any event, Markham's statement left him utterly indifferent.

"Mrs. Kenting's room," continued Markham, "as well as the window-sill and the ladder, was gone over thoroughly for finger-prints——"

"And none was found, of course, except the Sergeant's and mine."

"You're right," conceded Markham. "The person, or persons, must have worn gloves."

"Assumin' there was a person—or persons."

"All right, all right." Markham was beginning to be annoyed. "You're so damned cryptic about everything, and so reticent, that I have no way of knowing what prompted that last remark of yours. But, whatever you think, there must have been some one somewhere, or Mrs. Kenting could not have disappeared as she did."

"Quite true," returned Vance. "We can quite safely eliminate *a capella* accidents or amnesia or such things, in view of all the circumstances. I suppose all the hospitals have been checked as part of the pirouetting activities of Centre Street's master minds?"

"Naturally. And we drew a blank at every step. But if we failed in that respect we have, at least, disposed of the possibility."

"Amazin' progress," commented Vance. "There'll be finger-prints somewhere, so don't be downcast, old dear. But the signs-manual will be found, if at all, somewhere far removed from the Kenting house. Personally, I'd say you wouldn't find them till you have located the car in which Mrs. Kenting was probably driven away last night."

"What do you mean—what car?" demanded Markham.

"I haven't the slightest idea," said Vance laconically. "But I hardly think the lady walked out of sight. . . . And, by the by, Markham, speakin' of cars, what enormous array of information did you marshal about the green coupé that the energetic Sergeant found so conveniently waiting for him in the transverse? . . . Doubtless stolen—eh, what?"

Markham nodded glumly.

"Yes, Vance, that's just it. Belongs to a perfectly respectable spinster on upper West End Avenue. And a careful search of the car itself produced only the fact that there was a small sub-machine gun thrown into the tool chest under the seat."

"And the license plates?" asked Vance casually.

"Oh, those were stolen too." Markham spoke disgustedly.

"Plates didn't belong to the car, eh?" Vance smoked meditatively without stirring. "Very interestin'. Stolen car and stolen license plates. A car that doesn't belong to the fleeing occupants, and plates that don't belong to the car—well, well. Implies two cars, don't you know. Maybe it was the second car in which Mrs. Kenting was spirited away. Merely hazardin' a guess, don't y' know." He now uncrossed his knees and drew himself up slightly in his chair. "I rather imagine the dirty-green coupé was following Fleel around last night when Mrs. Kenting sallied forth to her assignation, and it was left to the other car to take care of the lady, as it were. Fairly well equipped gang."

"I don't follow you, Vance," Markham returned; "although I have a vague notion of the theory you're working out. But many other things might have happened last night."

"Oh, quite," agreed Vance. "As I said, I was merely hazardin' a guess. . . . What about Abe, the buddy of the chauffeur who drove us home last night? I suppose Heath or some of the Torquemadas in Centre Street put the poor devil through the requisite torture?"

"You read too many trashy books, Vance." Mark-

ham was indignant. "Heath talked to the driver of
the number one cab at Headquarters within an hour
of the time he left here last night. He merely cor-
roborated what our chauffeur told us—namely, that
he dropped the two men who came out of the
transverse at the uptown entrance of the Lexington Avenue subway. Incidentally, they didn't
wait for change but hurried down the stairs—they
were probably just in time to catch the last express."

Vance again sighed lightly. "Most helpful. . . .
Any other coruscatin' discoveries?"

"I spoke to the doctor who went over Kaspar's
body," Markham went on. "And there's little or
nothing to add to Snitkin's report of last night. The
exact location of the spot where he was found was
determined, and the ground was gone over carefully.
But there were no footprints or suggestive indications of any kind. McLaughlin heard and saw nothing last night around the Kenting house; Weem and
the cook both stick to the story that they were asleep
during that whole time; and two taxicab drivers who
were at the Columbus Avenue corner did not remember seeing Mrs. Kenting, whom they know by sight,
come down that way."

"Well, your information seems to be typically
thorough and typically useless," said Vance. "Did
any one do a bit of checkin' up to ascertain whether

there were any unaccounted-for semiprecious stones round town?"

Markham gave him a look of mild surprise and mock pity.

"Good heavens, no! What have your semiprecious stones to do with a case of kidnapping?"

"My dear Markham!" protested Vance. "I have told you—and I thought, in my naive way, that it had even been demonstrated to you—that this is *not* a case of kidnapping. Won't you even permit a subtle killer to set the stage for himself—to indulge in a bit of spectacular *décor*, so to speak? That collection of old Karl Kenting's gems has a dashed lot to do with the case. . . ."

"Well, suppose those pieces of colored glass do have something to do with the disappearances, what of it?" Markham interrupted aggressively. "I'm not worried as much about such vague factors in the case as I am about that attack on Fleel."

"Oh, that." Vance shrugged. "A mere bit of technique. And the operator of the sub-machine gun was kind enough to miss his target. As I told Fleel, he was very lucky."

"But whether Fleel survived or not," muttered Markham, "it was a dastardly affair."

"I quite agree with you there, Markham," said Vance approvingly.

At this moment Markham's secretary, coming

swiftly through the swinging leather door, interrupted the conversation.

"Chief," he announced, "there's a young fellow outside who's terribly excited and insists on seeing you at once. Says it's about the Kenting case. Gives his name as Falloway."

"Oh, send him in, by all means," said Vance, before Markham had time to answer.

The secretary looked interrogatingly at the District Attorney. Markham hesitated only a moment and then nodded. A few moments later Fraim Falloway was shown into the office. He came into the room with a frightened air, and bade Markham good morning. His eyes seemed larger and his face paler than when I had last seen him.

"Tell us what's on your mind, Mr. Falloway." Vance spoke softly.

The youth turned and noticed him for the first time.

"I'll tell you, all right," he said in quick, tremulous accents. "That—that beautiful alexandrite stone is gone from the collection. I'm sure it's been stolen."

"Stolen?" Vance looked at the youth closely. "Why do you say stolen?"

"I—I don't know," was the flustered reply. "All I know is that it is gone—how else could it have disappeared unless it was stolen? It was there two days ago."

Even I remembered the stone—an unusually large and beautifully cut octagonal stone of perhaps forty carats, which was in a place of honor, in the most conspicuous case, surrounded by other specimens of chrysoberyl. I had taken particular notice of it the morning of Kaspar Kenting's disappearance when Vance and I had looked over the various glass cases before ascending the stairs to Kaspar's room.

"I don't know anything about those stones in the collection," Falloway went on excitedly, "but I do know about this magnificent alexandrite. It always fascinated me—it was the only gem in the collection I cared anything about. It was a wonderful and beautiful thing. I used to go into the room often just to look at that stone. I could lose myself before it for an hour at a time. In the daytime it was the most marvellous green, like dark jade, with only touches of red in it; but at night, in the artificial light, it changed its color completely and became a thrilling red, like wine."

As Markham threw him a look of incredulity, Falloway hastened on.

"Oh, it was no miracle.—I looked it up in a book; I read about it. It had some strange and mystic quality which made it absorb and refract and reflect the light upon it in different ways. But I haven't feasted my eyes on it for two days—we've all been

so upset—, until last night—but that was in the
yellow artificial light—and it was a beautiful red
then."

Falloway paused and then hurried on ecstatically.

"But I like it most in the daylight when it turns
green and mysterious—that's when it recalls to me
Swinburne's great poem, *The Triumph of Time:*
'I will go back to the great sweet mother, mother and
lover of men, the sea.'—Oh, I hope you see what I
mean. . . ." He looked at each of us in turn. "So
this morning—a little while ago—I went downstairs
to look at it: I needed something—something . . .
But it wasn't green at all. It was still red, almost
purple. And after I had looked at it a while in
amazement, I realized that even the cutting was different. It was the same size and shape—but that was
all. Oh, I know every facet of that alexandrite. It
was not the same stone. It had been taken away and
another stone left in its place! . . ."

He fumbled nervously in his outside pocket and
finally drew out a large deep-colored gem, which can
best be described as deep red but with a very decided
purple cast. He held it out to Vance on the palm of
his shaking hand.

"That's what was left in the place of my beloved
alexandrite!"

Vance took the stone and looked at it a moment.
Still holding the gem he let his hand fall to his lap,

and looked up at Falloway with a comprehending nod.

"Yes, I see what you mean—quite," he said. "As good a substitution as possible. This is merely amethyst. Of comparatively little value. Similar to alexandrite, however, and often mistaken for it by amateurs. Any one would trade an amethyst for an alexandrite, the price of which has recently begun to soar. Can you say with any accuracy when the exchange was made?"

Falloway shook his head vaguely and sat down heavily.

"No," he said phlegmatically. "As I told you, I haven't seen it in daylight for two days, and last night I looked at it for just a second and didn't realize that it wasn't the .alexandrite. I discovered the truth this morning. The exchange might have been made at any time since I last saw the real stone in daylight."

Vance again looked at the stone and handed it back to Falloway.

"Return it to the case as soon as you reach home. And say nothing about it to any one till I speak to you again." He turned to the District Attorney. "Y' know, Markham, fine alexandrite is a very rare and valuable variety of chrysoberyl. It was discovered less than a hundred years ago, in the Urals, and it was named after the czarevitch who later became the conservative and reformative Alexander II, Czar of Russia, for it first came to light on his birthday. As Mr. Falloway rightly says, it is a curious dichroic gem. The light of the spectrum is reflected, absorbed and refracted in such a way that in the daylight it is quite green, and in artificial light, especially gas-light, it is a pronounced deep and scintillating red, slightly on the blue, or short wavelength end of the spectrum. A fine specimen of alexandrite the size of that stone would now be worth a small fortune. Such a specimen is the dream of every collector. I saw the stone when I glanced through the cases Wednesday morning and marvelled at old Karl's good luck. The other indifferent items in the collection were anything but consistent with that alexandrite; and when I spoke to Kenyon Kenting that morning, I entirely omitted any mention of that particular stone, for it takes more than one exceptional piece of chrysoberyl, no matter how beautiful, to constitute a well-rounded collection."

Vance paused a moment with a reflective look, and then continued.

"Amethyst, a variety of quartz, which likewise comes from Russia, although somewhat similar in shade to alexandrite, does not have that peculiar dichroic characteristic. Amethyst, d' ye see, has a structural dissimilarity from alexandrite. At times we find in the crystals a right-angular formation to the edge of the prism, shaped in sectoral triangles. This accounts for its bicoloration—the so-called white and purple tints, making it resemble two separate, fused stones. The fractural ripples and the feather-like effects—so apparent in amethyst—result from this peculiar laterality of structure. On the other hand, Markham, alexandrite——"

"Thanks for the lecture, but forgive me if I am not interested." Markham was irritated. "What I'd like to know is whether you see anything significant in the disappearance of the alexandrite and the substitution of the amethyst."

"Oh, yes—decidedly. You'd be amazed if you knew how highly significant it is." He turned quickly to Fraim Falloway, who had been listening with an eagerness of interest I had not seen him display at any previous time. "I think, Mr. Falloway, you would better return to your home at once and do exactly as I told you. We are grateful no end for your coming here and telling us about the missin' stone."

Falloway rose heavily.

"I'll put the stone back in place right away."

"Oh, by the by, Mr. Falloway." Vance drew himself up sharply. "If, as you have intimated, your favorite cutting of alexandrite was stolen, could you suggest the possible thief? Could it, for instance, have been any one you know?"

"You mean some one in the house?—or Mr. Quaggy or Mr. Fleel?" retorted Falloway with a show of indignation. "What would they want with my alexandrite?" He shook his head shrewdly. "But I have an idea who did take it."

"Ah!"

"Yes! I know more than you think I do." Falloway made a pitiful effort to thrust forward his narrow chest. "It was Kaspar—that's who it was!"

Vance nodded indulgently.

"But Kaspar is dead. His body was found last night."

"A damned good riddance!" Vance's announcement left Falloway unruffled. "I was hoping he wouldn't come back."

"He won't," interjected Markham laconically, staring at the youth with unmistakable disgust.

I doubt if Falloway even heard the District Attorney's remark: his attention was concentrated on Vance.

"But do you think you can ever find my beautiful alexandrite?" he asked. He seemed to regard the disappearance of the alexandrite as a personal loss.

"Oh, yes—I'm quite sanguine we shall recover it," Vance assured him.

The youth, greatly relieved, went toward the door with heavy, dragging feet.

Markham's secretary came again through the

leather door, just before Falloway reached it, and announced Kenyon Kenting.

"Send him in," said Markham.

Kenting and Falloway passed each other on the threshold. I was forcibly struck by the wordless exchange of hostility which passed between the elder and the younger man. Kenting bowed stiffly and muttered a word of greeting as he passed the other, with a stiff, elderly dignity in his manner. But Falloway did not respond as he went through to the outer office.

CHAPTER XVI

"THIS YEAR OF OUR LORD"

(*Friday, July 22; 11 a.m.*)

As Kenting stepped into the office it was obvious that he was in a perturbed state of mind. He nodded to Vance and to me, and, going to Markham's desk, dejectedly placed an envelope before the District Attorney.

"That came in the second mail this morning, to my office," Kenting said, controlling his excitement with considerable effort. "It's another one of those damn notes."

Markham had already picked up the envelope and was carefully extracting the folded sheet of paper from inside.

"And Fleel," added Kenting, "got a similar one in the same mail—at his office. He phoned me about it, just as I was leaving to come here. He sounded very much upset and asked me if I also had received a note from the kidnappers. I told him I had, and I read it to him over the phone. I added I was bringing it immediately to you; and Fleel said he would meet me here shortly and bring his own note with him. He hasn't, by any chance, come already?"

"Not yet," Markham answered, glancing up from the note. His face was unusually grave, and there was a deep, hopeless frown round his eyes. When he had finished his perusal of the note he picked up the envelope and handed them both to Vance.

"I suppose you'll want to see these, Vance," the District Attorney muttered distractedly.

"Oh, quite—by all means."

Vance, with his monocle already adjusted, took the note and the envelope with suppressed eagerness, glancing first at the envelope and then at the single sheet of paper. I had risen and was standing behind him, leaning over his chair.

The paper on which the note was written in lead pencil was exactly like that of the first note Fleel had received in the mail the day before. The disguised, deliberately clumsy chirography was also similar, but there was a distinct difference in the way it was worded. The spelling was correct, and the sentences grammatically constructed. Nor was there any pretense here in the means of expression. It was as if whoever wrote it had purposely abandoned such tactics so that there might be no mistake or misunderstanding of any kind regarding the import of the message. Vance merely read it through once—he did not seem greatly interested in it. But it was obvious that something about it annoyed and puzzled him.

The note read:

You did not obey instructions. You called in the police. We saw everything. That is why we took his wife. If you fail us again, the same thing will happen to her that happened to him. This is your last warning. Have the $50,000 ready at five o'clock today (Friday). You will get instructions at that time. And if you notify the police this time it is no dice. We mean business. Beware!

For signature there was the interlocking-squares symbol that had come to have such a sinister portent for us all.

"Very interestin' and illuminatin'," murmured Vance, as he carefully refolded the note, replaced it in the envelope, and tossed it back on Markham's desk. "The money is quite obviously wanted immediately. But I am not at all convinced that it was only the presence of the police that turned last night's episode in the park into a fiasco. However . . ."

"What shall I do—what shall I do?" Kenting asked, glancing distractedly from Vance to the District Attorney and back again.

"Really, y' know," said Vance in a kindly tone, "you can't do anything at present. You must wait for the forthcoming instructions. And then there's Mr. Fleel's *billet-doux* which we hope to see anon."

"I know, I know," mumbled Kenting hopelessly. "But it would be horrible if anything should happen to Madelaine."

Vance was silent a moment, and his eyes clouded. He showed more concern than he had since he had entered the Kenting case.

"One never knows, of course," he murmured. "But we can hope for the best. I realize that this waiting is abominable. But we are at a loss at present even as to where to begin. . . . By the by, Mr. Kenting, I don't suppose you heard the shots that were fired at Mr. Fleel shortly after you left your brother's house last night?"

"No, I didn't." Kenting seemed greatly perturbed. "I was frightfully shocked on hearing about it this morning. When I left you last night I was lucky enough to catch a taxicab just as I reached the corner, and I went directly home. How long after I left the house did Fleel go?"

"Just a few minutes," Vance returned. "But no doubt you had time to have got a taxi and have been well on your way."

Kenting considered the matter for a minute; then he looked up sharply with a frightened expression.

"Perhaps—perhaps——" he began in an awed voice which seemed to tremble with a sudden and uncontrollable emotion. "Perhaps those shots were intended for me! . . ."

"Oh, no, no—nothing like that," Vance assured him. "I'm quite sure the shots were not intended for you, sir. The fact is, I am not convinced that the shots were intended even for Mr. Fleel."

"What's that you say!" Kenting sat up quickly. "What do you mean by that? . . ."

Before Vance could answer, a buzzer sounded on Markham's desk. As the District Attorney pressed a key on the inter-communicating call-box a voice from the outer office announced that Fleel had just arrived. Markham had barely given instructions that Fleel be sent in when the lawyer came impatiently through the swinging door and joined us. He, too, looked pale and drawn and showed unmistakable traces of lack of rest,—he appeared to have lost much of his earlier self-confidence. He greeted all of us formally with the exception of Kenyon Kenting, with whom he shook hands with a silent, expressive grasp.

"A difficult situation," he said with a formal effort at condolence. "My deepest sympathy goes to you, Kenyon."

Kenting shrugged despondently.

"You yourself had a pretty close call last night."

"Oh, well," the other muttered, "at least I'm safe and sound enough now. But I can't understand that attack. Can't imagine who would want to shoot me, or what good it would do any one. It's the most incredible thing."

Kenting threw a sharp look at Vance, but Vance was busying himself with a fresh cigarette and seemed oblivious to the conventional interchange between the two men.

Fleel moved toward the District Attorney's desk.

"I brought the note I received in the mail this morning," he said, fumbling in his pocket. "There's no reason whatever why I should be getting anything like this—unless the kidnappers imagine that I control all the Kenting money and have it on deposit. . . . You can understand that I am greatly disturbed by this communication, and I thought it would be best to show it to you without delay, at the same time explaining to you that there's absolutely nothing I can do in the matter."

"There's no need for an explanation," said Markham abruptly. "We are wholly cognizant of that phase of the situation. Let's see the note."

Fleel had drawn an envelope from his inside coat pocket and held it out to Markham. As he did so his eyes fell on the note that Kenting had brought and which lay on the District Attorney's desk.

"Do you mind if I take a look at this?" he asked.

"Go right ahead," answered Markham as he opened the envelope Fleel had given him.

The note that Fleel turned over to Markham was not as long as the one received by Kenting. It was, however, written on the same kind of paper; and it was written in pencil and in the same handwriting.

The few brief sentences struck me as highly ominous:

> You have double-crossed us. You have control of the money. Get busy. And don't try any more foolishness again. You are a good lawyer and can handle everything if you want to. And you had better want to. We expect to see you according to instructions in our letter to Kenting today in this year of our Lord, 1936, or else it will be too bad.*

The interlocking, ink-brushed squares completed the message.

When Markham had finished reading it and handed it to Vance, Vance went through it quickly

---

* I have made one small and wholly immaterial change in transcribing this note. I have used the year in which I am actually writing the record of that memorable case, instead of stating the exact year in which it occurred (which, naturally, was the year given in the note); for I regard it as both unimportant and unnecessary to identify specifically the time at which the events herewith enumerated occurred. If that date has been forgotten, or if it is of any particular interest to the reader of this chronicle, it will not be difficult to find the year by referring to the back files of newspapers, for what has come to be known as the Kenting kidnap case received nation-wide publicity at the time.

but carefully and, sliding it into the envelope, laid it on Markham's desk beside the note which Kenting had brought in, and which Fleel had read and replaced without comment.

"I can say to you, Mr. Fleel," Vance told him, "only what I have already said to Mr. Kenting—that there is nothing to be done at the present moment. A rational decision is quite impossible just now. You must wait for the next communication—by whatever method it may come—before you can decide on a course of action."

He rose and confronted the two unstrung men.

"There is much to be done yet," he said. "And we are most sympathetic and eager to be helpful. Please believe that we are doing everything possible. I would advise that you both remain in your offices until you have heard something further. We will certainly communicate with you later, and we appreciate the cooperation you are giving us. . . . By the by,"—he spoke somewhat offhand to Kenting—"has your money been returned to you?"

"Yes, yes, Vance." It was Markham's impatient voice that answered. "Mr. Kenting received the money the first thing this morning. Two of the men in the Detective Division across the hall delivered it to him."

Kenting nodded in confirmation of the District Attorney's statement.

"Most efficient," sighed Vance. "After all, y'
know, Markham, Mr. Kenting couldn't give the
money out unless he had it again in his possession. . . . Most grateful for the information."

Vance addressed Fleel and Kenting again.

"We will, of course, expect to hear immediately
when you receive any further communication, or if
any new angle develops." His tone was one of polite
dismissal.

"Don't worry on that score, Mr. Vance." Kenting
was reaching for his hat. "As soon as either one of
us gets the instructions promised in my note, you'll
hear all about it."

A few moments later he and Fleel left the office
together.

As the door closed behind them Vance swung
swiftly about and went to Markham's desk.

"That note to Fleel!" he exclaimed. "I don't like
it, Markham. I don't at all like it. It is the most
curious concoction. I must see it again."

As he spoke he picked up the note once more and,
resuming his chair, studied the paper with far more
interest and care than he had shown when the lawyer
and Kenting had been present.

"You notice, of course, that both notes were can-
celled in the same post-office station as was yesterday's communication—the Westchester Station."

"Certainly I noticed it," Markham returned almost angrily. "But what is there significant about the postmark?"

"I don't know, Markham,—I really don't know. It's probably a minor point."

Vance did not look up: he was earnestly engaged with the note. He read it through several times, lingering with a troubled frown at the last two or three lines.

"I cannot understand the reference to 'this year of our Lord.' It doesn't belong here. It's out of key. My eyes go back to it every time I finish reading the note. It bothers me frightfully. Something was in the writer's mind—he had a strange thought at that time. It may be entirely meaningless, or it may have been written down inadvertently, like an instinctive or submerged thought which had struggled through in expression, or it could have been written into the note with some very subtle significance for some one who was expected to see it."

"I noticed that phrase, too," said Markham. "It *is* curious; but, in my opinion, it means nothing at all."

"I wonder. . . ." Vance raised his hand and brushed it lightly over his forehead. Then he got to his feet. "I'd like to be alone a while with this note. Where can I go—are the judges' chambers unoccupied?"

Markham looked at him in puzzled amazement.

"I don't know." His perturbed, questioning scrutiny of Vance continued. "By the way, Sergeant Heath should be here any minute now."

"Stout fella, Heath," Vance murmured. "I may want to see him. . . . But where can I go?"

"You can go into my private office, you damned prima donna." Markham pointed to a narrow door in the west wall of the room. "You'll be alone in there. Shall I let you know when Heath gets here?"

"No—no." Vance shook his head as he crossed the room. "Just tell him to wait for me." And, carrying the note before him, he opened the side door and went out of the room.

Markham looked after him in bewildered silence. Then he turned half-heartedly to a pile of papers and documents neatly arranged at one side of his desk blotter. He worked for some time on extraneous matters.

It was fully ten minutes before Vance emerged from the private office. In the meantime Heath had arrived and was waiting impatiently in one of the leather lounging chairs near the steel letter files in one corner of the room. When the Sergeant had stepped into the office Markham greeted him with simulated annoyance.

"Our pet orchid is communing with his soul in my private office," he explained. "He said he may want

to see you; so you'd better take a chair in the corner
and wait to see what his profound contemplation will
produce. Meanwhile, you might look at the note
Kenting received this morning." Markham handed
it to the Sergeant. "Another note, received by Fleel,
is being submitted to the searching monocle, as it
were."

Heath had grinned at Markham's sarcastic, but
good-natured, comments and sat down as the District
Attorney returned to his work.

When Vance re-entered the room he threw a quick
glance in Heath's direction. It was obvious he was
in an unusually serious mood and seemed unmindful
of his surroundings.

"Cheerio, Sergeant," he greeted Heath as he became fully aware of his presence. "I'm glad you
came in. Thanks awfully for waitin', and all that.
. . . I'm sure you've already read the note Kenting
received. Here's the one Fleel brought in."

And he tossed it negligently to me with a nod of
his head toward Heath. His eyes, a little strained
and with an unwonted intensity in them, were still
on Markham as I stepped across the room to Heath
with the paper.

Vance now stood in the centre of the room, gazing
down at the floor, deep in thought as he smoked.
After a moment he raised his head slowly and let his
eyes rest meditatively on Markham again.

"It could be—it could be," he murmured. And I felt that he was making an effort to control himself. "I want to see a detailed map of New York right away."

"On that wall—over there." Markham was watching him closely. "In the wooden frame. Just pull it down—it's on a roller."

Vance unrolled the black-and-white chart, with its red lines, and smoothed it against the wall. After a few minutes' search of the intersecting lines he turned back to Markham with a curious look on his face and heaved a sigh of relief.

"Let me see that yellow slip you had yesterday, with the official bound'ries of the Westchester Station post-office district."

Markham, still patiently silent, handed him the paper. Vance took it back to the map with him, glanced from the slip of paper to the chart and back again, and began to trace an imaginary zigzag line with his finger. I heard him enumerating, half to himself: "Pelham, Kingsland, Mace, Gunhill, Bushnell, Hutchinson River . . ."

Then his finger came to a stop, and he turned triumphantly.

"That's it! That's it!" His voice had a peculiar pitch. "I think I have found the meaning of that phrase."

"What in the name of Heaven do you mean?"

Markham had half risen from his chair and was leaning forward with his hands on the desk.

" 'This year of our Lord,' and the numerals. There's a Lord Street in that outlined section—up near Givans Basin—a section of open spaces and undeveloped highways. And the year 19—" and he gave the other two digits. "That's the house number —they run in the nineteen-hundreds over near the water on Lord Street. And, incidentally, I note that the only logical way to reach there is to take the Lexington Avenue subway uptown."

Markham sank slowly back into his chair without taking his eyes from Vance.

"I see what you mean," he said. "But——" He hesitated a moment. "That's merely a wild guess. A groundless assumption. It's too specious, too vague. It may not be an address at all. . . ." Then he added: "You may merely have stumbled on a co-incidence——" He stopped abruptly. "Do you think we ought to send some men out there—on a chance?"

"My word, no!" Vance returned emphatically. "That might wreck everything, providin' we've really got something here. Your myrmidons would be sure to give warning and bungle things; and only a moment would be needed for a strategic move fatal to our plans. This matter must be handled differently."

His face darkened; his eyelids drooped menacingly; and I knew that some new and overpowering emotion had taken hold of him.

"I'm going myself," he said. "It may be a wild-goose chase, but it must be done, don't y' know. We can't leave any possible avenue of approach untried just now. There's something frightful and sinister going on. And I'm not at all certain as to what will be found there. I'm a helpless babe, cryin' for the light."

Markham was impressed and, I believe, a little concerned at his manner.

"I don't like it, Vance. I think you should have protection, in case of an emergency——"

Heath had come forward and stood solemnly at one end of the desk.

"I'm going with you, Mr. Vance," he said, in a voice that was both stolid and final. "I got a feeling you may be needin' me. An' I sorta like the idea of that address you figured out. Anyhow, I'll have something to tell my grandchildren about learnin' how wrong you were."

Vance looked at the man a while seriously, and then slowly nodded.

"That will be quite all right, Sergeant," he said calmly. "I may need your help. And as for finding me wrong: I'm willin', don't y' know—like Barkis. But how are you going to have grandchildren when you're not even a benedick? * . . . In the meantime, Sergeant," he went on, dropping his jocular manner, and jotting down something on a small piece of yellow paper he had torn from the scratch-pad on Markham's desk, "have this carefully attended to— constant observation. You understand?"

Heath took the yellow slip, looked at it in utter amazement, and then stuffed it into his pocket. His eyes were wide and a look of skepticism and incredulity came into them.

"I don't like to say so, Mr. Vance, but I think you're daffy, sir."

"I don't in the least mind, Sergeant." Vance spoke almost affectionately. "But I want you to see to it, nevertheless." And he met the other's gaze coldly and steadily.

Heath moved his head up and down, his lips hanging open in disbelief.

"If you say so, sir," he mumbled. "But I still think——"

"Never mind making the effort, Sergeant." There was an irresistibly imperious note in Vance's tone. "But if you disobey that order—which, incidentally, is the first I've ever given you—I cannot proceed with the case."

---

* Sergeant Ernest Heath was what is popularly known as a confirmed bachelor. Even when he retired from the Homicide Bureau at fifty, he devoted himself not to a wife, but to raising wyandottes on his farm in the Mohawk valley.

Heath tried to grin but failed.

"I'll take care of it," he said. Though he was still awestricken, his tone was subdued. "When do we go?"

"After dark, of course," Vance replied, relaxing perceptibly. "It's misty and somewhat overcast to-day. . . . Be at my apartment at half-past eight. We'll drive up in my car."

Again the Sergeant moved his head up and down slowly.

"God Almighty!" he said. "I can't believe it: it don't make sense. Anyway," he added, "I'll string along with you, Mr. Vance. I'll be there at eight-thirty—heeled plenty."

"So you really believe I may be right," said Vance with a smile.

"Well, I ain't taking any chances—come what may."

CHAPTER XVII

SHOTS IN THE DARK

(Friday, July 22; noon.)

Vance remained in Markham's office only a short time after his enigmatic talk with Heath. (I did not regard that brief conversation as particularly momentous at the time, but within a few hours I learned that it was actually one of the most important conversations that had ever passed between these two widely disparate, but mutually sympathetic, men.)

Markham attempted repeatedly, with both cajolery and brusqueness, to draw Vance out. The District Attorney wished particularly to hear what significance Vance attached to the missing alexandrite, and what import he had sensed in the two notes which Kenting and Fleel had brought in. Vance, however, was unusually grave and adamant. He would give no excuse for not expressing freely his theory regarding the case; but his manner was such that Markham realized, as did I, that Vance had an excellent reason for temporarily withholding his suspicions from the District Attorney—and, I might add, from me as well.

In the end Markham was highly annoyed and, I think, somewhat resentful.

"I trust you know, Vance," he said in a tone intended to be coldly formal, but which did not entirely disguise his deep-rooted respect for the peculiar methods Vance followed in his investigation of a case, "that, as official head of the Police Department, I can compel Sergeant Heath here to show me that slip of paper you handed him."

"I fully appreciate that fact," Vance replied in a tone equally as frigid as Markham's. "But I also know you will not do it." Only once, during the investigation of the Bishop murder case, had I seen so serious an expression in Vance's eyes. "I know I can trust you to do nothing of the kind, and to forgo your technical rights in this instance." His voice suddenly softened and a look of genuine affection overspread his face as he added: "I want your confidence until tonight—I want you to believe that I have good and specific reasons for my seemingly boorish obstinacy."

Markham kept his eyes on Vance for several moments and then glanced away as he busied himself a little ostentatiously with a cigar.

"You're a damned nuisance," he mumbled, with simulated anger. "I wish I had never seen you."

"Do you flatter yourself, for one minute, Markham," retorted Vance, "that I have particularly enjoyed your acquaintance during the past fifteen years?"

And then Vance did something I had never seen him do before. He took a step toward Markham and held out his hand. Markham turned to him without any show of surprise and grasped his hand with sincere cordiality.

"After all," said Vance lightly, "you're only a District Attorney, don't y' know. I'll make due allowances." And he went from the room without another word, leaving the Sergeant and Markham in the room together.

Vance and I had luncheon at the Caviar Restaurant, and he lingered unconscionably long over his favorite brandy, which they always kept for him and brought out ceremoniously when he appeared at that restaurant. During the meal he spoke but infrequently—and then about subjects far removed from the Kenting case.

We went directly home after he had finished sipping his cognac, and Vance spent the entire afternoon in desultory reading in the library. I went into the room for some papers around four o'clock and noticed that he was engrossed in Erasmus' *Encomium Moriæ*.

As I stood for a moment behind him, looking discreetly over his shoulder, he looked up with a serious expression: he had settled into a studious mood.

"After all, Van," he commented, "what would the world be without folly? Nothing matters vitally—does it? Listen to this comfortin' thought:"—he ran his finger along the Erasmus passage before him and translated the words slowly—"'So likewise all this life of mortal man, what is it but a certain kind of stage play?' . . . Same like Shakespeare wrote in *As You Like It*, which came a century later—what?'"

Vance was in a peculiar humor, and I knew he was endeavoring to cover up what was actually in his mind; and for some reason, which I could not understand, I was prompted to quote to him, in answer, the famous line from Horace's *Epistles: Nec lusisse pudet, sed non incidere ludum.* However, I refrained, and went on about my work as Vance took up his book again.

A little before six o'clock Markham came in unexpectedly.

"Well, Vance," he said banteringly, "I suppose you're still indulging your flair for melodramatic reticence, and are still playing the part of *l'homme de mystère.* However, I'll respect your idiosyncrasies —with tongue in cheek, of course."

"Most generous of you," murmured Vance. "I'm overwhelmed. . . . What do you wish to tell me? I know full well you didn't come all the way to my humble diggin's without some sad message for me."

Markham sobered and sat down near Vance.

"I haven't heard yet from either Fleel or Kenting, . . ." he began.

"I rather expected that bit of news." Vance rose and, ringing for Currie, ordered Dubonnet. Then, as he resumed his seat, he went on. "Really, there's nothing to worry about. They have probably decided to proceed without the bunglin' assistance of the police this time—those last notes were pretty insistent on that point. Kenting undoubtedly has received his instructions. . . . By the by, have you tried to communicate with him?"

Markham nodded gravely.

"I tried to reach him at his office an hour ago, and was told he had gone home. I called him there, but the butler told me he had come in and had just gone out without leaving any instructions except that he would not be home for dinner."

"Not what you'd call a highly cooperative johnnie —what?"

The Dubonnet was served, and Vance sipped the wine placidly.

"Of course, you tried to reach him at the Purple House?"

"Of course I did," Markham answered. "But he wasn't there either and wasn't expected there."

"Very interestin'," murmured Vance. "Elusive chap. Food for thought, Markham. Think it over."

"I also tried to get in touch with Fleel," Markham continued doggedly. "But he, like Kenting it seems, had left his office earlier than usual today; nor was I able to reach him at his home."

"Two missin' men," commented Vance. "Very sad. But no need to be upset. Just a private matter being handled privately, I fear. District Attorney's office and the police not bein' trusted. Not entirely un-intelligent." He set down his Dubonnet glass. "But there's business afoot, or else I'm horribly mistaken. And what can you do? The actors in the tragic drama refuse to make an appearance. Most disconcertin', from the official point of view. The only thing left for you is to ring down the curtain temporarily, and bide your time. *C'est la fin de la pauvre Manon*—or words to that effect. Abominable opera. Incidentally, what are your plans for the evening?"

"I have to get dressed and attend a damned silly banquet tonight," grumbled Markham.

"It'll probably do you good," said Vance. "And when you make your speech, you can solemnly assure your bored listeners that the situation is under control, and that developments are expected very soon—or golden words to that effect."

Markham remained a short time longer and then went out. Vance resumed his interrupted reading.

Shortly after seven we had a simple home dinner which Currie served to us in the library, consisting of *gigot, rissoulées* potatoes, fresh mint jelly, asparagus *hollandaise*, and savarins *à la Medicis.*

Promptly at half-past eight the Sergeant arrived.

"I still think you're daffy, Mr. Vance," he said good-naturedly, as he took a long drink of Bourbon. "However, everything is being attended to."

"If I'm wrong, Sergeant," said Vance with pretended entreaty, "you must never divulge our little secret. The humiliation would be far too great. And I'm waxin' old and sensitive."

Heath chuckled and poured himself another glass of Bourbon. As he did so Vance went to the centre-table and, opening the drawer, brought out an automatic. He inspected it carefully, made sure the magazine was full, and then slipped it into his pocket.

I had risen and was now standing beside him. I reached out my hand for the other automatic in the drawer—the one I had carried in Central Park the night before—but Vance quickly closed the drawer and, turning to me, shook his head in negation.

"Sorry, Van," he said, "but I think you'd better bide at home tonight. This may be a very dangerous mission—or it may be an erroneous guess on my part. However, I rather anticipate trouble, and you'll be safer in your boudoir. . . ."

I became indignant and insisted that I go with him and share whatever danger the night might hold.

Again Vance shook his head.

"I think not, Van." He spoke in a strangely gentle tone. "No need whatever for you to take the risk. I'll tell you all about it when the Sergeant and I return."

He smiled with finality, but I became more insistent and more indignant, and told him frankly that, whether he gave me the gun or not, I intended to go along with him and Heath.

Vance studied me for several moments.

"All right, Van," he said at length. "But don't forget that I warned you." Without saying any more he swung about to the table, opened the drawer, and brought out the other automatic. "I suggest you keep it in your outside pocket this time," he advised, as he handed me the gun. "It's rather difficult to prophesy, don't y' know—though I'm hopin' you won't need the bally thing." Then, going to the window, he looked out for a moment. "It'll be dark by the time we get there." He turned slowly from the window and crossed the room to ring for Currie.

When the butler came into the room Vance looked at him for a while in silence, with a kindly smile.

"If you don't hear from me by eleven," he said, "go to bed. And *schlafen Sie wohl!* If I am not back in the morning, you will find some interesting legal documents in a blue envelope with your name on it, in the upper right-hand drawer of the secret'ry. And notify Mr. Markham." He turned round to Heath with an air of exaggerated nonchalance. "Come along, Sergeant," he said. "Let's be on our way. Duty calls, as the sayin' goes. *Ich dien*, and all that sort of twaddle."

We went down to the street in silence—Vance's instructions to Currie had struck me as curiously portentous. We got into Vance's car, which was waiting outside, Heath and I in the tonneau and Vance at the wheel.

Vance was an expert driver, and he handled the Hispano-Suiza with a quiet efficiency and care that made the long, low-slung car seem almost something animate. There was never the slightest sound of enmeshing gears, never the slightest jerk, as he stopped and started the car in the flow of traffic.

We drove up Fifth Avenue to its northern end, and there crossed the Harlem River into the Bronx. At the far side of the bridge Vance stopped the car and drew a folded map from his pocket.

"No need to lose ourselves in this maze of criss-crossing avenues," he remarked to us over his shoulder. "Since we know where we're going, we might as well mark the route." He had unfolded the map and was tracing an itinerary at one side of it. "Westchester Avenue will take us at least half of the way to our destination; and then if I can work

my way through to Bassett Avenue we should have
no further difficulties."

He placed the map on the seat beside him and
drove on. At the intersection of East 177th Street
he made a sharp turn to the left, and we skirted the
grounds of the New York Catholic Protectory. After
a few more turns a street sign showed that we were
on Bassett Avenue, and Vance continued to the north.
At its upper end we found ourselves at a small stretch
of water,* and Vance again stopped the car to con-
sult his map.

"I've gone a little too far," he informed us, as he
took the wheel again and turned the car sharply to
the left, at right angles with Bassett Avenue. "But
I'll go through to the next avenue—Waring, I think
it is—turn south there, and park the car just round
the corner from Lord Street. The number we're looking for should be there or thereabouts."

It took a few minutes to make the detour, for the
roadway was unsuitable for automobile traffic. Vance
shut off all his lights as we approached the corner,
and we drove the last half block in complete darkness, as the nearest street light was far down Waring
Avenue. The gliding Hispano-Suiza made no sound
under Vance's efficient handling; even the closing of
the doors, as we got out, could not be heard more
than a few feet away.

* This, I later learned, was Givans Basin.

We proceeded on foot into Lord Street, a narrow thoroughfare and sparsely inhabited. Here and there was an old wooden shack, standing out, in the darkness of the night, as a black patch against the overcast sky.

"It would be on this side of the street," Vance said, in a low, vibrant voice. "This is the even-number side. My guess is it's that next two-story structure, just beyond this vacant lot."

"I think you're right at that," Heath returned, *sotto voce*.

When we stood in front of the small frame dwelling, it seemed particularly black. There was no light showing at any of the windows. Until we accustomed our eyes to the darkness it looked as if the place had no windows at all.

Heath tiptoed up the three sagging wooden steps that led to the narrow front porch and flashed his light close to the door. Crudely painted on the lintel was the number we sought. The Sergeant beckoned to us with a sweeping gesture of his arm, and Vance and I joined him silently before the wooden-panelled front door with its nondescript peeling paint. At one side of the door was an old-fashioned bell-pull with a white knob, and Vance gave it a tentative jerk.

There was a faint tinkle inside, and we stood waiting, filled with misgivings and not knowing what to expect. I saw Heath slip his hand into the pocket where he carried his gun; and I too—by instinct or imitation—dropped my hand into my right outside coat pocket and, grasping my automatic, shifted the safety release.

After a long delay, during which we remained there without a sound, we heard a leisurely shifting of the bolts. The door then opened a few inches, and the pinched yellow face of an undersized Chinaman peered out cautiously at us.

As I stood there, straining my eyes through the partly open door at the yellow face that looked inquisitively out at us, the significance of the imprint of the Chinese sandals at the foot of the ladder, as well as of the Sinological nature of the signatures of the various ransom notes, flashed through my mind. I knew in that brief moment that Vance had interpreted the address correctly, and that we had come to the right house. Although I had not doubted the accuracy of Vance's prognostication, a chill swept over me as I stared at the flat yellow features of the small man on the other side of the door.

Vance immediately wedged his foot in the slight aperture and forced the door inward with his shoulder. Before us, in the dingy light of a gas jet which hung from the ceiling far back in the hall, was a Chinaman, clad in black pajamas and a pair of sandals. He was barely five feet tall.

"What you want?" he asked, in an antagonistic,

falsetto voice, backing away quickly against the wall
to the right of the door.

"We want to speak to Mrs. Kenting," said Vance,
scarcely above a whisper.

"She not here," the Chinaman answered. "Me no
know Missy Kenting. Nobody here. You have wrong
house. Go away."

Vance had already stepped inside, and in a flash
he drew a large handkerchief from his outer breast
pocket and crushed it against the Chinaman's mouth,
pinioning him against the wall. Then I noticed the
reason for Vance's act:—only a foot or so away was
an old-fashioned push-bell toward which the Chinaman had been slyly reaching. The man stood back
against the wall under Vance's firm pressure, as if
he felt that any effort to escape would be futile.

Then, with the most amazing quickness and dexterity, he forced his head upward and leaped on
Vance, like a wrestler executing a flying tackle, and
twined his legs about Vance's waist, at the same time
throwing his arms round Vance's neck. It was an
astonishing feat of nimble accuracy.

But, with a movement almost as quick as the
Chinaman's, Heath, who was standing close to
Vance, brought the butt of his revolver down on the
yellow man's head with terrific force. The Chinaman's legs disentangled themselves; his arms relaxed; his head fell back; and he began slipping

limply to the floor. Vance caught him and eased him down noiselessly. Leaning over for a moment, he looked at the Chinaman by the flame of his cigarette lighter, and then straightened up.

"He's good for an hour, at least, Sergeant," he said in a hoarse whisper. "My word! You're so brutal. . . . He was trying to reach that bell signal. The others must be upstairs." He moved silently toward the narrow carpeted stairway that led above. "This is a damnable situation. Keep your guns handy, both of you, and don't touch the banister— it may creak."

As we filed noiselessly up the dimly-lit stairs, Vance leading the way, Heath just behind him, and I bringing up the rear, I was assailed by a terrifying premonition of disaster. There was something sinister in the atmosphere of that house; and I imagined that grave danger lurked in the deep shadows above us. I grasped my automatic more firmly, and a sensation of alertness seized me as if my brain had suddenly been swept clear of everything but the apprehension of what might lie ahead. . . .

It seemed an unreasonably long time before we reached the upper landing—a sensation like a crazy hasheesh distortion—and I felt myself struggling to regain a sense of reality.

As Vance stepped into the hallway above, which was narrower and dingier than the one downstairs, he stood tensely still for a moment, looking about him. There was only one small lighted gas jet at the rear of the hall. Luckily, the floor was covered with an old worn runner which deadened our footsteps as we followed Vance up the hall. Suddenly the muffled sound of voices came to us, but we could not distinguish any words. Vance moved stealthily toward the front of the house and stood before the only door on the left of the corridor. A line of faint light outlined the threshold, and it was now evident that the voices came from within that room.

After listening a moment Vance tried the doorknob with extreme care. To our surprise the door was not locked, but swung back easily into a long, narrow, squalid room in the centre of which stood a plain deal table. At one end of the table, by the light of an oil lamp, two illy dressed men sat playing casino, judging by the distribution of the cards.

Though the room was filled with cigarette smoke, I immediately recognized one of the men as the shabby figure I had seen leaning against the bench in Central Park the night before. The lamp furnished the only illumination in the room, and dark grey blankets, hanging in full folds from over the window-frames, let no ray of light escape either at the front or side window.

The two men sprang to their feet instantaneously, turning in our direction.

"Down, Van!" ordered Vance; and his call was submerged under two deafening detonations accompanied by two flashes from a revolver in the hand of the man nearest us. The bullets must have gone over us, for both Heath and I had dropped quickly to the floor at Vance's order. Almost immediately—so quickly as to be practically simultaneous—there came two reports from Vance's automatic, and I saw the man who had shot at us pitch forward. The thud of his body on the floor coincided with the crash of the lamp, knocked over by the second man. The room was plunged in complete darkness.

"Stay down, Van!" came the commanding voice of Vance.

Almost as he spoke there was a staccato exchange of shots. All I could see were the brilliant flashes from the automatics. To this day I cannot determine the number of shots fired that night, for they overlapped each other in such rapid succession that it was impossible to make an accurate count. I lay flat on my stomach across the door-sill, my head spinning dizzily, my muscles paralyzed with fear for Vance.

There was a brief respite of black silence, so poignant as to be almost palpable, and then came the crash of an upset chair and the dull heavy sound of a human body striking the floor. I was afraid to move. Heath's labored breathing made a welcome noise at my side. I could not tell, in the blackness of the room, who had fallen. A terrifying dread assailed me.

Then I heard Vance's voice—the cynical, nonchalant voice I knew so well—and my intensity of fright gave way to a feeling of relief and overpowering weakness. I felt like a drowning man, who, coming up for the third time, suddenly feels strong arms beneath his shoulders.

"Really, y' know," his voice came from somewhere in the darkness, "there should be electric lights in this house. I saw the wires as we entered."

He was fumbling around somewhere above me, and suddenly the Sergeant's flashlight swept over the room. I staggered to my feet and leaned limply against the casing of the door.

"The idiot!" Vance was murmuring. "He kept his lighted cigarette in his mouth, and I was able to follow every move he made. . . . There must be a switch or a fixture somewhere. The lamp and the blankets at the window were only to give the house the appearance of being untenanted."

The ray from Heath's pocket flash moved about the walls and ceiling, but I could see neither him nor Vance. Then the light came to a halt, and Heath's triumphant voice rang out.

"Here it is, sir,—a socket beside the window." And as he spoke a weak, yellowed bulb dimly lit up the room.

Heath was at the front window, his hand still on the switch of a small electric light socket; and Vance stood near-by, to all appearances cool and unconcerned. On the floor lay two motionless bodies.

"Pleasant evening, Sergeant." Vance spoke in his usual steady, whimsical voice. "My sincerest apologies, and all that." Then he caught sight of me, and his face sobered. "Are you all right, Van?" he asked.

I assured him I had escaped the mêlée unscathed, and added that I had not used my automatic because I was afraid I might have hit him in the dark.

"I quite understand," he murmured and, nodding his head, he went quickly to the two prostrate bodies. After a momentary inspection, he stood up and said:

"Quite dead, Sergeant. Really, y' know, I seem to be a fairly accurate shot."

"I'll say!" breathed Heath with admiration. "I wasn't a hell of a lot of help, was I, Mr. Vance?" he added a bit shamefacedly.

"Really nothing for you to do, Sergeant."

Vance looked about him. Through a wide alcove at the far end of the room a white iron bed was clearly visible. This adjoining chamber was like a small bedroom, with only dirty red rep curtains dividing it from the main room. Vance stepped quickly between the curtains, and switched on a light just over the wooden mantel near the bed. At the rear of the room, near the foot of the bed, was a door standing half ajar. Between the mantel and the bed with its uncovered mattress, was a small bureau with a large mirror swung between two supports rising from the bureau itself.

Heath had followed Vance into the room, and I trailed weakly after them. Vance stood before the bureau for a moment or so, looking down at the few cigarette-burnt toilet articles scattered about it. He opened the top drawer and looked into it. Then he opened the second drawer.

"Ah!" he murmured half aloud, and reached inside.

When he withdrew his hand he was holding a neatly rolled pair of thin Shantung-silk pajamas. He inspected them for a moment and smiled slightly.

"The missin' pajamas," he said as if to himself, though both Heath and I heard every word he spoke. "Never been worn. Very interestin'." He unrolled them on the top of the bureau and drew forth a small green-handled toothbrush. "And the missin' toothbrush," he added. He ran his thumb over the bristles. "And quite dry. . . . The pajamas, I opine, were rolled quickly round the toothbrush and the comb, brought here, and thrown into the drawer. The comb, of course, slipped out into the hedge as the Chinaman now prostrate below descended the ladder from Kaspar Kenting's room." He re-rolled the pajamas, placed them back into the drawer, and resumed his inspection of the toilet articles on the bureau top.

Heath and I were both near the archway, our eyes on Vance, when he suddenly called out, "Look out, Sergeant!"

The last word had been only half completed when there came two shots from the rear door. The slim, crouching figure of a man, somewhat scholarly looking and well dressed, had suddenly appeared there.

Vance had swung about simultaneously with his warning to Heath, and there were two more shots in rapid succession, this time from Vance's gun.

I saw the poised revolver of blue steel drop from the raised hand of the man at the rear door: he looked round him, dazed, and both his hands went to his abdomen. He remained upright for a moment; then he doubled up and sank to the floor where he lay in an awkward crumpled heap.

Heath's revolver too dropped from his grip. When the first shot had been fired, he had pivoted round as if some powerful unseen hand had pushed him: he staggered backward a few feet and slid heavily into a chair. Vance looked a moment at the contorted figure of the man on the floor, and then hastened to Heath.

"The baby winged me," Heath said with an effort. "My gun jammed."

Vance gave him a cursory examination and then smiled encouragingly.

"Frightfully sorry, Sergeant,—it was all the fault of my trustin' nature. McLaughlin told us there were only two men in that green car, and I foolishly concluded that two gentlemen and the Chinaman would be all we should have to contend with. I should have been more far-seein'. Most humiliatin'. . . . You'll have a sore arm for a couple of weeks," he added. "Lucky it's only a flesh wound. You'll probably lose a lot of gore; but really, y' know, you're far too full of blood as it is." And he expertly bound up Heath's right arm, using a handkerchief for a bandage.

The Sergeant struggled to his feet.

"You're treating me like a damn baby." He stepped to the mantel and leaned against it. "There's nothing the matter with me. Where do we go from here?" His face was unusually white, and I could see that the mantel behind him was a most welcome prop.

"Glad I had that mirror in front of me," murmured Vance. "Very useful devices, mirrors."

He had barely finished speaking when we heard a repeated ringing near us.

"By Jove, a telephone!" commented Vance. "Now we'll have to find the instrument."

Heath straightened up.

"The thing's right here on the mantel," he said. "I've been standing in front of it."

Vance made a sudden move forward, but Heath stood in the way.

"You'd better let me answer it, Mr. Vance. You're too refined." He picked up the receiver with his left hand.

"What d' you want?" he asked, in a gruff, officious tone. There was a short pause. "Oh, yeah? O.-K., go ahead." A longer pause followed, as Heath listened. "Don't know nothing about it," he shot back, in a heavy, resentful voice. Then he added: "You got the wrong number." And he slammed down the receiver.

"Who was it, do you know, Sergeant?" Vance spoke quietly as he lighted a cigarette.

Heath turned slowly and looked at Vance. His eyes were narrowed, and there was an expression of awe on his face as he answered.

"Sure I know," he said significantly. He shook his head as if he did not trust himself to speak. "There ain't no mistaking *that* voice."

"Well, who was it, Sergeant?" asked Vance mildly, without looking up from his cigarette.

The Sergeant seemed stronger: he stood away from the mantelpiece, his legs wide apart and firmly planted. Rivulets of blood were running down over his right hand which hung limply at his side.

"It was——" he began, and then he was suddenly aware of my presence in the room. "Mother o' God!" he breathed. "I don't have to tell *you*, Mr. Vance. You knew this morning."

CHAPTER XVIII

THE WINDOWLESS ROOM

(*Friday, July 22; 10:30 p.m.*)

Vance looked at the Sergeant a moment and shook his head.

"Y' know," he said, in a curiously repressed voice, "I was almost hoping I was wrong. I hate to think——" He came suddenly forward to Heath who had fallen back weakly against the mantel and was blindly reaching for the wall, in an effort to hold himself upright. Vance put his arm around Heath and led him to a chair.

"Here, Sergeant," he said in a kindly tone, handing him an etched silver flask, "take a drink of this—and don't be a sissy."

"Go to hell," grumbled Heath, and inverted the flask to his lips. Then he handed it back to Vance. "That's potent juice," he said, standing up and pushing Vance away from him. "Let's get going."

"Right-o, Sergeant. We've only begun." As he spoke he walked toward the rear door and stepped over the dead man, into the next room. Heath and I were at his heels.

The room was in darkness, but with the aid of his flashlight the Sergeant quickly found the electric light. We were in a small box-like room, without windows. Opposite us, against the wall, stood a narrow army cot. Vance rushed forward and leaned over the cot. The motionless form of a woman lay stretched out on it. Despite her disheveled hair and her deathlike pallor, I recognized Madelaine Kenting. Strips of adhesive tape bound her lips together, and both her arms were tied securely with pieces of heavy clothes-line to the iron rods at either side of the cot.

Vance dexterously removed the tape from her mouth, and the woman sucked in a deep breath, as if she had been partly suffocated. There was a low rumbling in her throat, expressive of agony and fear, like that of a person coming out of an anæsthetic after a serious operation.

Vance busied himself with the cruel cords binding her wrists. When he had released them he laid his ear against her heart for a moment, and poured a little of the cognac from his flask between her lips. She swallowed automatically and coughed. Then Vance lifted her in his arms and started from the room.

Just as he reached the door the telephone rang again, and Heath went toward it.

"Don't bother to answer it, Sergeant," said Vance.

"It's probably the same person calling back." And he continued on his way, with the woman in his arms.

I preceded him as he carried his inert burden down the dingy stairway.

"We must get her to a hospital at once, Van," he said when we had reached the lower hallway.

I held the front door open for him, my automatic extended before me, ready for instant use, should the occasion arise. Vance went down the shaky steps without a word, just as Heath joined me at the door. The Chinaman still lay where we had left him, on the floor against the wall.

"Drag him up to that pipe in the corner, Mr. Van Dine," the Sergeant told me in a strained voice. "My arm is sorta numb."

For the first time I noticed that a two-inch water pipe, corroding for lack of paint, rose through the front hall, behind the door, a few inches from the wall. I moved the limp form of the Chinaman until his head came in contact with the pipe; and Heath, with one hand, drew out a pair of handcuffs. Clamping one of the manacles on the unconscious man's right wrist, he pulled it around the pipe and with his foot manipulated the Chinaman's left arm upward till he could close the second iron around it. Then he reached into his pocket and drew out a piece of clothes-line which he had obviously brought from the windowless room upstairs.

"Tie his ankles together, will you, Mr. Van Dine?" he said. "I can't quite make it."

I slipped my gun back into my coat pocket and did as Heath directed.

Then we both went out into the murky night, Heath slamming the door behind him. Vance, with his burden, was perhaps a hundred yards ahead of us, and we came up with him just as he reached the car. He placed Mrs. Kenting on the rear seat of the tonneau and arranged the cushions under her head.

"You can both sit in front with me," he suggested over his shoulder, as he took his place at the wheel; and before Heath and I were actually seated he had started the engine, shifted the gear, and got the car in motion with a sudden but smooth roll. He continued straight down Waring Avenue.

As we approached a lone patrolman after two or three blocks, Heath requested that we stop. Vance threw on his brakes, and honked his horn to attract the patrolman's attention.

"Have I got a minute, Mr. Vance?" asked Heath.

"Certainly, Sergeant," Vance told him, as he drew up to the curb beside the officer. "Mrs. Kenting is fairly comfortable and in no immediate danger. A few minutes more or less in arrivin' at a hospital will make no material difference."

Heath spoke to the officer through the open window, identified himself, and then asked the man, "Where's your call-box?"

"On the next corner, Sergeant, at Gunhill Road," answered the officer, saluting.

"All right," returned Heath brusquely. "Hop on the running-board." He leaned back in the seat again and we went on for another block, stopping at the direction of the officer.

The Sergeant slid out of the car, and the patrolman unlocked the box for him. Heath's back was to us, and I could not hear what he was saying over the telephone, but when he turned he addressed the officer peremptorily:

"Get up to Lord Street"—he gave the number, and added: "The second house from the corner of Waring—and stay on duty. Some of the boys from the 47th Precinct station will join you in a few minutes, and a couple of men from the Homicide Bureau will be coming up a little later—as soon as they can get here. I'll be returning myself inside of an hour or so. You'll find three stiffs in the joint and a Chink chained up to a water pipe in the front hall. There'll be an ambulance up before long."

"Right, sir," the officer answered, and started on the run up Waring Avenue.

Heath had climbed into the car as he spoke, and Vance drove off without delay.

"I'm heading for the Doran Hospital, just this

side of Bronx Park, Sergeant," Vance said, as we sped along. In about fifteen minutes, ignoring all traffic lights and driving at a rate far exceeding the city speed limit, we drew up in front of the hospital.

Vance jumped from the car, took Mrs. Kenting in his arms again, and carried her up the wide marble steps. He returned to the car in less than ten minutes.

"Everything's all right, Sergeant," he said as he approached the car. "The lady has regained consciousness. Fresh air did it. Her mind is a bit misty. Nothing fundamentally wrong, however."

Heath had stepped out of the car and was standing on the sidewalk.

"So long, Mr. Vance," he said. "I'm getting in that taxi up ahead. I gotta get back to that damn house. I got work to do." He moved away as he spoke.

But Vance rushed forward and took him by the arm.

"Stay right here, Sergeant, and get that arm properly dressed first."

He led Heath back, and accompanied him up the hospital steps.

A few minutes later Vance came out alone.

"The noble Sergeant is all right, Van," he said, as he took his place at the wheel again. "He'll be out before long. But he insists on going back to Lord

Street." And Vance started the car once more, and headed downtown.

When we reached Vance's apartment Currie opened the door for us. There was relief written in every line of the old butler's face.

"Good heavens, Currie!" said Vance, as we stepped inside. "I told you, you might tuck yourself in at eleven o'clock if you hadn't heard from me—and here it is nearing midnight, and you're still up."

The old man looked away with embarrassment as he closed the door.

"I'm sorry, sir," he said in a voice which, for all its formality, had an emotional tremolo in it. "I—I couldn't go to bed, sir, until you returned. I understood, sir,—if you will pardon my saying so—your reference to the documents in the drawer of the secretary. And I've taken the liberty this evening of worrying about you. I'm very glad you have come home, sir."

"You're a sentimental old fossil, Currie," Vance complained, handing the butler his hat.

"Mr. Markham is waiting in the library," said Currie, like an old faithful soldier reporting to his superior officer.

"I rather imagined he would be," murmured Vance as he went up the stairs. "Good old Markham. Always fretting about me."

As we entered the library, we found Markham

pacing up and down. He stopped suddenly at sight of Vance.

"Well, thank God!" he said. And, though he attempted to sound trivial, his relief was as evident as old Currie's had been. He crossed the room and sank into a chair; and I got the impression, from the way he relaxed, that he had been on his feet for a long time.

"Greetings, old dear," said Vance. "Why this unexpected pleasure of your presence at such an hour?"

"I was merely interested, officially, in what you might have found on Lord Street," returned Markham. "I suppose you found a vast vacant space with a real estate sign saying 'Suitable for factory site.'"

Vance smiled.

"Not exactly that, don't y' know. I had a jolly good time—which will probably make you very angry and envious."

He turned round and came to where I had seated myself. I felt weak and shaky. I was only then beginning to feel the reaction from the excitement of the evening. I realized now that in the brief space of time we had spent on Lord Street, I had become too keyed up physically to apprehend completely the dread possibilities of the situation. In the quiet and safety of familiar surroundings, the flood of reality suddenly overwhelmed me, and it was only with great effort that I managed to maintain a normal attitude.

"Let's have your gun, Van," said Vance, in his cool, steadying voice, holding out his hand. "Glad you didn't have to use it. . . . Horrible mess—what? Sorry I let you come along. But really, y' know, I myself was rather surprised and shocked by the turn of affairs."

A little abashed, I took the unused automatic from my pocket and handed it over to him: it was he who had assumed the entire brunt of the danger, and I had been unable to be of any assistance. He stepped to the centre-table and pulled open the drawer. Then he tossed my automatic into it, laid his own beside it, and, closing the drawer meditatively, rang the bell for Currie.

Markham was watching him closely but restrained his curiosity as the old butler entered with a service of brandy. Currie had sensed Vance's wish and had not waited for an order. When he had set down the tray and left the room, Markham leaned forward in his chair.

"Well, what the hell *did* happen?" he demanded irritably.

Vance sipped his cognac slowly, lighted a *Régie*, took several deep inhalations, and sat down leisurely in his favorite chair.

"I'm frightfully sorry, Markham," he said, "but I fear I have made you a bit of trouble. . . . The fact is," he added carelessly, "I killed three men."

Markham leaped to his feet as if he had been shot upward by the sudden release of a powerful steel spring. He glared at Vance, in doubt whether the other was jesting or in earnest. Simultaneously he exploded:

"What do you mean, Vance?"

Vance drew deeply again on his cigarette before answering. Then he said with a tantalizing smile:

"*J'ai tué trois hommes—Ich habe drei Männer getötet—Ho ucciso tre uomini—He matado tres hombres—Három embert megöltem—Haragti sheloshah anashim.* Meanin', I killed three men."

"Are you serious?" blurted Markham.

"Oh, quite," answered Vance. "Do you think you can save me from the dire consequences? . . . Incidentally, I found Mrs. Kenting. I took her to the Doran Hospital. Not a matter of life and death, but she required immediate and competent attention. Rather upset, I should imagine, by her detention. A bit out of her mind, in fact. Frightful experience she went through. Doin' nicely, however. Under excellent care. Should be quite herself in a few days. Can't co-ordinate just yet. . . . Oh, I say, Markham, do sit down again and take your cognac. You look positively perturbed."

Markham obeyed automatically, like a frightened child submitting to his parent. He swallowed the brandy in one gulp.

"For the love of God, Vance," he pleaded, "drop this silly ring-around-the-rosy stuff and talk to me like a sane human being."

"Sorry, Markham, and all that sort of thing," murmured Vance contritely. And then he told Markham in detail everything that had happened that night. But I thought he too greatly minimized his own part in the tragic drama. When he had finished his recital he asked somewhat coyly:

"Am I a doomed culprit, or were there what you would call extenuatin' circumstances?—I'm horribly weak on the intricacies of the law, don't y' know."

"Damn it! forget everything," said Markham. "If you're really worried, I'll get you a brass medal as big as Columbus Circle."

"My word, what a fate!" sighed Vance.

"Have you any idea who these three men were?" Markham went on, in tense seriousness.

"Not the groggiest notion," admitted Vance sadly. "One of them, Van Dine tells me, was watchin' us from the footpath in the park last night. Two of the three were probably the lads McLaughlin saw in the green coupé outside the Kenting domicile Wednesday morning. The other one I have never had the exquisite pleasure of meetin' before. I'd say, however, he had a gift for tradin' in doubtful securities on the sly: I've seen bucket-shop operators who resembled him. Anyhow, Markham old dear, why fret about it tonight? They were not nice persons, not nice at all. The geniuses at Headquarters will check up on their identities. . . ."

The front door-bell rang, and a minute later Heath entered the library. His ordinarily ruddy face was a little pale and drawn, and his right arm was in a sling. He saluted Markham and turned sheepishly to Vance.

"Your old saw-bones at the hospital told me I had to go home," he complained. "And there's nothing in God's world the matter with me," he added disgustedly. "Imagine him puttin' this arm in a sling!—said I had to take the weight offen it, that it would heal quicker that way. And then had to go and make my other arm sore by stickin' a needle in it! . . . What was the needle for, Mr. Vance?"

"Tetanus antitoxin, Sergeant," Vance told him, smiling. "Simply has to be done, don't y' know, with all gun-shot wounds. Nothing to cause you any discomfort, though. Reaction in a week—that's all."

Heath snorted. "Hell! If my gun hadn't jammed——"

"Yes, that was a bad break, Sergeant," nodded Markham.

"The doc wouldn't even let me go back to the house," grumbled Heath. "Anyway, I got the report from the local station up there. They took the three stiffs over to the morgue. The Chink'll live. Maybe we can——"

"You'll never wangle anything out of him," put in Vance quietly. "Your beloved hose-pipes and water-cures and telephone directories will get you nowhere. I know Chinamen. But Mrs. Kenting will have an interestin' story to tell as soon as she's rational again. . . . Cheer up, Sergeant, and have some more medicinê." He poured Heath a liberal drink of his rare brandy.

"I'll be on the job tomorrow all right, Chief," the Sergeant asserted as he put down the glass on a small table at his side. "Just imagine that young whipper-snapper of an intern at the Doran Hospital tryin' to make a Little Lord Fauntleroy outa me! A sling!"

Vance and Markham and Heath discussed the case from various angles for perhaps a half hour longer. Markham was getting impatient.

"I'm going home," he said finally, as he rose. "We'll get this thing straightened out in the morn-ing."

Vance left his chair reluctantly.

"I sincerely hope so, Markham," he said. "It's not at all a particularly nice case, and the sooner you're free of it, the better."

"Is there anything you want me to do, Mr. Vance?" Heath's tone was respectful, but a little weary.

Vance looked at him with commiseration.

"I want you to go home and have a good sleep. . . . And, by the by, Sergeant, how about rounding everybody up and invitin' them to the Purple House tomorrow, around noon?" he asked. "I'm speakin' of Fleel, Kenyon Kenting, and Quaggy. Mrs. Falloway and her son will, I'm sure, be there, in any event."

Heath got to his feet and grinned confidently.

"Don't you worry, Mr. Vance," he said. "I'll have 'em there for you." He went toward the door, then suddenly turned round and held out his left hand to Vance. "Much obliged, sir, for tonight——"

"Oh, please ignore it, my good Sergeant,—it was merely a slight nuisance, after all," returned Vance, though he grasped the Sergeant's hand warmly.

Markham and Heath departed together, and Vance again pressed the bell for Currie.

When the old man had entered the room Vance said:

"I'm turning in, Currie. That will be all for to-night."

The butler bowed, and picked up the tray and the empty cognac glasses.

"Very good, sir. Thank you, sir. Good night, sir."

CHAPTER XIX

THE FINAL SCENE

(Saturday, July 23; 9 a.m.)

Vance was up and dressed in good season the next morning. He seemed fairly cheerful but somewhat distrait. Before he sat down to his typical meager breakfast he went into the anteroom and telephoned to Heath. It was rather a long conversation, but no word of it reached me where I sat at the desk in the library.

As he returned to the room he said to me: "I think, Van, we're in a position now to get somewhere with this case. The poor Sergeant!—he's practically a ravin' maniac this morning, with the reporters houndin' him every minute. The news of last night's altercation did not break soon enough for the morning editions of the papers. But the mere thought of reading of our escapade in the noon editions fills me with horror." He sipped his Turkish coffee. "I had hoped we could clear up the beastly matter before the news venders began giving tongue. The best place to conclude the case is in the Purple House. It's a family gathering-place, as it were. Every one connected with the family, don't y' know, is rather intimately concerned, and hopin' for illumination. . . ."

Late in the forenoon Markham, haggard and drawn, joined us at the apartment. He did not ask Vance any questions, for he knew it would be futile in the mood Vance was in. He did, however, greet him cordially.

"I think you're going to get that medal, whether you like it or not," he said, lighting a cigar and leaning against the mantel. "All three men have been definitely identified, and they have all been on the police books for years. They've been urgently wanted at Headquarters for a long time. Two of them have served terms: one for extortion, and the other for manslaughter. They're Goodley Franks and Austria Rentwick—no, he didn't come from Austria. The third man was none other than our old elusive friend, Gilt-Edge Lamarne, with a dozen aliases—a very shrewd crook. He's been arrested nine times, but we've never been able to make the charges stick. He's kept the local boys, as well as the federal men, awake nights for years. We've had the goods on him for eight months now, but we couldn't find him."

Markham smiled at Vance with solemn satisfaction.

"It was a very fortunate affair last night, from

every point of view. Everybody's happy; only, I fear you're about to become a hero and will have ticker-tape rained on you from the windows whenever you go down Broadway."

"Oh, my Markham, my Markham!" wailed Vance. "I won't have it. I'm about to sail to South America, or Alaska, or the Malay Peninsula. . . ." He got to his feet and went to the table where he finished his old port. "Come along, Markham," he said as he put his glass down. "Let's get uptown and conclude this bally case before I sail for foreign parts where ticker-tape is unknown."

He went toward the door, with Markham and me following him.

"You think we can finish the case today?" Markham looked skeptical.

"Oh, quite. It was, in fact, finished long ago." Vance stopped with his hand on the knob and smiled cheerfully. "But, knowin' your passionate adoration for legal evidence, I have waited till now."

Markham studied Vance for a moment, and said nothing. In silence we went out and descended the stairs to the street.

We arrived at the Kenting residence, Vance driving us there in his car, fifteen minutes before noon. Weem took our hats and made a surly gesture toward the drawing-room. Sergeant Heath and Snitkin were already there.

A little later Fleel and Kenyon Kenting arrived together, followed almost immediately by Porter Quaggy. They had barely seated themselves when old Mrs. Falloway, supported by her son Fraim, came down the front stairs and joined us.

"I'm so anxious about Madelaine," Mrs. Falloway said. "How is she, Mr. Vance?"

"I received a telephone call from the hospital shortly before I came here," he replied, addressing himself to the others in the room, as well as to the old woman who, with Fraim's help, had now seated herself comfortably at one end of the small sofa. "Mrs. Kenting is doing even better today than I would have expected. She is still somewhat irrational —which is quite natural, considering the frightful experience she has been through—but I can assure you that she will be home in two or three days, fully recovered and in her normal mind."

He sat down by the window leisurely, and lighted a cigarette.

"And I imagine she will have a most interestin' tale to unfold," he went on. "Y' know, it was not intended that she return."

He moved slightly in his chair.

"The truth is, this was not a kidnapping case at all. The authorities were expected to accept it in that light, but the murderer made too many errors— his fault lay in trying to be excessively clever. I think I can reconstruct most of the events in their chronological order. Some one wanted money— wanted it rather desperately, in fact,—and all the means for an easy acquisition were at hand. The plot was as simple as it was cowardly. But the plotter met a snag when some of the early steps failed rather dismally, and a new and bolder procedure and technique became necess'ry. A damnable new technique, but one that was equally encumbered by the grave possibility of error. The errors developed almost inevitably, for the human brain, however clever, has its limitations. But the person who mapped out the plot was blinded and confused by a passionate desire for the money. Everything was sordid. . . ."

Again Vance shifted his position slightly and drew deeply on his cigarette, expelling the smoke in curling ribbons, as he went on.

"There is no doubt whatever that Kaspar Kenting made an appointment for the early morning hours, after he had returned from his evening's entertainment at the casino with Mr. Quaggy. He came in and went to his room, changed his suit and his shoes, and kept that appointment. It was a vital matter to him, as he was deeply in debt and undoubtedly expected some sort of practical solution of his problem to result from this meeting. The two mysterious and objectionable gentlemen whom Mrs. Kenting described to us as callers here earlier in the week, were

quite harmless creatures, but avid for the money
Kaspar owed them. One of them was a book-maker,
the other a shady fellow who ran a *sub-rosa* gambling
house—I rather suspected their identity from the
first, and verified it this morning: I happened to rec-
ognize one of the men through Mrs. Kenting's
description.

"When Kaspar left this house early Wednesday
morning, he was met at the appointed place not by
the person with whom he had made his appointment,
but by others whom he had never seen before. They
struck him over the head before he so much as
realized that anything was amiss, threw him into a
coupé, and then drove off with him to the East River
and disposed of him, hoping he would not be found
too soon. It was straight, brutal murder. And the
persons who committed that murder had been hired
for that purpose and had been instructed accord-
ingly. You will understand that the plotter at the
source never intended anything less than murder for
the victim—since there was grave risk in letting him
live to point an accusing finger later. . . . The slender Chinaman—the *lobby-gow* of the gang, who now
has concussion of the brain from the Sergeant's blow
last night—then returned to the house here, placed
the ladder against the window—it had been left here
previously for just that purpose—entered the room
through the window, and set the stage according to

instructions, taking the toothbrush, the comb, and the pajamas, and pinning the note to the window-sill, generally leaving mute but spurious indications that Kaspar Kenting had kidnapped himself in order to collect the money he needed to straighten out his debts. Kaspar's keeping of the appointment at such an hour naturally implied that the rendezvous was with some one he thought could help him. I found the pajamas and toothbrush, unused, in the Lord-Street house last night. It was the Chinaman that Mrs. Kenting heard moving about in her husband's room at dawn Wednesday. He was arranging the details in which he had been instructed."

Vance continued in a matter-of-fact voice.

"So far the plot was working nicely. The first set-back occurred after the arrival in the mail of the ransom note with the instructions to take the money to the tree. The scheme of the murderer to collect the money from the tree was thwarted, makin' necess'ry further steps. The same day Mrs. Kenting was approached for an appointment, perhaps with a promise of news of her husband—obviously by some one she trusted, for she went out alone at ten o'clock that night to keep the appointment. She was awaited —possibly just inside Central Park—by the same hard gentlemen who had done away with her husband. But instead of meeting with the same fate as Kaspar Kenting, she was taken to the house on Lord

Street I visited last night, and held there as a sort of hostage. I rather imagine, don't y' know, that the perpetrator of this fiendish scheme had not yet been able to pay the price demanded for the neat performance of Kaspar's killing, thereby irking the hired assassins. The lady still alive was a very definite menace to the schemer, since she would be able, if released, to tell with whom she had made the appointment. She was, so to speak, a threat held over one criminal by another criminal who was a bit more clever.

"Mrs. Kenting undoubtedly used, that evening, a certain kind of perfume—emerald—because it had been given to her by the person with whom she had the rendezvous. Surely, being a blonde, she knew better than to use it as her personal choice. That will explain to you gentlemen why I asked you so seemingly irrelevant a question the night before last. . . . Incidentally," he added calmly, "I happen to know who gave Mrs. Kenting that Courtet's emerald."

There was a slight stir, but Vance went on without a pause:

"Poor Kaspar! He was a weak chappie, and the price for his own murder was being wangled out of him without his realizing it. Through the gem collection of old Karl Kenting, of course. He was depleting that collection regularly at the subtle instigation of some one else, some one who took the gems and gave him practically nothing compared to what they were actually worth, hopin' to turn them over at an outrageous profit. But semiprecious stones are not so easy to dispose of through illegitimate channels. They really need a collector to appreciate them—and collectors have grown rather exactin' regarding the origin of their purchases. A shady transaction of this nature would naturally require time, and the now-defunct henchmen who were waiting for settlement were becoming annoyed. Most of the really valuable stones, which I am sure the collection contained originally, were no longer there when I glanced over the cases the other morning. I am quite certain that the balas-ruby I found in the poor fellow's dinner coat was brought back because the purchaser would not give him what he thought it was worth—Kaspar probably mistook the stone for a real ruby. There were black opals missing from the collection, also exhibits of jade, which Karl Kenting must undoubtedly have included in the collection; and yesterday morning the absence of a large piece of alexandrite was discovered——"

Fraim Falloway suddenly leaped to his feet, glaring at Vance with the eyes of a maniac. There was an abnormal color in the young man's face, and he was shaking from head to foot.

"I didn't do it!" he screamed hysterically. "I didn't have Kaspar killed! I tell you I didn't—I *didn't!* And you think I'd hurt Madelaine! You're a devil. I didn't do it, I say! You have no right to accuse me." He reached down quickly and picked up a small, but heavy, bronze statue of Antinoüs on the table beside him. But Heath, who was standing at his side, was even quicker than Falloway. He grasped the youth's shoulder with his free arm, just as the other lifted the statue to hurl at Vance. The figurine fell harmlessly to the floor, and Heath forced young Falloway back into his chair.

"Put your pulse-warmers on him, Snitkin," he ordered.

Snitkin, standing just behind Fraim Falloway's chair, leaned over and deftly manacled the youth, who sank back limply in his chair, breathing heavily.

Mrs. Falloway, who had sat stoically throughout the entire unexpected scene in the drawing-room, now looked up quickly as Snitkin placed the handcuffs on her son. She leaned forward with horror in her eyes. I thought for a moment she was going to speak, but she made no comment.

"Really, Mr. Falloway," Vance admonished in a soothing voice, "you shouldn't handle heavy objects when you're in that frame of mind. Frightfully sorry. But just sit still and relax." He drew on his cigarette again and, apparently ignoring the incident, went on in his unemotional drawl:

"As I was sayin', the disappearance of the stones

from the collection was an indication of the identity of the murderer, for the simple reason that the hirin' of thugs and the underground disposal of these gems quite obviously suggested that the same type of person was involved in both endeavors: to wit, both procedures implied a connection with undercover characters—fences and assassins. Not that the reasonin' was final, you understand, but most suggestive. The two notes yesterday were highly enlightenin'. One of them was obviously concocted for effect; the other was quite genuine. But boldness—usually a good technique—was, in this case, seen through."

"But who," asked Quaggy, "could possibly have fulfilled the requirements, so to speak, of your vague and amusing theory?" The smile on his lips was without mirth—it was cold and self-satisfied. "Just because you saw two black opals in my possession——"

"My theory, Mr. Quaggy, is not nearly so vague as you may think," Vance interrupted quickly. "And if it amuses you, I am delighted." Vance looked at the man with steady, indifferent eyes. "But, to answer your question, I should say that it was some one with an opportunity to render legal service, with legal protection, to members of the underworld. . . ."

Fleel, who was sitting at the small desk at the front of the room, quickly addressed Vance.

"There is a definite implication in your words, sir," he said, with his customary judicial air. (I could not resist the impression that he was pleading for a client in a court of law.) "I'm a lawyer," he went on, with ostentatious bitterness, "and I naturally have certain contacts with the type of men you imply were at the bottom of this outrage." Then he chuckled sarcastically. "However," he added, "I shall not hold the insult against you. The fact is, your amateurish ratiocinations are highly amusing." And, leaning back in his chair, he smirked.

Vance barely glanced at the man, and continued speaking as if there had been no interruption.

"Referrin' again to the various ransom notes, they were dictated by the plotter of Kaspar's murder—that is, all but the one received by Mr. Fleel yesterday—, and they were couched in such language that they could be shown to the authorities in order to side-track suspicion from the actual culprit and at the same time impress Mr. Kenyon Kenting with the urgent necessity of raising the fifty thousand dollars. I had two statements as to the amount of money which Kaspar himself was demanding for his debts—one, an honest report of fifty thousand dollars; the other, no doubt a stupidly concocted tale of thirty thousand dollars—again obviously for the purpose of diverting suspicion from the person connected with the crime."

Vance looked thoughtfully at Fleel and continued.

"Of course, it is possible that Kaspar asked you for only thirty thousand dollars, whereas he had just asked his brother for fifty thousand. But it is highly significant that he first asked his brother for fifty thousand dollars and then asked you for a different amount, whereas the ransom note called for the fifty thousand. This discrepancy between Mr. Kenting's report and your report of the amount would certainly have a tendency to point toward the brother and not toward you—which could easily be interpreted, in view of everything, as another clever means of your pointing suspicion away from yourself in case you were suspected. Certainly Mr. Kenyon Kenting was not lying about the amount, and there could be little or no reason to think that Kaspar's brother was guilty of the crime, for in such a case the money would have had to come from him—and people, don't y' know, do not ordinarily commit crimes in order to impoverish themselves—eh, what? Summing it up, there was no reason for Mr. Kenyon Kenting to lie about the amount demanded by Kaspar, whereas there was a definite reason for you to lie about it."

Vance moved his eyes slowly round the startled group.

"The second note received by Mr. Fleel, was not, as I have already intimated, one of the series written at the instructions of the guilty man—it was a genuine document addressed *to* him; and the recipient felt that he not only could use it to have the ransom money paid over to him, but to disarm once more any suspicion that might be springing up in the minds of the authorities. It did not occur to him that the address, cryptically written in for his eyes alone, could be interpreted by another. Oh, yes, it was a genuine message from the unpaid minions, demanding the money they had earned by disposing of Kaspar."

He turned slowly to Fleel again and met the other's smirk with a cold smile.

"When I suspected you, Mr. Fleel," he said, "I sent you from the District Attorney's office Thursday before Mr. Markham and I came here, in order to verify my expectation that you would urge Mr. Kenyon Kenting to request that all police interference be eliminated. This you did, and when I learned of it, after arriving here with Mr. Markham, I definitely objected to the proposal and counteracted your influence on Mr. Kenting so that you could not get the money safely that night. Seeing that part of your plan hopelessly failing, you cleverly changed your attitude and agreed to act for us—at my request through Sergeant Heath—as the person to place the money in the tree, and went through with the farce in order to prove that no connection existed between you and the demand for money. One of your henchmen had come to Central Park to pick up the package if everything went according to your pre-arranged schedule. Mr. Van Dine and I both saw the man. When he learned that you had not been successful with your plans, he undoubtedly reported your failure, thereby throwing fear into your hirelings that they might not be paid—which accounts for their keeping Mrs. Kenting alive as an effective threat to hold over you till payment was forthcoming."

Fleel looked up slowly with a patronizing grin.

"Aren't you overlooking the possibility, Mr. Vance, that young Kaspar kidnapped himself—as I maintained from the beginning—and was murdered by thugs later, for reasons and under circumstances unknown to us? Certainly all the evidence points to his self-abduction for the purpose of acquiring the money he needed."

"Ah! I've been expecting that observation," Vance returned, meeting the other's cynical stare. "The self-kidnapping setup was very clever. Much too clever. Overdone, in fact. As I see it, it was to have been your—what shall we call it?—your emergency escape, let us say, if your innocence in the matter should at any time be in doubt. In that event how easy it would have been for you to say just what you have said regarding the implications of a self-motivated pseudo-crime. And I am not overlooking the significant fact that you have consistently advised Mr. Kenyon Kenting to pay over the money in spite of the glaring evidence that Kaspar had planned the kidnapping himself."

Fleel's expression did not change. His grin became even more marked; in fact, when Vance paused and looked at him keenly, Fleel began to shake with mirth.

"A very pretty theory, Mr. Vance," he commented. "It shows remarkable ingenuity, but it entirely fails to take into consideration the fact that I myself was attacked by a sub-machine gunner on the very night of Mrs. Kenting's disappearance. You have conveniently forgotten that little episode since it would knock the entire foundation from under your amusing little house of cards."

Vance shook his head slowly, and though his smile seemed to broaden, it grew even chillier.

"No. Oh, no, Mr. Fleel. Not conveniently forgot —conveniently remembered. Most vivid recollection, don't y' know. And you were jolly well frightened by the attack. Surely, you don't believe your escape from any casualty was the result of a miracle. All quite simple, really. The gentleman with the machine-gun had no intention whatever of perforating you. His only object was to frighten you and warn you of exactly what to expect if you did not raise the money instanter to pay for the dastardly services rendered you. You were never safer in your life than when that machine-gun was sputtering away in your general direction."

The smirk slowly faded from Fleel's lips; his face flushed, and he stood up, glowering resentfully at Vance.

"Your theory, Mr. Vance," he said angrily, "no longer has even the merit of humor. Up to this point I have been amused by it and have been able to laugh at it. But you are carrying a joke too far, sir. And I wish you to know that I greatly resent your remarks." He remained standing.

"I don't regard that fact as disconcertin' in the least," Vance returned with a cold smile. "The fact is, Mr. Fleel, you will be infinitely more resentful when I inform you that at this very minute certified public accountants are at work on your books and that the police are scrutinizing most carefully the contents of your safe." Vance glanced indifferently at the cigarette in his hand.

For two seconds Fleel looked at him with a serious frown. Then he took a swift backward step and, thrusting his hand into his pocket, drew forth a large, ugly looking automatic. Both Heath and Snitkin had been watching him steadily, and as Fleel made this movement Heath, with lightning-like speed, produced an automatic from beneath the black sling of his wounded arm. The movements of the two men were almost concurrent.

But there was no need for Heath to fire his gun, for in that fraction of a second Fleel raised his automatic to his own temple and pulled the trigger. The weapon fell from his hand immediately, and his body slumped down against the edge of the desk and fell to the floor out of sight.

Vance, apparently, was little moved by the tragedy. However, after a deep sigh, he rose listlessly and stepped behind the desk. The others in the room were, I think, like myself, too paralyzed at the sudden termination of the case to make any move. Vance bent down.

"Dead, Markham,—quite," he announced as he rose, a moment or so later. "Consid'rate chappie— what? Has saved you legal worry no end. Most gratifyin'." He was leaning now against the corner of the desk, and, nodding to Snitkin, who had rushed forward with an automatic in his hand, jerked his head significantly toward Fraim Falloway.

Snitkin hesitated but a moment. He slipped the gun back into his pocket and unlocked the handcuffs on young Falloway.

"Sorry, Mr. Falloway," murmured Vance. "But you lost your self-control and became a bit annoyin'. . . . Feelin' better?"

The youth stammered: "I'm all right." He was

alert and apparently his normal self now. "And Sis will be home in a couple of days!" He found a cigarette, after much effort, and lighted it nervously.

"By the by, Mr. Kenting," Vance resumed, without moving from the desk, "there's a little point I want cleared up. I know that the District Attorney is aching to ask you a few questions about what happened yesterday evening. He had not heard from you and was unable to reach you. Did you, by any chance, give that fifty thousand dollars to Fleel?"

"Yes!" Kenting stood up excitedly. "I gave it to him a little after nine o'clock last night. We got the final instructions all right—that is, Fleel got them. He called me up right away and we arranged to meet. He said some one had telephoned to him and told him that the money had to be at a certain place —far up in the Bronx somewhere—at ten o'clock that night. He convinced me that this person on the telephone had said he would not deal with any one but Fleel."

He hesitated a moment.

"I was afraid to act through the police again, after that night in the park. So I took Fleel's urgent advice to leave the police out of it, and let him handle the matter. I was desperate! And I trusted him— God help me! I didn't telephone to Mr. Markham, and I wouldn't speak to him when he called. I was afraid. I wanted Madelaine back safe. And I gave the money to Fleel—and thought he could arrange everything. . . ." *

"I quite understand, Mr. Kenting." Vance spoke softly, in a tone which was not without pity. "I was pretty sure you had given him the money last night, for he telephoned to the Lord-Street house while we were there, obviously to make immediate arrangements to pay off his commissions, as it were. Sergeant Heath here recognized his voice over the wire. . . . But, really, y' know, Mr. Kenting, you should have trusted the police. Of course, Fleel received no message of instructions last night. It was part of his stupid technique, however, to tell you he had, for he needed the money and was at his wit's end. He too was desperate, I think. When Mr. Markham told me he was unable to get in touch with you, I rather thought, don't y' know, you had done just what you have stated. . . . Fleel was far too bold in showing us that note yesterday. Really, y' know, he shouldn't have done it. There were references in it which he thought only he himself could understand. Luckily, I saw through them. That note, in fact, verified my theory regarding him. But he showed it to us because he wished to make an impression on you. He needed that money. I rather think he had gambled away, in one way or another,

* The practice of turning over ransom money to outsiders, in the hopes of settling kidnap cases, is not an unusual one. There have been several famous instances of this in recent years.

the money he held in trust for the Kenting estate. We sha'n't know definitely till we get the report from Stitt and McCoy,* the accountants who are goin' over Fleel's books. It is quite immaterial, however."

Vance suddenly yawned and glanced at his watch.

"My word, Markham!" he exclaimed, turning to the District Attorney, who had sat stolidly and non-plused through the amazing drama. "It's still rather early, don't y' know. If I hasten, old dear, I'll be able to catch the second act of *Tristan and Isolde*."

Vance went swiftly across the room to Mrs. Fallo-way and bowed over her hand solicitously with a murmured adieu. Then he hurried out to his car waiting at the curb.

.   .   .   .   .

When the reports from the accountants and the police came in at the end of the day on which Fleel had shot himself, Vance's theory and suppositions were wholly substantiated. The accountants found that Fleel had been speculating heavily on his own behalf with the funds he held in trust for the Kenting estate. His bank had already called upon him to cover the legitimate investments permitted him by law as the trustee of the estate. The amount he had embezzled was approximately fifty thousand dollars,

* This was the same firm of certified public accountants whom Markham had called in to inspect the books of the firm of Benson and Benson in the investigation of the Benson murder case.

and as he had long since lost his own money in the same kind of precarious bucket-shop transactions, it would have been but a matter of days before the shortage caused by his extra-legal operations would have been discovered.

In his safe were found practically all the gem-stones missing from the Kenting collection, including the large and valuable alexandrite. (How or when he had acquired this last item was never definitely determined.) The package of bills which Kenyon Kenting had so trustingly given him was also found in the safe.

All this happened years before the actual account of the case was set down here. Since then, Kenyon Kenting has married his sister-in-law, Madelaine, who returned to the Purple House the second day after Fleel's suicide.

Less than a year later Vance and I had tea with Mrs. Falloway. Vance had a genuine affection for the crippled old woman. As we were about to go, Fraim Falloway entered the room. He was a different man from the one we had known during the investigation of what the papers persisted in calling the Kenting kidnap case (perhaps the alliteration of the nomenclature was largely the reason for it). Fraim Falloway's face had noticeably filled in, and his color was healthy and normal; there was a vitality in his eyes, and he moved with ease and determined alacrity. His whole manner had changed. I learned later that old Mrs. Falloway had called in the endocrinologist whose name Vance had given her, and that the youth had been under observation and treatment for many months.

After our greetings that day Vance asked Falloway casually how his stamp collecting was going. The youth seemed almost scornful and replied he had no time for such matters any more—that he was too busy with his new work at the Museum of Natural History to devote any of his time to so futile a pursuit as philately.

It might be interesting to note, in closing, that Kenyon Kenting's first act, after his marriage to Madelaine Kenting, was to have the exterior of the Purple House thoroughly scraped and sand-blasted, so that the natural color of the bricks and stones was restored. It ceased to be the "purple house," and took on a more domestic and *gemütlich* appearance, and has so remained to the present day.